JUBA'S CUP

by
Luella Dow

Luella Dow

8.20-2011

BOOKS BY LUELLA DOW:

Fire In Her Soul

Bird In The Hand

Of Cabbages And Kings

Juba's Cup

Book design by Pine Orchard. Visit us on the internet at www.pineorchard.com

Printed in Canada.

9 8 7 6 5 4 3 2 1

ISBN 0-9658786-3-5

Library of Congress Control Number: 2003100431

DEDICATION

This book is dedicated to all
who have had an impossible dream
and made it come true.

ACKNOWLEDGMENTS

Blessings to Jerrelene Williamson, President
of Spokane Black Pioneers, for her constant
encouragement and helpful suggestions from the
first page of this book to the last.

Many thanks to Norma and Larry Danielson
for "on the spot" information about Negro Creek.

A hearty handshake to Donnitta Warren, Bill
Wynd, Rocky Salts, Larry Gilliam, Chris Kaplan,
Donna Berg, and Cheney Public Library for
tidbits of authenticity.

INTRODUCTION

This is a work of fiction.

It is based, however, on the true story of a black slave who escaped from a Southern plantation in the 1850's and established a dairy near Rock Lake, Whitman County, Washington State.

All that remains to remind us of his presence is Negro Creek, a meandering stream that flows from a hillside and quietly murmurs: "He was here, he was here."

"He was here" in eastern Washington, south of Spokane.

FOREWORD

And Jesus said unto them, "You shall indeed drink of the cup that I drink of."—*Mark 10:39*

Juba's Cup is an American saga, the story of a slave yearning to be free.

Although the tin cup, given to him by a friend, holds cool, sweet water, it is a symbol of the hopes, dreams, bitterness, hate, adventure, despair, caring and love that Juba encounters on his journey to freedom.

Will Juba survive the obstacles thrown in his way? Will he be reunited with his beloved Meggie, the young slave that he left behind?

Luella Dow has written with great warmth and compassion, and gives a descriptive view of the Northwest and its inhabitants when the Northwest was mostly wilderness. The author brings out the good and the bad of each character in her book in an exciting and compelling way—almost as if she were right there.

Juba's Cup is a book worthy of a great deal of attention, not only because of its historic background, but because it is an American tale of survival and love.

—JERRELENE WILLIAMSON
President of *Spokane Northwest Black Pioneers*
Recipient of the *Jefferson Award for Community Service in Washington State*

JUBA'S CUP

CHAPTER 1

Juba watched the whip rear back. He heard the sharp crack as it sliced through the air. Leather ripped flesh. Reuben, roped to the whipping post, cried out. The whip reared again and again, marking its path in blood.

Juba clenched his fists so tight his fingers ached. He squinted his eyes shut. He could not look. The scar on his temple turned bright pink. It gave him away—every time.

Pilcher, the overseer, bellowed, "Everybody watch. Ain't nobody gonna get away with not looking. Not unless you want a whipping too."

With slightly lowered lids, Juba glanced at the slaves circling the whipping post. They all looked scared. Mighty scared. They stared in horror at Reuben's back, now striped and criss-crossed with blood.

"Twenty-eight—twenty-nine—thirty." Pilcher counted the last of the lashes. He reached for a bucket of brine and sloshed it over Reuben's back.

Reuben screamed as the salty vinegar water bit into the mangled skin of his back.

"Take him down, boys. Next one pulls the same stunt gets the same prize." A smirk played at the corners of Pilcher's mouth. He turned and dragged the whip in the dust to grind off the blood.

Most of the slaves hurried away. The low murmur of their voices rose and fell, droning like a hundred bumblebees.

Juba ran to Reuben and helped untie him. "Easy, brother, easy now."

As the rope loosened from around Reuben's wrists, freeing him from the splintery post, his knees gave way. Great sobs heaved his shoulders.

"Got my arm around you, Reub. Mose is on the other side. We'll get you to your cabin. Hold on, now. A few more steps."

They half-carried him into his shack and gently lowered him to the blanket-covered plank that was his bed. "Rest easy, now." Juba comforted. "You're gonna be all right."

Somebody set a can of warm water on the floor. Juba stared at the clean strip of rag that floated, then gradually sank to the bottom of the can. Anonymous hands reached around the doorway and offered a cracked teacup filled with deer tallow. Juba looked up. Dark eyes gazed into his, a silent affirmation, a slight nod, and he was again alone with Reuben. Reuben moaned.

Juba knelt beside him and lifted the dripping rag from the can. "This's gonna hurt some more, I reckon. But we gotta wash these cuts 'cause—"

"What'sa use?" Reuben's voice was thick with shock. "I'se gonna die anyway."

"No, you're not."

Reuben flinched as the water penetrated the cuts. "How d'you know so much?"

Juba squeezed the water from the rag across Reuben's back and let it dribble onto the floor. "You gotta heal up, Reub. For Lizzie's sake."

"What good is it? Pilcher ain't gonna let me see her. Not now, not for a long time. I just wanna die, Juba. I just wanna die."

Juba dug his fingers into the warm deer tallow and began to spread it over Reuben's back. The tallow turned pink with blood. Bits of cut flesh mingled with the tallow that coated Juba's fingers. "Tallow'll help," he said. "Start the healing. You rest 'til morning, you'll feel better."

"I don't wanna feel better. I wanna die. There ain't no other way outta this misery. Ain't no other way outta slavery. Just ta die, tha's all."

"God knows you're hurting, Reub. God knows." Juba began to hum a low soothing melody. A song of hope and better times. *You're a liar*, his conscience goaded him. *A liar, and you know it.*

The smoke from cooking fires wafted through the air. Supper time. Overseers knew when to hold whippings. After the day's work was done, before folks ate, so they'd forget while they chewed their hoecakes. During the night, the mangled back would begin to scab over, hiding the deep bruises. Get more work out of the slaves that way.

Juba shook his head in silence. The beating was brutal. And all because Reuben's wife was sold to another plantation owner and Reuben sneaked out, just to be with her. Juba didn't know who the snitch was that told on Reuben. He clenched his fists. Anger boiled in his chest and clogged his throat. How could anybody be so low as to tell on a man longing for his wife? And for what reward? A handful of cornmeal?

Reuben was quiet now, his eyes closed. The tallow covering the cuts on his back glistened in the fading light. Juba stood in the open doorway of the cabin and watched the stars appear in the sky. The longing to be free was in every man. To give up was to die inside. Juba glanced back at Reuben. If he had a wife on a neighboring plantation, he'd risk everything too, just to hold her for a few minutes.

Meggie was on his mind a lot these days. He loved her. Loved her with all his being. If ever they were to have a life together… Juba leaned his head against the doorframe.

Reuben groaned and Juba turned back into the cabin. "Easy, brother," he soothed. He stepped outside and turned his face to the sky. "Freedom," he whispered. Somehow, somewhere. Was Reuben right? There had to be another way out of slavery besides dying.

A few days earlier, Juba had overheard Massah Robinson talking. "That Juba's twenty years old, right in his prime." Juba wrinkled his nose. Prime, huh? Talking about a man like he was some herd sire. Well, he wasn't an animal. He was a man and he wanted to live like one.

He looked toward the big house. Only three of its white porch pillars were visible, gleaming in the moonlight through the sheltering curtain of cypress trees. Slave quarters were set well back from the mansion. Wouldn't do for Massah's guests to catch a glimpse of the slave shacks. Juba set his jaw and stared hard at the portico of the mansion, a gesture he would not dare to repeat if someone were watching. *Freedom*. There had to be a way. Somehow, he'd find it …

CHAPTER 2

Sunday afternoon, Juba sat on the bank of the Pearl River, fishing. He wished Meggie was there to hold his hand. But Miss Lorinda, Massah Robinson's daughter, was having a lady's tea and Meggie had to serve.

The gentle lap of the water and the occasional buzz of a fly made Juba drowsy. His eyes closed. The stranger slashing through the weeds and swamp grass startled him. As the man came into view, Juba decided he was old, considering his lined face and the stiffness he displayed as he bent to set his can of worms on the ground.

"Howdy," the man said.

Juba nodded and continued to work his worm onto the hook.

"Catching anything?"

"Yassah. Two good-sized ones here." Juba held his catfish up for inspection.

The man settled himself on the ground about ten feet away, spat into the river, and threaded a line through his bamboo pole.

Juba shot him a quick glance. There was grime on the man's ragged shirt cuffs. His frayed collar was the same color as his skin, a mottled gray. Juba's lip curled. The man stank.

"Name's Wilbur," the man said. "Not that it makes a particle of difference to anyone. I sometimes change it if I get the notion." He turned to look straight at Juba. From under bushy brows, his eyes twinkled like bright blue marbles. He smiled broadly over tobacco-stained teeth. "You wondering why I'm here?"

"No, suh."

"No? Well, you ought to. I'm a traveling tinsmith. Just been to the big house. Sold 'em a sixteen-inch boiler and brought back a kettle I fixed last month. Had the handle broken a while back."

"Yassah," Juba swallowed. A flicker of apprehension made him clear his throat. If the man wasn't here to fish, what was his purpose?

"That all you got to say? Yassah? No, suh?"

Juba tried to smile. "Just trying to be respectful's all." His lips trembled.

The old man spat into a clump of swamp grass. He hitched himself along until he was close enough to touch. "Look at me, Juba," he muttered. "Look me in the eye. I saw you walking out here. Saw you last time I was at the big house too. And the time before that. Don't you ever get a yearning to see the world?"

Startled, Juba's eyes grew wide. "N-no-no, suh."

The old man swung his arm. His line followed a perfect cast to the middle of the river. "Most folks'd like to see what's beyond their own back fence. 'Course you don't have a back fence to look past."

"No, suh."

"How d'you suppose I know your name?"

Juba shrugged. "Don't know, suh."

The old man's laugh sounded like a fingertip scratched on a weathered board. "I asked. That's how." His eyes held Juba's gaze. He would not let it go. "I travel all over the country. See lots of folks. Ain't a one of 'em, black or white, don't want to be free of something. Lest it's a poor old colored man so beaten down he don't care no more."

Juba's heart began to pound. He glanced over his shoulder.

"Don't worry. There ain't nobody around to hear us. I made sure of that."

For an instant, Juba thought about jumping up and running. He'd heard of set-ups, of traps where the slave was fooled into following directions supposedly to gain freedom. Then, when he was caught, he was beaten and chained. Juba laid down his pole. He shifted his leg.

The old man went right on as if he hadn't noticed. He gazed out over the water. "Ever see a river that ain't full of 'gators like this ol' Pearl and water so cold it makes yer toes ache?"

"N-no, suh."

"Ever see land so flat you can walk for miles and never get to the end of it?"

Juba shook his head. A muscle in his calf twitched.

"Ever see the Rocky Mountains?"

"R-Rocky Mountains? No, suh."

"Yep. Prettiest sight on earth, them mountains with snow on 'em, touching the sky."

"Yassah."

The old man jabbed a grimy finger at Juba and spoke so rapidly Juba jumped. "Ever want to see 'em?"

Juba looked away. His hands curled into fists.

"There's white folks starting west all the time up in territory around Missouri. Get 'em a span of oxen or mules and a wagon. Stretch a canvas across the top. Dozens of 'em. Call 'em wagon trains. Going across that prairie I told you about. Seeing them mountains." He shook his pole a time or two. "Ever hear of Missouri?"

"No, suh."

The old man spat into the river again. "Reckon a feller might hire on, mebbe as a mule skinner, ya know? Congregating at Independence. That's where they start from. Might join up with 'em myself, one of these days."

He reeled in his line and tugged a fish from the hook. "Still don't trust me, do ya? Can't help that. Don't blame you, neither."

Juba clamped his lips shut. He grasped a handful of grass and pulled it up by the roots.

The old man slowly unfolded himself and stood. He said, still in that coarse whisper, "Underground railroad's kinda shut down right now. Folk's gettin' caught right and left." He stuck his worm can into a torn pocket. "Ain't no rule saying a man can't strike out on his own. Well, there is. But you know what I mean. Some rules meant to be broke."

He lifted a greasy hat and scratched his head with the same hand holding the fish. "Best be getting on. Got another delivery over to Jensen's plantation." He stared at Juba. "Thank your lucky stars you ain't a slave over there. Bad business on that place. Bad business."

The old man turned as if to walk away, then spun around. Juba was surprised at his sudden agility. He leaned toward Juba and whispered, "Ain't often the fox outruns the dogs. A smart one can— sometimes. Reckon you might."

He sauntered away. He stretched out his arm in a backhanded wave and disappeared into the tall grass. Juba stared after him. For a minute or so, he traced the old man's progress by the swarm of gnats that hovered above his head.

Juba's knees trembled. A shiver ran down his spine. The fish on the end of his line wriggled, unnoticed. It was then he spied a crumpled piece of paper on the ground. Had the old man dropped it? Juba reached for it, then jerked his hand back as if the paper might burn him. He looked furtively about and snagged it with a finger. Holding it close to his chest, he smoothed the wrinkles and peeked at it.

What he saw jolted him clear to his toes. He frowned. A steady pounding began in his chest. The old man had drawn a picture of the countryside. Juba's finger traced the curving line of the Pearl River.

If he hadn't been so agitated, he might have smiled. The old man had drawn fish jumping in it. Nearby, was Bournby's swamp with mean looking alligators hiding in the mud. A series of arrows followed the river until it came to a sharp bend. At that point, the line crossed the river and zigzagged north. And near the top of the paper, just like the old man said, was a row of wagons pulled by oxen, heading west.

Juba drew in a sharp breath. If anybody saw this map, if anybody knew he had it, he was doomed. Anger at the old man flared. What did the old man have against him? To put him in danger like this, to upset his whole life, single him out for suspicion and whippings and—reason asserted itself. The old man had put himself in jeopardy as well. Why? Why had he done this?

Juba had seen the tinsmith's wagon before, loaded with pots and pans clanging together. Every few weeks, it clattered around to the kitchen door of the big house. Once he saw the old man sitting on a wood block near the stables, smoking with Pilcher. Never thought anything of it. A visiting tinsmith smoking with the overseer; nothing strange about that. Or a farrier come to shoe the horses. Or a wheel-wright.

Then he remembered what the old man said about Jensen's plantation and a stab of dread clenched his stomach. There'd been a rumor circulating among the slaves a couple of weeks ago that Massah Robinson might trade for a couple of Jensen's slaves. Sometimes money figured into the deal, if one slave was worth more than another. You never knew who might be sold. Your life was not your own. It was not your right to say what was done with it. Slaves, bought and sold like cattle. Juba gritted his teeth.

He swallowed and flexed the shoulder muscles that had begun to cramp with tension. What was it the old man said? *Ain't a man, black or white, don't want to be free of something.* He was right on that point. And hadn't Juba dreamed of freedom? Of course. Lots of times. Only, he'd never figured how to make it happen.

It was getting late. He'd better head back. He glanced at the map again. Could be a trap after all. What if somebody was watching right now, sneaking around in the tall swamp grass, waiting to see what he would do. And yet, there was something about the old man that he wanted to trust. Just a feeling. It told him the old man wouldn't be a party to a slave trap.

Juba shook his head. Naw, it was too risky. *Quit your dreaming, Juba.* Better get rid of the map. He folded it in half and gripped it with both hands. Better tear it into tiny pieces and throw it into the river. Then he paused. The old man had come to him on purpose, hadn't he? Walked out here in the swamp grass. Risked his own neck. Must have been planning all along on catching Juba alone sometime.

Half-ashamed for doubting, half-frightened for believing, he fiddled with the edges of the paper. Maybe he could keep it for now. Hide it somewhere. Stuff it in a fish's mouth? No. If he'd had shoes on he could have laid it flat under the soles of his feet. Finally, with a shrug, he folded it into a tiny square and tucked it into his mouth next to his cheek He reeled in his last fish, picked up the other two, and headed back to slave quarters.

With his first step through the tall grass, a powerful elation took hold of him. It made him want to jump and shout hallelujah and wave his arms. He could hardly keep his feet from skipping the rest of the way to his cabin. He had to bite his lips lest he grin from ear to ear. In the dusty yard marked with thousands of prints from the slaves' bare feet, he handed the fish to old Tessie. There she stood, by the big kettle in which she cooked the mess of grub on Sunday evenings for anybody who wanted it.

"Why, thank you, Juba," she crooned.

Juba muttered, "Welcome," his tongue sliding past the paper in his cheek. He ducked through his cabin doorway and took the paper from his mouth. Under his bunk was a loose board at the base of the wall. He had discovered it one day while hunting for a button that came off his shirt and rolled under his bed. He scooted under the bunk on his belly and stuffed the paper behind the board. Perfect! Nobody'd ever know.

"Hey, Juba! Whatcha doing under there?"

The voice in the doorway made him jump and bump his head on the underside of his bunk. Sweat broke out on his brow and trickled down the scar on his temple. His tongue glued itself to the roof of his mouth. Stiff as a broom handle, he lay there, his legs sticking out across the floor of his tiny cabin.

"Juba? I said whatcha doing?" Bare feet nudged his leg.

Juba eyed the feet. They belonged to Jim. Fella who hoed alongside him in the fields. He blew out his pent-up breath. Jim had caught him. No getting around it. He wriggled from under the bunk and sat on it.

"Oh, 'lo, Jim." His voice shook and he coughed to cover it. His hands seemed as big as shovels. Could Jim see how they trembled? He looked at the floor. "I-I ain't doing nothing. Been trying to find where—where a mouse gets in, is all." He made himself take a deep breath. He could tell Jim didn't believe him. He saw the suspicion in Jim's eyes.

"Go fishing this afternoon?"

Instantly defensive, Juba shot back, "Yeah, what about it?"

"Hey, brother, whatcha so jumpy about? Just wondering 's all. Didn't see you around 's all."

Anxious to head off more questions, Juba blurted, "Fella's got a right to sit on the river bank if he wants an'. . . ." He let the sentence dangle, reached down and began to pick at a callus on his heel. When he looked up, Jim was leaning on the doorframe, frowning at him. Jim's tone was as gentle as leaves rustling in a warm breeze.

"You in trouble, Juba?"

"Tr-trouble?"

Jim hunkered down in front of Juba. "Look, brother, whatever it is, I'll stand by you. We all got to depend on each other, you know. Ain't nobody else gonna look out for us."

"Yeah," Juba said on a sigh. For the first time, he looked directly into Jim's eyes. He saw genuine friendship there and worry. He touched Jim's arm. "Just give me a little time, okay? I gotta sort something out."

Jim stood. "Sure, brother, sure." Jim stooped as he went through the low doorway. He turned and seemed about to say something, thought better of it, and loped out of sight.

Juba's shoulders slumped. His hands hung down over the edge of the bunk. He had never before had a secret so profound. It was a promise of new life and a death sentence all at the same time. He wanted desperately to share it with Meggie. Somehow he had to find a way to be alone with Meggie.

The excitement of it began to bubble within him once more. He had an impulse to jump off the bunk and yell. The next instant, a terror shook him, so cold it took his breath away. He covered his face with his hands and cowered next to the wall.

In his mind, Juba pictured the map waving like a flag outside his cabin door. There was no hiding it. Everyone could see it, even Pilcher. He envisioned folks pointing at him and laughing. *"This nigger thinks he's gonna run away to freedom."* While Pilcher, advancing with his whip, laughed the loudest of all. *"C'mon, Juba, the only freedom you're gonna see is the flogging I'll give you."*

He thought about the old man who had left the map in the grass down by the river. He remembered every detail of the drawing. Together, he and Meggie would slip away. Together, they would follow the map to freedom. He scrunched up his face, thinking, willing ideas and plans to surface.

A shock wave ran through Juba's body. He found himself again on the floor, not knowing how he got there. He scanned the wall under his bunk to make sure no corner of the paper stuck out for somebody to glimpse. "Oh, Lawd." It was half prayer, half an utterance of desperation. Yet, a warmth touched him, as if a reassuring hand lay on his shoulder. He turned, expecting to see someone bending over him. There was no one.

CHAPTER 3

Meggie was sixteen years old. She had been Miss Lorinda's house slave for ten years. Secretly, Meggie regarded Miss Lorinda as a pampered, useless person who couldn't put on her own shoes if she had to. Meggie had perfected a mask of complacency so that Miss Lorinda would never know her true feelings. She was well aware that Miss Lorinda thought of her as a possession. Meggie's role in life was to obey every whim of her mistress.

While Juba worked in the fields, Meggie picked up the dresses Miss Lorinda discarded on the floor. She fetched cool drinks or sugary pastries from the oven. Meggie ironed Miss Lorinda's clothes and opened or shut windows as Miss Lorinda required. Meggie said, "Yes, ma'am," or "No, ma'am," a hundred times a day and sometimes stood behind Miss Lorinda waving a fan for a whole hour if that was what Miss Lorinda wanted.

When Miss Lorinda was out with a beau, Meggie worked in the kitchen. She knew a great deal about stirring blackberry jam or stringing beans or chopping beets into dainty cubes.

Meggie didn't mind all the fetching and carrying, the running up and down stairs more times than she could count. That was the easy part. The hard part was staying out of Massah Robinson's clutches. Miss Lorinda's father had a yen for black girls. Meggie had seen him charm a hapless young lady into his buggy and race for the cover of the distant trees. She had also seen him strong-arm a Negro girl, silencing her screams with a firm hand over her mouth as he shoved her into a vacant cabin. With his wife dead three years past and Miss Lorinda so self-absorbed, who was there to protest?

When the Massah was at home, Meggie peeked around corners and listened at closed doors before venturing afoot. She studied and timed the Massah's habits. And if she happened to meet him in a hallway, she dropped something just so she could stoop to pick it up as he passed by.

This morning, he caught her alone in the kitchen when Hester went down to the cellar for a bowl of peaches. Meggie, at the stove, stirred vanilla pudding for Miss Lorinda's supper.

Massah Robinson stood close. He casually laid a hand on her shoulder, then slid it down her back. "Pudding looks good, Meggie. How about a taste?"

Meggie's heart beat like a spoon on a tin pan. She quickly turned and backed into the stove so that his hand touched the hot surface.

"Ow! You little vixen!"

"Sorry, massah, sorry."

Robinson ran to the water bucket and plunged his hand into the cool water. "You did that on purpose."

"Sorry, massah."

"I ought to have you whipped."

"Sorry, massah." Meggie shoved the pudding to the back of the stove and escaped to the front parlor where Reba dusted the lamps. Reba raised a questioning brow. Meggie held a finger to her lips and, panting with fright, slipped behind the heavy drapes.

Massah poked his head in the parlor doorway. "Reba, have you seen Meggie?"

Reba lowered her gaze to his feet. "No, suh, I ain't seen Meggie for a couple hours."

Meggie heard Massah mumble something to himself. Then his patent leather shoes slapped the oiled oak floor as he went on down the hallway.

Reba glanced toward the doorway and whispered, "You better get outta here."

Meggie sneezed in the dust that filtered from the drapes. "Thanks for not telling on me, Reba."

"I understand, hon, but you gotta find another way."

"How? What way is there?"

Reba wrapped a rag around a broom and, standing on tiptoe, gently drew it across the chandelier hanging from the ten-foot ceiling. "I dunno." Her face creased into a wide smile. "Get old, like me, with a middle big as a washtub. That'll do it."

Upstairs, the bell in Miss Lorinda's room rang twice. Meggie started for the door. "Gotta go. Miss Lorinda wants me to pin up her hair 'cause Josiah Thornburg's coming calling tonight."

Reba straightened from polishing the base of a gas lamp. "That young scamp? That'll solve your problem."

"How?"

"Simple. Ain't you Miss Lorinda's personal servant?"

"Yeah, you know it."

"Honey, she'll be taking you along when she gets married."

Meggie paused at the parlor door. A sudden revelation made her heart slam against her chest. "Then, me' n' Juba, we won't—" She sucked in her breath. She had not thought about being separated from Juba. As she climbed the stairs, a prayer formed on her lips. "Please, God, don't let Miss Lorinda get married for the longest, longest time."

CHAPTER 4

Juba and Meggie sat on the river bank. The swamp grass tickled their legs as they dangled their feet in the tepid water.

Juba lay back in the grass. "I been thinking, Meggie, thinking hard."

They were partially hidden from prying eyes. Juba pulled Meggie down to lie beside him, turned and whispered in her ear. "Meg, let's run away."

"What!" She sat up, her eyes flashing fear as she looked all around.

"Meg?"

"I heard you."

"Well?"

"Well, what?"

"We stay here, life's gonna swallow us up. Won't get no better. On the outside, we got a chance, chance to be free—"

"Juba, you mustn't—"

"No, I want—"

She stopped him with a kiss. "I love you, Juba. Don't ever think of something so scary. Pilcher'd kill you and I'd—I'd be all alone. I couldn't stand that."

"Not if we escaped," he said, his jaw set stubbornly.

"We'd never make it. You know Massah's hounds. Have you forgotten what happened to Skeet?"

"Skeet was dumb. He told everybody. Pilcher pays fellas to snitch. Easiest thing in the world to catch Skeet."

"He does?" Meggie's eyes were round. Her mouth made a perfect O.

Juba frowned. "Huh?"

"What you said. About Pilcher. Pays fellas to snitch?"

"Yeah."

"How'd you know?"

Juba tangled his fingers in the grass beside him and tugged. "Known it a long time."

"That's why Hobie ended up in the river? Why they found him with his hands tied?"

"Yeah."

In the silence, crickets kept up a steady sawing. Out in the middle of the river, a catfish broke the surface.

Meggie shuddered. "Awful, awful," she whispered.

Juba sat up. He yanked a blade of grass by the root and chewed it. "Snitches don't deserve to live," he murmured. He drew the grass gently over her arm. Her flesh was warm, the color of dark honey. He caught the fragrance of vanilla.

Meggie jerked away. "Did—did you help with Hobie?"

"No, but I would if they'd asked me to. Meg?" He squeezed her hand. "We'd be together. Nobody could separate us."

"No."

"Stay here, Massah might sell you or me. Never see each other again."

"No, Juba. He wouldn't."

"How d'you know?"

"'Cause he—"

"Yeah, I know how he's always eyeing you. Probably like to see me dead."

"Never! You're too good a worker, Juba. You're one of the best."

"Worth more money, huh? Like a prize stallion. Get your head out of the clouds, Meg. You living in a dream land." Her hair tickled his face. Their cheeks touched. "We could run at night. Wouldn't be missed till daylight. Could be miles away by then."

Meggie began to tremble. "Don't, Juba. Scares me something awful to think of it."

"We could make it together. I got a plan. Say you'll come with me, Meg." He watched a beetle trying to climb a grass stem. It fell to the ground and started up again. Over and over, it climbed and fell, climbed and fell. Juba smashed it between thumb and finger. He had power over the beetle like Pilcher had power over the slaves.

He knew Pilcher was itching for him to make a mistake. Just one mistake. So he could peel the flesh off Juba's back. Peel it off, stripe by stripe, until the whip was coated with his blood and the other slaves were so terrified they wouldn't even dare to breathe without permission. Pilcher enjoyed the smell of blood.

The horn sounded. Juba and Meggie scrambled to their feet.

"Please, Meg," Juba whispered. "Let's do it. Let's run away."

"Juba, Juba, gotta think on something like that. Can't just—"

Juba kissed her. "Love you, hon." He ran to the cotton field.

Meggie followed the path to the big house, where she would spend three hours ironing the ruffles on Miss Lorinda's dresses. Perfectly calm outwardly, Meggie found her thoughts, like ocean waves, crashing against the rocks of indecision.

Night came. Juba lay on his board bed, the threadbare blanket under him. He dozed and awoke with a snore. A star shone through the knothole in the roof of his cabin. He'd have to cram a rag in that knothole before the fall rains came. Or would he be far away by then? Meggie'd go with him, wouldn't she? A longing so intense began in his throat and quivered the length of his body. She had to. He couldn't live without Meggie. He pounded his fists together. How did a man get so tangled up in his dreams? Juba sat up and leaned against the splintery boards of the cabin wall. He squeezed his eyes shut tight. Images whirled in his mind like tumbleweeds before the wind. He saw the two of them, he and Meggie, slipping through the woods and outfoxing the hounds. They were sitting on a distant river bank in the sunshine, tasting *freedom* with every breath.

CHAPTER 5

Juba and Meggie strolled, hand in hand, along the dusty path that led to the cotton field. Juba stood still and gazed all around.

Meggie spoke softly. "Whatcha looking for, Juba?"

"Looking for eyes that might see and ears that might hear."

"You got something that important to tell me?"

"Yeah, I do." Juba scratched the back of his neck. He gnawed at a fingernail. "I love you," he said. His lips quivered.

Meggie wrinkled her brow. "What's making you so nervous?"

Juba dug his toes into the dirt and drew a circle. "You—you know what we were talking about last week?" His voice dropped to a mumble. "About running away?"

Meggie gasped. "Running—" She clapped her hand over her mouth. "Shhh," she whispered. "Yeah, how could I forget it? You scared me something awful and I—"

Juba reached inside his shirt and brought out a folded piece of paper. His hand covered it as he held it to his chest. "C'mon. Let's walk into the cotton rows. Don't want nobody to see this."

"What is it, Juba? Where'd you get it?"

Juba looked her straight in the eyes. "When I was talking to you about running away?"

Meggie nodded, her mouth slightly open.

"I had this already. The old tinsmith gave it to me. It's a map—a map for getting outta here."

"A map? But how? Where?" Meggie pressed against his side as Juba carefully unfolded the paper and traced the lines with his finger. "Look here, and here."

"Oh, my!" Meggie shook her head. "You mustn't—"

"The day you had to serve for Miss Lorinda's tea party?"

"Yeah?"

"I was fishing. Somehow, the old man followed me. Sat right down next to me 'side the river. Got a feeling he'd been trying to catch me alone. Musta had his eye on me for a while."

"Black man or white man?"

"White man, hon."

"Juba, you can't trust somebody like that!"

"Well, I did. White man's not all devils. Just some. He was trying to tell me, Meggie. There's hope. We can do it."

Meggie grabbed a handful of his shirt. "No, Juba, no. It's too scary." She leaned against him and trembled.

Juba drew her into his arms. "I've thought and thought about it, Meg. We could do it. If you'd go with me. Together, we could do it."

Meggie shook her head. She frowned.

"Just look at the map, Meg. See where the trail goes? See?"

"But—you don't know how far that is or—"

Juba tucked the paper back inside his shirt. "We could find out as we're going along."

Meggie took a step backward. "I'm not going anywhere alone with you 'less we're married."

He grinned at her. "Best thing I've heard all day."

"I mean it, Juba."

"We could jump the broom anytime, Meg. Betcha the preacher could fix us up next Sunday."

Meggie caressed his face. Her fingers gently traced the scar on his temple. "Love you, Juba. I'm not scared about marrying you. But, this other, it—I don't know—what if we—"

He kissed her, wanting to love all the doubts away. She had to believe in him. She had to go with him. They could be married soon and then they'd light out . . .

CHAPTER 6

The slaves stood in line, waiting to have their cotton bags weighed. Reuben nudged Juba with his elbow. "Ya heard?" He spoke under the commotion of shuffling feet and the slaves' grunts and groans as bags were lifted onto the scales. Pilcher's commands echoed in the big shed.

"Heard what?" Juba put up a hand to shield his mouth.

"Massah's bought another cotton plantation somewheres else."

"Yeah?"

"Think some of us are staying here and some of us are going along to work it."

"Which ones?"

"Don't know."

"When?"

"Don't know that either. Pretty soon, though. Saw those two good-for-nothing snitches over there in the corner fixing up a wagon yesterday to hold twenty slaves."

They pushed along, dragging their bags toward the head of the line.

Juba scratched his chin. "Must be down the road a piece, else field hands would walk."

Reuben reached up, pretending to scratch his head. His arm hid his mouth. "Heard Massah's bought three more spans of mules to go along too."

Juba felt his stomach clench. "I gotta know."

"Can't do nothing about it."

"I just gotta know, that's all."

"What if it's us, Juba? What if we're the ones?"

"Tha's why I gotta know."

"Wanna ask Pilcher?"

Juba snorted.

All the slaves' bags of cotton were weighed. Juba had picked thirty pounds more than his quota. He rubbed the ball of his thumb over the three pennies he received and listened to the scolding Pilcher gave those who had not reached their quota. Some of them would face a beating. Juba knew old Joss's rheumatism was hurting him bad. He could hardly walk. Couldn't Pilcher understand an old man like Joss did the best he could? Naw, Pilcher didn't care.

Pilcher's voice rang out. "Now listen up, boys. I ain't gonna tell this only once. Master Robinson's bought another plantation. Long ways from here. We're moving. All of us. He grinned, "You got a little missy on the side, in the bushes somewhere? Better tell her, bye-bye. Now get out of here. Got lots to do before morning. Getting ready to move."

Juba whispered to Reuben, "Then who's taking our places here?"

As if he'd heard the question, Pilcher shouted, "Fresh load of hands coming in tomorrow. Clear out yer cabins."

Juba and Meggie sat whispering in the weeds behind the slave shacks. "We're loading up tonight, Meggie. I'm supposed to go with the rest of 'em in the morning. If only we'd known . . . You and me, we gotta run away tonight!"

"But, Juba—"

"I know, honey, but we don't have a choice now. It's either strike out or—"

Tears ran down Meggie's cheeks. "Going off together, you'n'me. I haven't hardly had time to think about it. And you said we'd get married first and—"

"Can't help that now. We can get married along the way. Please, Meg. Oh, please."

Meggie was silent.

Juba waited impatiently. He fisted his hands. He scratched his head. He knuckled his knees. "Just you'n'me, Meg. That's all we got. We have to make our own decisions. What's best for us."

Meggie sniffed and pressed her palms over her eyes.

Juba said, "Meggie? I only got a few more minutes. Just say yes, Meg. Please, Meg. I gotta go. Don't want no trouble with Pilcher tonight."

Meggie lifted her face to him. "I love you, Juba. Want you to know that. Gotta be by myself a little while. Gotta think—"

"Sure, Meg, sure. Now, remember what I said? Remember the signal?"

Meggie nodded. "Juba?"

"Yes, honey?"

She shrugged. "Guess it's nothing. I'm just scared, that's all."

Juba rose. "That's my girl." He gave her a quick kiss on the cheek. "Pilcher's hurrying us hard to get everything packed before dark." He bounded away.

CHAPTER 7

The light in Master Robinson's room had gone out an hour ago. And Pilcher was at the other end of the plantation engrossed in a poker game, a jug of white lightning by his elbow. When Reuben brought the mules in from the far field, he told Juba that Pilcher would probably be at it most of the night. Reuben silently touched Juba's arm, his dark eyes mirroring depths of friendship and a wordless goodbye. Reuben knew. Reuben would not tell.

Juba crouched in the shadows beside the smokehouse. An owl swooped low, not twenty feet away, and snatched a mouse from the grass. The owl rose noiselessly. Juba wished he could be that quiet. Wished he had wings to whisk himself away.

In another hour, the first bright light of the rising moon would begin to silhouette the distant trees. Time to move fast. Time to carry out his plans. His heart accelerated. He swallowed. Would Meggie be ready?

Juba crawled through the weeds on hands and knees, silently counting each slave shack as he passed. He came to Meggie's and Granny Em's. How many slave children had Granny Em been mamma to? She'd cuddled him when his own mamma was sold and done the same for most of the rest, he guessed. Wiping noses and telling stories to those too young to work in the fields. Sewing on buttons and patches for the others. He'd miss Granny Em and he couldn't even tell her goodbye. Dasn't dare.

Juba spread his hand on the still warm, splintery boards. He curled his fingers into a fist and thumped the wall in the prescribed spot. Once, pause, twice, pause, once again. His legs cramped and he sat back to ease the muscles. He wiped the sweat from his face. He waited. There was no response. His brow furrowed. Again, he thumped the wall.

Meggie appeared around the corner of the shack. "Shh, Juba," she whispered. "You'll wake everybody."

Juba grinned. Excitement and joy filled his chest. He curved his arm forward in an arc. "Let's go." He slid ahead on his knees, then looked back, frowning. "Where's your bundle?"

Meggie crossed her arms over her chest. "I'm not—"

"What?"

She scooted forward and touched his ear with her lips. "I'm not going, Juba."

"You got to, Meggie!"

"Shh. No—I'm staying here."

"Meggie, no, no."

"Shh."

"But, Meg, you said—"

"I can't. I'm scared. What if—"

"I'll protect you. Promised I would."

"I can't, Juba. I just can't."

"Don't let me down, Meggie. Not now. Thought we had this all—"

"Oh, oh, oh, Juba." Sobbing, Meggie threw her arms around him and buried her face in his chest. Her tears washed the front of his shirt. "Love you, Juba. Love you so."

"Then come. Quick, grab something. Gotta go."

Meggie rose on tiptoe and pressed her face close to his. "No, Juba. Love you forever." She kissed him and slipped away, barefoot and silent, into the gloom.

Juba stood, too shocked to move. An errant breeze dried Meggie's tears on his cheeks. Her kiss lingered on his lips. "Meggie?" he whispered. There was no reply.

He could not stand here, a target for Pilcher's scouts. But Meggie was his life. He could not leave without her. All the joy of a few moments earlier evaporated. Juba's disappointment was a stone in his chest. He took one indecisive step forward and looked back. If he did not run now, he might not ever have another chance. Meggie?

Tears raced down his cheeks. He could not go without her. He had to. No, not without Meggie. No, no! But he must.

Juba knotted a fist and slammed the air. Oh Lawd! Surely, he could feel his heart tearing in two. The pain of Meggie's desertion made him gasp. He fell to his knees, arms outstretched, and silently screamed his despair. *Meggie!* Then, with a firm grip on his bundle, he stumbled away from the slave shacks, away from Meggie, away from the only life he had ever known.

Every three or four steps, Juba stopped to listen, eyes wide as he peered into the darkness. He crouched and darted from bush to bush. At the mule pen, he climbed the fence and murmured for Jack. The mule's hooves made muffled slapping sounds in the churned-up dirt of the corral as Jack came near and nuzzled Juba's hand. "Good fella, Jack," he whispered.

Something caught his eye, a movement, beyond the pen. He waited, heart drumming. Were his eyes playing tricks on him? He blinked and stared at a dark form. Jack's breath whuffled against his sleeve as he rubbed his head on Juba's arm. A breeze sprang up and the dark form, beyond the pen, changed shape. Branches waved and bent. Juba sagged with relief.

Slowly, carefully, Juba led Jack through the gate. At the spot where the gate usually squeaked when someone shut it, he paused. He held his breath and moved the gate, inch by inch, toward the latch post. *Come on, come on*, he scolded himself. *You're taking too long*. Jack pushed against him, and the gate rammed the post with a thunk. Sweat broke out on Juba's brow. He fumbled with the hook, dropped it, and finally drove the point of it into the eyebolt.

Juba led the mule along a path at the edge of a cotton field. "Gotta hurry, ole mule," he whispered. "You'n'me's taking a trip." His voice broke on the last word. If only Meggie had . . . He turned, half expecting to glimpse her running after him. But he saw only the dim shadows of bushes and roof lines of buildings, now far across the field.

Juba urged Jack into the brush that outlined the river. Thorns dragged at the legs of his overalls and scratched the mule's hide. The marshy ground sucked at the mule's hooves, leaving deep pockets half filled with water.

In spite of the gloom, Juba found a trail where deer had floundered through the brush. He whispered, "C'mon, Jack. We gotta move." A twig cracked. He flinched. Those dark shapes over there. Surely they were—blackened stumps. A low-slung branch slapped him in the face. He hunched down over Jack's back. As he passed beneath the trees, Spanish moss combed through his hair. His shoulders were so tense that his back muscles ached.

Now, the air reverberated with a shout, a rifle shot, and the baying of hounds.

"Oh Lawd, gotta get in the river, mule. Get in the river!"

Another shot rang out. Juba felt the searing jolt in his thigh before he heard the rifle report. The mule coughed, stumbled, and went to its knees. Juba barely had time to grab an overhead branch and hold on as the mule rolled away from under him. Its hind legs flailed the air. One hoof grazed his ankle, peeling back the skin.

Juba lay beside the tree, gasping. Terror raced through his nerves. The wound in his thigh began to burn. He heard the mule thrash through the brush as it slid down an incline, a splash when it hit the water. Juba's heartbeat thundered in his ears. The woods were silent.

"Killed your own mule, Massah Robinson," Juba whispered, "you white devil." His pulse pounded like a hammer. He couldn't swallow. They'd be on him in a minute. Better get to the river. He felt about for a stick and levered himself to his feet. His pant leg stuck to the wound. Sticky blood slithered down his leg. The hurt made tears spring to his eyes. His breath rasped, his chest so tight he thought it would burst.

Something crashed through the thicket behind him. He froze. A frightened deer raced past, leaping wildly through the night. The moon momentarily reflected in its black eye, its pale body a blur.

Sliding, stifling groans, stumbling, Juba eased into the river. He heard the men shout to one another. "This way, Eb. Come this way." That was Pilcher's voice, leading the hunt. Had Pilcher known about his escape the whole time? Had Pilcher's stool pigeons been watching?

Just before Juba ducked under the water, the tepid river rolling over his head, he heard the hounds. The yelping, baying hounds, after their prey. After a runaway slave.

The water stung Juba's wound. It shocked and buoyed him into action. *Please, Lawd, no 'gators prowling tonight.* He swam to the middle of the river and dived as his pursuers reached the bank, holding their lanterns high to scan the water. Juba broke the surface to draw in air and heard a horse nicker, a man curse. The light swept past him.

"Damn nigger, took my best mule too."

"Thought you gave it to him, Eb."

"Well, I did. But the nigger belonged to me, didn't it? So I figure anything he had was mine too."

"He's drowned now, Eb. That's for certain. 'Gators'll get 'im. Lost 'em both, I reckon. Tough luck."

"Yeah, but I'll get another one next week."

"Oh? You going to the slave auction over at Bethel?"

"Naw, I was talking about buying another mule from McKindrick. He's got the best stock. Y'know, that nigger mightta got away after all. I ain't gonna stumble around in the dark. If he's out there, I'll get the bounty hunter to bring him in." Their voices faded as they walked away. Darkness swallowed the lantern light. A dog bayed once, followed by the sharp faraway command of its master.

Careful not to splash, Juba swam silently to the opposite side of the river. A fallen cypress lay at the water's edge. He worked around it and struggled up the bank. His leg throbbed. Trembling and panting, he felt for his poke. It was gone, lying in the mud where the mule tumbled into the river. He stood on shaking legs. This was no place to rest, still within shouting distance of the plantation. Within jaw reach of a 'gator.

The moon rose above the trees. Its light was small help. Juba was surrounded by brush and thickets of thorn-tipped bushes. He held his arms up for protection as he stumbled along. His face was scratched and bleeding. Vines tangled around his legs and tripped him.

Three times he fell, knocking the breath out of him. He crawled over protruding tree roots and rotted logs. He sank to his ankles in the marshy ground. A moon-silvered branch, broken from a tree by the wind, lay across some low bushes. Juba snatched it up. The stick steadied him as he plunged through undergrowth and slogged around mud holes.

He knew he should be watching out for pursuers. But how could he be alert to suspicious movement or noise, when he could not see ten feet in front of him? When he made enough racket himself for all but the deaf to hear? He had lost all sense of direction. Exhausted, his muscles quivering, he hobbled past giant-girthed trees until the gray mist of dawn swirled around him and the ache in his thigh demanded rest.

Juba's legs collapsed and tumbled him to the ground. He had no idea how far he had come or where he was. Hunched over, wanting to cry, he sat, panting, until his pounding heart settled down. Wearily, he floundered to the water in the first light and washed the wound in his thigh. Soon he must find a yarrow plant and lay the leaves over the wound and gather willow bark to bind it.

A cluster of woodbine vines trailed up the trunk of a gnarled oak tree. One side of the trunk curved like a wing-tipped chair. Juba crawled through the vines and settled into the curve. He brought his knees up to his chest and hugged himself with his hands in his armpits. Did he dare to close his eyes? He could not go on without rest. There had been a twist of jerky and a slab of bread in his poke. Best not to think of it now. Maybe later, he could find some berries. Could he snare a rabbit? Maybe, but it would take precious time. He swallowed. And although tremors occasionally ran the length of his body, exhaustion pulled him into sleep.

CHAPTER 8

A twig crackled. Blackbirds resting in the trees whirred into flight. Juba opened his eyes. He heard the rustle of someone moving through the brush. Silently, ever so slowly, Juba sat up. He set his jaw against a groan as he moved his stiffened legs.

Not a hundred feet away, a man spoke. "He ain't anywhere's around."

"How d'you know?" another voice said.

"'Cause you can smell 'em. Ain't you ever noticed?"

"Naw, never did."

"Well, you ain't got much of a smeller then. I can smell a nigger a mile away."

Juba tried to clamp his hand over his face to smother the sound of his breathing. But he was shaking so hard he could not hold it there. His heart began to hammer again. It seemed to vibrate through his whole body right into the ground. Two men out there. He recognized the voice of the one who claimed to smell slaves. Peel. Hezekiah Peel, the bounty hunter.

Juba knew Peel struck fear in the heart of every slave for miles around. Peel could sneak up behind a man, shoot him to disable him, then tell the massah he caught the slave trying to run away. Peel was a rich man. Peel, the bounty hunter, rich and hated.

"Tell you what," Peel was saying, "you make a big circle around that way and I'll sneak off this way and we'll meet by that cypress knee just yonder."

"But, if he ain't anywhere's near here, why—"

"Quit whining and get on with it."

"But which cypress knee, Peel. There's a bunch of 'em."

"You didn't watch where I pointed. That big one stickin' up. The size of yer two legs. Now, hurry up."

Juba heard the partner move away, heard him thrash through bushes, splash in shallow water. Then, a scuffling sound made his heart stop. It was Peel, pushing into the thicket on the other side of Juba's tree. He heard Peel chuckle to himself as he followed the progression of the other man through his sights. "Just light enough to track ya," he mumbled to himself. "Idiot. Think I'd share a nigger bounty with you?"

Juba thought he would be sick. He swallowed frantically to control a tickle in his throat that threatened to build toward a cough. His wounded thigh tightened in a cramp. He was dizzy. Escape plans flashed across his brain, none of them workable. Every second brought more daylight. If Peel should glance his way . . .

The blast of the rifle made Juba cry out in terror. His scream was drowned out by Peel's whoop of triumph. As Juba cowered in the curve of the tree trunk, he heard Peel fight free of the thicket. Juba chanced a look and saw Peel's back disappear into a stand of tall marsh grass.

Terror propelled Juba from behind the oak tree. He clawed at the woodbine. His trembling hands and quaking knees carried him in an awkward crabwalk to the shelter of a magnolia tree. *Gotta keep moving,* he told himself. *No use making it easy for Peel.* Trying to take deep, even breaths, he crawled farther away to a large cypress and peeked around it. He saw Peel count money taken from his partner's clothes. Peel slipped a gold watch from the man's pocket and put it in his own.

Keep moving, keep moving. Don't stay here, run. Get behind those trees over yonder. Whatcha waiting for? He did not know. Something held him back, goaded him. It was wicked what Peel was doing. *Of course, it was wicked. But, don't be a fool, Juba, just run. No. Somebody ought to stop Peel. What makes you think you can do it? I gotta try. No, he'll kill you. Gotta try. Gonna die anyway. Whatsa use?* He could never run far enough or fast enough. Peel would find him. *Gotta try*, he whispered to himself. *Gotta try*.

As precious seconds ticked away, Juba felt along the ground for a heavy stick. His hands closed around a sturdy limb with a knot on the end of it. He wiped the sweat from his eyes and crept silently toward Peel. Two steps—three—four—five—

Juba stood directly behind Peel. He raised the stick. Peel must have sensed the motion. He whirled around. Juba brought the stick down with all his strength. He stared straight into Peel's astonished eyes. The stick cracked against Peel's skull. Peel's gun roared. The ball sang past Juba's ear and buried itself with a thunk in the trunk of a tree behind him. In slow motion, Peel began to fall. A buckled knee, an arm thrust awkwardly, shoulders slumped, chin bobbing on his chest, at last he lay sprawled at Juba's feet.

Deafened by the blast of the gun, Juba stood there, panting and shaking. Sweat ran over his pink scar, down his face, and soaked his shirt. He looked at Peel. Peel did not move. Juba hunkered down and gazed at Peel's body. Had he killed him? What was this numbness in his soul? This void? As if he could kill a man, shrug his shoulders, and go on his way. Just like Peel.

Peel's fingers twitched. A moan escaped from his lips. Juba fell back on his haunches. Fear gripped him once more. He shivered. A voice shouted in his head: *Get outta here!*

Juba stood and scuffed the dirt. He leaned forward, took a halting step, and looked back. Peel's leg moved. Peel had on high laced boots. Juba said, "Huh!" He fumbled with the laces. They tangled in knots before he finally ripped them free. Gingerly, he touched Peel's hands. The feel of the man's flesh made his stomach turn. Peel groaned.

The laces tangled again in Juba's trembling grasp. *Hurry up with it and get out of here*. He turned Peel over, pressed his wrists together, and cinched the laces around them.

Peel began to kick. Juba jumped back. He almost stumbled over the fallen partner. Partner of the bounty hunter, shot without a qualm. Juba mashed his lips together. He ripped the laces from the dead man's boots, grabbed Peel's flailing legs, and knelt on them to keep them still. He wrapped the laces around several times and tied them in knots. Peel began to mumble.

What if the laces didn't hold? As Peel bucked and groaned, Juba unfastened Peel's belt. He glanced at the buckle. Fancy. Only the best for the rich bounty hunter. Juba slipped the belt underneath

Peel's arms and dragged him to a small tree. He fastened the belt around the backside of the tree, then picked up a stick and wedged it between the rough bark and the belt. Peel was cursing now.

One more thing to do. One more, before Juba's shaking legs collapsed, before he lost his resolve. Juba grabbed Peel's rifle and limped around the tree to face him. He pointed the rifle at Peel's chest. He ached to pull the trigger. It was his right, wasn't it? To avenge all the crimes Peel had committed. "I could kill you," he said. His ears still rang. His voice seemed to come from the bottom of a barrel. "But, I'm no killer. All I want is my *freedom*."

He looked square into Peel's eyes and stared down the hatred he saw there. His fingers felt pinched and he became aware of his awful grip on the rifle. He should take it with him. It could come in mighty handy. But into his mind flashed images of the way Peel had used it and he almost dropped it. It seemed to burn his palm. Could Peel's wickedness have seeped into the rifle? Then it would be tainted, tainted with the same evil Peel's hands had done.

Juba shuddered and held it away from his body as if it were contaminated, then he hoisted it above his head and threw it as hard as he could. Somewhere, out of sight, they heard it slam into a tree and break apart. Peel would never kill another man with that rifle.

Juba's gaze fell on Peel's slain partner. He grabbed the man under the arms, dragged him and laid him gently in front of Peel.

Peel's eyes widened. He stammered, "Wha—what you doing?"

Juba did not answer. There was blood on his hands. He bent near and wiped the blood on Peel's clothes. Peel twisted and strained against his bonds. He screamed, "You cussed nigger. You cussed nigger!" He tried to spit on Juba, but the spittle dribbled down his own chin.

Juba turned and limped away. After he had gone fifty feet, his stomach revolted and he retched, holding onto a tree lest his trembling legs give way. Peel's screams and threats followed him as he set a stumbling course around briar patches and over fallen logs. "You'll hang for this, nigger. I'll get you yet. I ain't gonna die out here."

Juba kept on, his back straight and chin determined. By the time he had put a couple of briar patches between himself and Peel, the muscles in his legs no longer felt like dishwater. Today, for a while, he had looked hate in the eye and conquered it. Removed from the ordeal a little, he wondered how he had found the strength to do it.

Don't get to feeling uppity now, Juba. 'Bout the time you think you're home free, Peel'll grab the back of your neck. Just the thought made him turn and look all around, the fear nagging him again.

He knew Peel would get loose. Anybody with half a brain would figure out how to untie the knots behind his back. It would take him a while and he might have to work at it mighty hard. Well, it was about time Peel didn't have everything so easy.

Eyes wide open as he trudged along, Juba whispered, "Wanted to kill him. Wanted to so bad. It would have been easy." He wondered at the resolve that had kept him from it.

He paused and listened. He could no longer hear Peel's screams. With a glance in the general direction of the plantation, he mumbled, "You ain't got me yet." He let a grin tease the corners of his lips. "I'm still *free*, ya hear?" He would have added a few more words, but Meggie's face came to mind and choked up his throat.

It was slow going among the ferns and vines and brush. Juba's feet sunk deeper and deeper into the muck. As he pulled one foot out of the mud, the other foot plunged in farther. The trees formed a canopy that shut out the very air. The atmosphere turned oppressive. It smelled of decay.

He took another step and abruptly sank to his knees in tea-colored water. Something bumped against his leg. He started. What was it? His heart began a slow heavy rhythm as if it too were weighed down. The swamp grew darker. A dirty twilight pervaded the area. He looked up, searching the canopy for a glimpse of the sky. Instead, he caught the gaze of a cottonmouth inches above his head, dangling from a tree. He struggled forward. Underwater vines clung to his legs like shackles. He could not get clear of them and dragged them along.

Another faltering step and a moment later, murky water lapped at his chest. He reached down, trying to free his feet, lost his balance, and fell backwards. The water closed over his head. In panic, he floundered and writhed as more vines wrapped around his arms and clung to his neck. Eyes wide open, he saw leaves and twigs floating on the water, worms wriggling suspended, and insects flitting across the oily surface. Finally, he got his feet under him and rose above it. Choking and gagging, he gasped for air. Slimy mud stung his eyes. He shook his head and swiped at the mud.

The familiar slave mentality of helplessness taunted him and made a hollow in his stomach. It chanted: *Give up. You can't make it.*

You're gonna fail. He'd drown here. This would be the end of him. He should never have left the plantation. He was a fool to try.

The old man's words, spoken beside the Pearl River, came back to him: "Sometimes the fox outruns the hounds. Reckon you might." But the old man didn't know. He'd never been a slave. It was too hard. He couldn't . . .

A black snake swam alongside Juba. Startled, he jumped. The snake passed him and veered away. One of his feet slipped on slime. The water rose to his chin. He shuddered and heard himself panting from the breath he hadn't known he was holding.

Then he saw it, swimming across from the other side. Only the eyes were visible above the water. Alligator! Come to close his sharp-toothed maw around Juba's body. Come to drag him under the water. Come to drown him and never let him go.

CHAPTER 9

Frozen with terror, Juba watched the alligator inch closer and closer. A surge of rage made him clench his fists. He bellowed, "Nooo!" He slapped the water with both hands, stirring up a muddy froth and splashing it high. A scream tore at his throat. He raised his legs as far as they would go, pulling on the vines that bound his feet. The movement dislodged some of the tangled stems. He thrashed about. The alligator, in relentless pursuit, was almost upon him. "No, no!" he yelled again. Desperate, with slim chance of escape, he clambered onto a cypress knee, dragging the vines behind him. He lunged for a limb hanging over the water and caught it with thumb and three fingers. "Dear Lawd," he cried out as his hand began to slip.

The alligator's snout grazed his foot at the very moment he swung his other hand up and secured the limb in his grasp. "Get out of here," he yelled. "Leave me alone!" As if in reply, the alligator's cavernous mouth opened wider. Juba managed to hook one arm over the limb and, dangling within inches of death, stared into the beast's throat.

Minutes dragged by like hours and finally the alligator slipped away in search of other prey. The muscles in Juba's arms trembled with fatigue as he worked his way off the limb and into the crotch of the tree. His hands could scarcely grip the bark as he searched in the dim light for more predators. Behind the tree was a soggy knoll, a curtain of vines and higher ground leading to a cluster of sweet gum trees. Still trembling, Juba climbed out of the cypress, splashed through shallow water alive with gnats and stumbled onto the knoll. He was lost. His wound throbbed. He was weak from hunger and fright. "Oh Lawd," he cried, "why'd you ever let me run away from the plantation?" Beatings and unrelenting toil were better than starving, lost and alone, and succumbing to the terror of an alligator's jaws.

Slowly, reason asserted itself. It had been his own idea to run away. And wasn't freedom a dream dearer than life? He labored onto still higher ground.

Night came and through an opening in the trees, he glimpsed the rising moon. He watched it climb and a saying whispered among the slaves came to him: "Look for the drinking gourd." How could he have forgotten? There it was: the North Star shining like a diamond at the tip of the Little Dipper's handle. The drinking gourd, pointing the way north. Juba knelt in thankfulness, sank to the ground and slept.

The sun had not yet risen on the following morning when Juba limped through the misty shadows to a willow tree, peeled away some bark and applied it to his wound. A strip from the hem of his overalls kept it in place.

He worked the map out of his back pocket. It was still wet from the swamp. He had to be careful as he unfolded it and straightened the soggy creases. As the sky grew lighter, he frowned and studied it. Slogging through the swamp had thrown him off course. He nodded to himself. The swamp was on his right. He needed to veer left. It was peaceful here. Birds trilled in the trees. Squirrels chased one another from limb to limb. Juba's stomach growled. He was so hungry he could almost eat a squirrel raw. *Best get moving, Juba. And don't get lulled into not watching your step or looking out for bounty hunters.*

He took up a stick and dug a couple of dandelions from the moist earth. They were a far cry from a tasty mess of collard greens and he grimaced as he began to chew. He ate it all, leaves and root. One of Granny Em's sayings came to mind. When he was about six years old, she had told him and the other little boys who crowded around her waiting for a story, that dandelion, in a pinch, would keep their teeth from falling out. How they had giggled and nudged one another, mimicking toothless old Amos who had been, to their minds, at least a hundred.

Juba leaned on his stick with every step and threaded his way through the brush. He came to a river. It had to be the still winding Pearl, he was sure of it. Ahead, he saw a good-sized woods of loblolly pines. Better walk over there. Better get smart. Long ways to go if he intended to stay free.

Hours later, gnats swarmed around him in the heat. The river made a wide sweep. Juba limped around the corner and stopped in his tracks. "Huh!" He dropped to the ground. Panic skittered his pulse. Not three hundred yards off, at the bend in the river, stood a farmhouse. A corn patch rustled in the breeze. Beyond, Juba saw a field of turnips.

As he watched, a woman came out of the house and banged the screen door. She began to hang clothes on a line to dry. Juba shifted his gaze and caught sight of a man unhitching a team from a plow. A waggy-tailed dog stood nearby. Juba heard the clink of the harness and clatter of the double tree. Faintly, carried over the field, came the voice of the man urging the horses forward out of the traces.

Juba eyed the spotted dog. If that dog caught a whiff of Juba, he was a goner. But the corn and turnip patches set his mouth to watering. He couldn't go much farther without food. Maybe if he holed up until dark . . .

Juba's head snapped up at the woman's screech. He saw her run from the clothesline. A three-hundred-pound sow lumbered after her. "Herb! Help, help! Get her away from me, Herb!" The woman ran around the house with the sow in pursuit. The man slapped the horses on their rumps and headed them in the direction of the barn, then joined the chase. The barking dog rushed after them all, caught up with the sow and nipped at her side.

Juba limped as fast as his leg would let him into the stand of corn and began to rip ears from the stalks. In his hurry, more cobs slid from his arms than he could hold on to. He stuffed a few down his shirt front and was about to head back to the woods when he heard snorting and snuffling, and saw the corn stalks ahead of him shake violently. He glimpsed a flash of blue. It was the woman, still yelling, "Herb, Herb, she'll ruin the corn!"

The sow was now in the lead and coming straight at him. Juba flung himself to one side. The sow thrashed past him, the dog nipping at her tail. The woman, coming in third, tripped and fell headlong beside Juba. Spitting dirt, she raised her head and saw him. Her scream reverberated in his ears. He lunged to his feet and tore through the corn, hoping desperately he was running toward the river. Dried razor-sharp leaves scratched his face as he crashed from row to row and finally emerged from the patch.

Somewhere in the middle of the patch the woman still screamed and sobbed. Juba risked a glance backward and saw the man running through the adjacent field with a rifle in his hand.

Juba scuttled down the riverbank, his injured thigh protesting all the way. Just as he jumped into the water, the man's rifle went off over his head. He ducked under and held his breath until his lungs would surely burst. As he cautiously breached the surface, he saw the farmer and wife a considerable distance downstream, arguing.

The woman shook her finger in her husband's face. "I know what I saw, Herb. He warn't two feet from me. It was a black boy as sure as shooting. An' he was sitting there right in the middle of the corn patch."

The farmer aimed tobacco juice toward the river. "Now, that don't make no sense. What's a black boy doing sitting in our corn patch?"

"How do I know? But there he was."

"Looks to me, Hildie, you just landed too hard and it scrambled your brains fer a while."

"Well, if you didn't see him, what'd you shoot for?"

"Why, 'cause you yelled 'shoot,' that's what for."

A chuckle bubbled in Juba's throat. He clamped his lips shut and did not wait to hear the rest of the tale. He sank beneath the surface.

Hidden in a clump of cattails on the far side of the river, he watched the sow amble from the corn patch, the dog alongside. Shoulder to shoulder, like two friends, they headed for the farm buildings. The farmer and his wife still argued as they entered the house. The screen door slammed behind them.

An hour later and several miles farther on, Juba sat beneath the shade of a willow tree. He reached inside his shirt and pulled out the remaining corncobs. They had saved his life. He could go on now. He could walk a few more miles.

The memory of the astonished woman so close to him in the corn patch pulled a grin at the corners of his mouth. "Didn't mean to scare you, ma'am," he murmured. "Thanks for the—" He was asleep before he could finish the sentence. A magpie, swinging from a branch of the willow scolded him, cocked its head and flew away.

CHAPTER 10

It was a road of sorts. Saw grass and tules were fast reclaiming it. Every time it rained, a little more of the clay on the shoulders sloughed off into the ditches. Juba jogged along, leaping over washouts, keeping near the encroaching brush in case he should have to duck out of sight. His ears were tuned to the slightest noise. His eyes continually probed for someone hiding in the bushes, for someone waiting to pounce on him.

Up ahead, a couple of hundred feet, he heard a commotion. He rounded a bend and saw a wagon of corn fodder overturned where the ditch was steep. An elderly farmer's mule was tangled in the traces. The more the farmer railed at the mule, the more it floundered and the wagon slid down hill.

Juba crouched behind a bush and watched. He'd best get over there and help that old man. *Yeah, and have him yell at me same's he's yelling at the mule.* Well, wouldn't be the first time a farmer yelled at him. No, and once he got a good look at Juba, he'd start asking questions and then Juba'd get turned in for being a runaway. *Sure, boy, just hop right over there and jump into the fire.*

As Juba argued with his conscience, the farmer lost his footing and fell. The agitated mule slid sideways, dragging the wagon toward the old man. Juba sprang up, raced to the mule and grabbed his halter. "Whoa, whoa there."

The farmer struggled to his feet. "Where'd you come from?"

"I—I was just passing by, massah."

The farmer squinted at him and tried to brush some of the mud from his clothes. He studied Juba's face. "Passing by, huh? Twenty miles from nowhere and just passing by." His mouth turned up in a funny little twitch.

"Uh—yes, massah."

"Suppose you got your pass in your pocket?"

Juba tensed. "Uh—guess I—" He shifted his weight. He could easily outrun this old man if he had to.

The farmer's mouth twitched again. "Yep," he said. "Well, I'm mighty glad you came along. This consarned mule was fixing to bury me."

"Yes, massah."

"You go ahead and pull him forward a bit. See if we can untangle this mess."

"Yes, massah."

As Juba began to coax the mule forward, they heard several horsemen pounding up the trail. The old farmer glanced up, shielded his eyes and swore. "Speculator," he said and spat. He grabbed a straw hat from under the seat of his wagon and jammed it onto Juba's head. "See to the mule."

The riders pulled up in a clatter of hooves. The speculator spoke. "Morning, old feller."

The farmer hitched his overall straps. "Morning."

"We're looking for a runaway slave. About fits the description of the one you got there. Is that your nigger?"

Juba held his breath. He lifted the mule's front hoof and poked at it.

"'Course, it's my nigger," the farmer said. "Bought him years ago." He dug his thumbs into his overall pockets, lowered his head, and took a step toward the speculator. Juba's heart lurched as the old man's voice thundered, "Just because I got one nigger don't mean he ain't mine. Not every man in this here country's so rich he can afford a hundred. This'n's mine and I aim to keep him."

Juba stole a glance at the farmer. The old man turned on him. "Quit yer gawking and git them rocks outta that mule's hoof."

"Yassah."

The speculator pressed on. "You see any runaways last couple days?"

"Nope."

"The one we're looking for has a price on him. Two hundred for the man that turns him in."

Juba closed his eyes. Look at what helping had got him. The old man would not resist accepting that much money. Defeat sat on his chest.

The old man's quick retort startled him. "Told ya I ain't seen a runaway."

The speculator dismounted. "Mind if I look at your nigger?"

The old man shrugged. "Look if you want but I ain't selling."

The speculator approached Juba. He pinched his arm in a vice-like grip. "Stand up, nigger."

Juba kept his eyes downcast.

"What's yer name, boy?"

"A-Abe, massah."

"That the name you've always had?"

"Yassah."

"What's your master's name, boy?"

Juba swallowed. The old man stomped over. "See here, you trying to scare the daylights outta my nigger? Name's Humbolt, if it's any a'your business." He waved his arms. "Now be off with you. We got work to do."

The speculator wrenched Juba's chin. "Look at me," he ordered." He put his finger to his lips and scowled at Juba. "You got a brother, boy? Down the track a-piece? Belong to Master Robinson?"

"R—Robinson? No, suh." Juba locked his knees to still their trembling.

"Dead ringer," the speculator said. He gave Juba's arm a shove and backed away. "Dead ringer," he said again. He mounted his horse and the other riders turned. As an afterthought, the speculator called over his shoulder, "Harboring runaways's a crime, you know, old man."

The farmer shouted back, "That's why I only got me one nigger. One's enough trouble."

Juba let down the mule's muddy foot and stood beside it. He buried his face in its neck and waited for his body to quit shaking. When he looked up, the farmer was sitting on the upturned side of the wagon, spinning one of the wheels that stuck up in the air. He grinned at Juba." Reckon we got by there pretty good, eh?" He jerked his chin in the direction of the departed speculator. "Them fools." He jumped off the wagon. "Let's see if we can git this wagon back on the track and the fodder loaded. Tie my mule to that bush yonder for the time being."

As they worked, Juba said, "Thank you, Massah, for saving my life."

"Warn't nothing," the farmer said. "Besides, I didn't want those buggers poking around anyhow." He trotted back into the ditch and dug into the spilled pile of corn fodder. He pulled out a gallon jug of moonshine wrapped in a gunnysack. "Whee, this'n's all right. Got ten of 'em in there if they're not broken. Worth a couple dollars a piece, by cracky. Made it myself. Tell ya something, mule can carry 'bout four bushel corn off the field. But he can carry more'n four times that in the jug. Offer you some, but I got a customer waiting up the road apiece." His mouth twitched.

Juba tried to be respectful, to keep his gaze on the ground. But a laugh started low in his chest and bubbled into his throat. He couldn't stop it. He looked up. The farmer nodded. His mouth twitched again. Juba laughed until tears ran down his cheeks. The farmer sat down in the track and snickered with him.

"Here," the farmer held out his bandana handkerchief. "Wipe the mud off your face. I'm particular to keep my niggers clean."

Juba did as he was told. The farmer squinted at him. "Got quite a scar there on your face, ain't ya?"

"Yassah."

"Reckon the speculator was looking for that scar? Couldn't see it, plastered with mud."

The two of them finished reloading the wagon's cargo. They buried the moonshine deep out of sight. The farmer climbed onto the wagon seat. "Gotta make up for wasted time now."

Juba stepped away from the wagon. "Mighty thankful, Massah. I best be walking in the trees now." He began to lope to the far side of the track.

"Hey! Where you going?" the farmer called. "Come back here."

The old familiar fear squeezed Juba's chest. Had he gauged the farmer wrong? He paused, his legs tensed to run. "Massah?"

"No use walking when you can ride. I'll take you as far as the bend in the road and dump you off. Folks'll think you're mine as long as you ride in the back of the wagon. You know where you are, don't you?"

"No, suh, not for sure."

"You're on the Natchez Trace, what's left of it, anyhow. You fixing to head north, ain'tcha?"

"Yassah."

"Well, track angles off up here a ways. C'mon."

Juba pursed his lips in a silent "whew." He climbed into the back of the wagon and sat with his legs dangling over the edge. The farmer turned around. Juba saw the now familiar twitch in his face. "Besides, you're still wearing my hat. Git up, old mule."

They bounced and jiggled no more than two miles when the old farmer said, "Whoa."

Juba twisted around, "Time to get off, massah?"

"No. I got something to tell you. Come on up here so we can talk."

Juba jumped off the back of the wagon and climbed up beside the old farmer. "Yes, massah?"

"And don't call me 'massah.'"

"Yes, mas—uh, suh."

"That's better. You see, I don't believe in anybody being a master over somebody else. And I'm gonna tell you why." The old farmer tickled the reins over the mule's back. The wagon wheels groaned and began to roll. Juba waited patiently. All of a sudden the farmer said "whoa" again. He pulled to a stop. His mouth made the quirk that was becoming familiar. "Get down," he said.

Bewildered, Juba said, "Massah? Er—suh?"

"Come around to this side and drive my mule. That makes it look like—well, you know what it looks like. You're doing the work and I'm just riding along."

Juba grinned and jumped down. "Yassah."

Once more on their way, the old farmer began to tell his tale. "I was a little boy, mebbe five or six. My mamma died. My pa hired a housekeeper 'cause they was five of us younguns, two sisters and two brothers 'sides me. Well, as things happen, my pa married the housekeeper. Now then, she warn't housekeeper no more." He smacked his hands together. "She was boss."

Juba glanced at the old farmer. There was the quirk in his mouth but his eyes reflected smoldering coals.

"So, here we was, my brothers and sisters. Mamma gone to heaven, Pa out in the fields all day, and we was home with the boss." He nudged Juba with an elbow. "I said boss, but I meant somethin' else. She warn't a man, so I can't call her a master, but she warn't no lady, you can be sure."

The old farmer reached out as the wagon lumbered by and snatched a long stem of grass. He broke it into three lengths and began to braid it. "Well, it was fetch this, tote that, all day long. And we was just little ones. If we didn't fetch fast enough, we felt the willow switch she kept behind the door. And believe me, she used it plenty. My legs and backside was sore most of the time."

He held the braided grass up as if admiring it, then threw it over the side. "Well," he began again, "my brother and sister older'n me said they wasn't takin' no more of that and ran out to help pa in the fields. They picked up rocks and wrestled stumps and piled brush all day. Came in of an evening looking like they hadn't had a bath since Christmas, but they was happy. Pa worked 'em, but he was kind.

Sometimes he sang songs with them or played with them a few minutes out in the field."

Juba said, "But, didn't your pa—?"

The old farmer held up a finger. "I'm a-getting to what happened next. My pa was so tired when he'd come in of an evening, he never noticed how unhappy his little ones was. He was just trying to make a living, to keep us together. Well, one day I got my little sister and brother out behind the house. They was about four'n'five then. I says to them, let's run away. So we sneaked around. Put some bread 'n' salt pork in a cloth sack. Didn't have no extra clothes to take along. And we lit out. We hadn't gone more'n a mile till here the boss come, galloping on a old horse my pa had. She had the switch in her hand and fire in her eye. She jumped down from the horse and took after me."

The old farmer stopped to rub his eyes and clear his throat. "Well, she catched me and she whaled me something awful, screeching all the while how I was a cussed sinner bound for hell. My little brother and sister just stood there and cried their hearts out. Never will forget how they sounded."

He paused again to rub his eyes and clear his throat. He looked at Juba. "You ever see a overseer tie a slave on beside his horse and make the feller run to keep up?"

Juba said, "Yassah."

"Well, that's what she did. She tied me and the little ones to a rope and made us run behind the horse all the way home. 'Course, we all fell down. Our legs couldn't run fast enough, so she drug us the rest of the way. 'That'll teach you,' she yelled. 'You won't never run away again. Now git up and do yer chores.' 'Course we was too tuckered out and banged up to do anything."

Juba looked at the floorboards of the wagon and shook his head.

The old farmer said, "Well, my pa come in from the field about that time. He saw me and my little sister and brother all scratched up and bloody and crying like we'd never stop. And he went up to that woman and yelled right in her face, 'Git out an' never come back.'"

Juba nodded in agreement.

The old farmer said, "But, that warn't the end of it. That woman went in the house and came back out with the gun. She was gonna shoot us all, I guess. She started hollering something awful at my pa. An' he just walked right up to her, rifle pointed at his chest an'all. Had a rock in his hand. Hit her upside the head with it. She dropped

right there, in the doorway. Never moved a muscle. He handed the
rifle to my older brother, then drug her out behind the house so we
wouldn't have to see her. Then he gathered us all in front of him and
told us how sorry he was."

The old farmer paused to blow his nose. "Seems like yesterday,"
he said.

Juba said, "What'd he do with her, suh?"

The old farmer shrugged. "Never did find out. Didn't want to ask.
I heard something in the night, but I was too tired and sore to git up
to see. All I know is, we never saw her again." He harrumped. "Now,
what I been hankering to tell you is this. Sometime later, my pa took
us to a plantation and we saw first hand how the overseer used his
whip. We saw a slave running beside a horse while the master sat
there so prim and proper. It was like watching ourselves all over agin
when we was little tots. And I vowed I'd never treat a body that
way."

He laid a hand on Juba's arm. "I never have."

"Thank you, suh."

"'Course, I've seen some good masters too. Ain't all of 'em
wicked."

"No, suh."

"Well, lookie here, we've come to the turn." He pointed. "Now,
you want to start off that-a-way."

Juba handed the reins to the old man and jumped off the wagon.
"Thank you, suh."

"By the by, what's your real name? Ain't Abe, I reckon."

"No, suh. I'm Juba. 'Allas have been. 'Allas will be."

The old farmer stuck out his hand. Juba shook it. The old farmer
said, "Pleased to make your acquaintance, Juba. But, I'll be
dadburned if I ever saw a runaway slave on this road. Did you?"

Juba grinned. "No, suh, never did."

The old farmer's mouth quirked once more. "Now then, give me
back my hat."

CHAPTER 11

After the old farmer let him off the wagon, Juba traveled more
than thirty miles on foot, skirting patches of sharp saw grass and
loping around scrub cedar. The old man had given him good

directions. The moon appeared above the trees. Deep in the woods, among the loblolly pines, he sat down to rest. He dozed off.

A terrible ruckus woke him. He opened his eyes. Lanterns dipped and swayed. Men shouted. He heard a woman's high keening wail. A baby screamed. The report of a rifle shot echoed from tree to tree and sent Juba sprawling into some brush for cover. He peered cautiously around twigs sprouting thorns.

He had not noticed earlier a trail about two hundred feet off that wound through the trees. Dark figures climbed from a straw-filled wagon. Several men with rifles surrounded them while another held a lantern high.

Juba's breath caught. His heart thudded. "Fugitive roundup," he whispered.

"Count 'em. Count 'em," one man ordered.

"Get the driver," another yelled. "Don't let him get away."

As Juba watched, a man limped from the front of the wagon. Streaks of blood on his face shone in the light of a lantern. Behind him walked a cocky fellow who waved a rifle in the air, then poked him in the back with it. His voice rang through the trees, "Whoopee, whoopee, caught me a traitor."

"Shut up, Cal," one of the men at the back of the wagon yelled. "We got 'em all?"

"Lucky tip. Them Quakers oughta thank us for taking 'em off their hands," another man rasped.

"What'll we do with 'em now?" came a soft, whining voice.

"Do with 'em? They're all going to jail, that's what. Get me a head count. Threaten that driver with his life. How many niggers supposed to be in this wagon?"

The frightened fugitives huddled together. Lights from the lanterns bobbed and flashed among the trees. The men's legs scissored back and forth against the light as they milled around their captives. Juba felt his throat tighten in pity as the woman swayed and sobbed, trying to comfort her crying baby. He could do nothing to help them. They would be chained together and taken back to their masters for whippings.

One of the captors ran from the other side of the wagon. "We only got six. There's supposed to be seven aboard. Fan out," he shouted. "Fan out. Nigger's on the loose!"

Juba's heart lurched. He gasped. They were coming straight toward him. He tore out of the brush and began to run. "He's over there,"

someone yelled. "I hear him. See? Hold that lantern higher. There
he goes! Get the horses."

Panic propelled Juba over fallen trees and into tangled vines. He
tore at them with his hands, forcing his way through. Protruding
roots tripped him. He crashed headlong through bushes. There was
just enough moonlight filtering through the woods for him to make
out shapes. Heavy footsteps pounded behind him, gaining on him.
He zigzagged left, then right. He almost ran nose-first into a tree.
His lungs were on fire. A sob broke on his next breath. He fell. His
pulse pounded in his temples. There was no more strength in him.
They'd get him and they hadn't even known he was here.

Juba lay on the ground, too exhausted to cry. All his struggles had
been for nothing. The taste of defeat was incredibly bitter. In an
agony of spirit and overwhelming anger at the fickleness of fate, he
doubled his fist and pounded the pine needles beneath his chest. His
arm grazed a log. His eye caught a glimmer of light. The moon shone
part way inside the log. It was hollow.

Very close behind now, heavy boots crackled the underbrush. Still
on his stomach, Juba felt for a stick and threw it. It landed against a
tree farther on. He heard one of the men call, "This way. I heard him
over in those bushes."

Juba inched into the log on elbows and knees and lay still. He put
a hand over his mouth to muffle the panting he could not control
while his heart hammered a tattoo against the mealy remains beneath
him that beetles had discarded.

The posse ran past. A deep voice said, "Sure I heard him farther
on. Dad gum it, don't hear nothing now." The lantern light swept
over the log and went on. A man on horseback thundered past. The
pounding footsteps and the shouts faded into the distance. Juba
scrunched his eyes shut and waited. The log was like a moldy coffin.

He must have fallen asleep. Morning light filtered into the end of
the log. Juba's cramped hands and arms were numb. He listened for
a few minutes and heard only bird calls and mice rustling in the
fallen brown needles under the trees. Inch by inch, he worked his
way out of the log and sat up. He wondered what happened to the
other fugitive the posse thought they were chasing. He could only
hope the man got away. Mighty close to catching him by mistake. He
shuddered at the thought and looked up. And then he saw the eyes.

They were staring straight at him. Intelligent eyes. The face was obscured by pine branches. How long had the feller been watching him? Suppose he thinks he's got me like a sitting duck. Well, it was true.

The eyes never wavered. Juba scrambled to his feet. Did the feller have a bead on him? Probably the minute he took a step he'd be shot. A breeze stirred the tree. Juba stared, mouth open in astonishment. He said, "Oh Lawd," and released a sigh. "You's a 'coon. Just a 'coon. Up in that tree, staring at me. A 'coon." He grinned and shook his head. "Lucky you ain't bubbling in some pot for my breakfast." No time to stare down a 'coon. He'd better move on. Speculator might still be lurking in these woods somewhere. Speculator might be up a tree staring down at him too. Speculators were almost as smart as 'coons.

He knew where he was headed. The Mississippi River. Maybe he could stowaway on a sternwheeler. He'd heard folks talking about how those sternwheelers carried cargo north. Reckoned he was just as good a'cargo as the next thing.

CHAPTER 12

Water lapped and gurgled against the *Silver Lady*. Her mooring ropes creaked. She waited for dawn just off the landing at Beulah with a sizable load of cotton bales, thirty casks of sorghum, and a small mountain of coiled and tagged hemp rope. The sky was overcast on this moonless night. A mist enveloped the river. The only lights were flickering lanterns fore and aft.

Juba had sneaked aboard at dark, stepping onto the spongy woodwork just above the water line of the sternwheeler. He slept wedged among the cotton bales. A cough nearby roused him.

"Hey," a man whispered. Juba felt a nudge. He sat up quickly, his muscles tense. "Shh," the man said and coughed again.

"Yeah?" Juba whispered back. The lantern swayed in the rocking of the ship. Its shadowy light passed across the face of the whisperer. Juba recognized the man as the Negro who stoked wood into the steam boiler.

"You lookin' fer a job?"

Juba frowned. He stared at the man in the flickering light. "Whatcha mean?"

The man coughed again, trying to muffle it with both hands. "I'se sick. Gonna go under if'n I don't get off this boat. Sides, my fambly's back there. Back at the last landing." He waved beyond the boat. "Cap'n made me come aboard, said, 'You keep the fire box full.' Guess the last stoker 'fore me jumped ship. I seen you first thing." He paused to cough. "You ain't hid good 'nuff. You kin take my place. Won't need to hide."

Juba said, "What you talking about? You take off, Cap'n'll know the difference between you and me. He'll know—"

The man covered his mouth and signaled for Juba to wait. His whisper was hoarse when he tried to speak again, "Naw, he won' even know the difference. Whiteys think we blacks all look alike. They don' pay no attention. You'n'me the same size. Even got a scar 'bout the same. Look." He turned his head. Juba leaned forward, squinting in the lantern light. Sure enough, a scar near his temple did resemble Juba's.

The man whispered in his ear again. " 'Sides, you gonna get found out here. Cap'n's coming through in the morning, just looking for fellas sneaking on board. Allas looks 'round the cotton bales. That's where they all hide." He bowed his head and gasped for breath. "Wanna see my fambly 'fore I go under."

Juba studied the man's feverish eyes. "What's your name? What's Cap'n call you?"

"Calls me 'boy.' What else? They don't know we got names. You don't need to know mine neither. Wanna see my fambly." The man sidled toward the railing. His body weaved uncertainly as he balanced there.

Juba said, "Wait! How—how do you put the wood in the boiler?"

The man's laugh was full of phlegm. "Just throws it in, tha's all."

"But—" Juba heard a gentle splash and stumbled to the rail. The man had disappeared. The mist swirled above the murky water. The only sound was the gentle wash of waves caressing the side of the boat.

Juba gripped the railing. He filled his lungs with the river's mist, the smell of sea grass and fish. Below him, the dark water nudged the boat. Juba shook his head and crawled back into his cubbyhole between the cotton bales. So now he was the wood stoker. He smiled. Got an official reason for being on this boat. He closed his eyes and tried to visualize himself stoking the firebox: sweaty back bent over the open firebox door, the fierce heat reaching out to sear a too-close body. Had the man worn gloves? Probably not. Captains and overseers did not think about such luxuries. Juba rubbed his palms together. They'd lost their familiarity with a hoe and shovel. They'd gone soft. Blisters. That's what he'd have. Blisters.

Before he climbed aboard, clinging to the side with just his head above the water, Juba had overheard the Captain telling somebody the *Silver Lady* was headed for St. Louis in the state of Missouri. After he found a nest between the cotton bales, he wondered if he had made a wise choice. Sure couldn't tell which direction a body was headed by the thousand twists and turns in the ol' Mississippi.

Missouri, that's where Independence was, what they called the jumping off place. The start of the trail across the prairie toward Oregon.

Prairie? What was a prairie? Guess he'd find out if he didn't go plum dizzy on this boat. His thoughts turned to the tinker back on the plantation. Seemed like a hundred years since the man had passed him the map. He had it still. It was faded and tattered, smeared and torn in the creases. Juba fished it out of his pocket and held it up to the lantern light. He squinted as he put his finger on the x where the tinker had drawn wagons, a whole bunch of them in a row, traveling west.

Juba's heart leaped. West was free territory. A man was a man in the West. Not a slave or a "boy." Best get some sleep. When dawn came, he was fixing to receive some blisters.

At daylight, Juba was up and standing beside the boiler. The Captain barely glanced at him. "Get this thing red hot, boy," he said. "We need a lot of pressure today. First thing, we'll slip through the chutes up yonder slow and easy."

Juba bent to the task.

The Captain said, "Don't put the wood in that way. Thought I told you yesterday. Can't you remember from one day to the next?"

Juba ducked his head. "No, massah."

The Captain whistled through his teeth. "Look. Lay it in like this at first. See? Later on, you just need to shove it in fast. Hold off on the pitch, once it gets a head of steam going."

"Yas, massah."

The Captain studied the pressure gauge. "Coming up good. Pile more on, boy. See that needle? When it jumps to there," he pointed with a pudgy finger, "hold it there. Don't take your eyes off it, you hear? We can't cast off till the steam is up."

Juba nodded, "Yas, massah."

The Captain eyed him curiously. "Sounds like the catarrh you had yesterday's much better."

"Yas, massah." Juba hid his face and chucked more wood into the firebox.

The Captain watched him for a minute. He said, "You're livelier too. Thought last night I might have to leave you off at some landing. Sick nigger's no good to me."

"No, massah."

Juba heard boots scuffing the waterlogged floor. The Captain turned away. "Oh, good morning, Laughton. What do you think of my boat now? Ain't she a workhorse? Just wait till you see her go through the chutes up yonder."

Laughton said, "Come down on your price any?"

Captain said, "I can let you have her for a hundred-ten-thousand and terms."

Juba, back bent before the firebox, heard Laughton's voice, "I'm still considering it. Throw in the stoker?"

Juba saw the Captain shrug. The Captain laughed. "You're full of humor this morning, Laughton. Don't matter to me. Picked him up off the landing a couple of days ago, myself." He cleared his throat. "She's a hundred-and-ninety tons with an unloaded draft of about fourteen inches. Carries twelve passengers in the style they're accustomed to, of course. I've been plying these waters with her for two years. Lots of wear left in her."

Laughton twirled the ends of his waxed moustache. He inspected his buffed fingernails. He said, "You got the new worn off her, Captain."

"Naw, just well broken in." Then to Juba, "Mind the gauge, boy. Remember I showed you this speaking tube yesterday?"

Juba glanced at the strange object and felt a pang of apprehension. He had wondered what the thing was for. "Yes, massah."

" If I call down from the wheelhouse for more steam, you pour on the wood. Understand?"

"Yes, massah."

The Captain turned back to his guest, "Come on, Laughton, I'll show you how easy it is to make repairs. She's got a right nice shallow draft and I . . ." The Captain's voice faded as the two men ambled away.

Juba watched the needle on the pressure gauge. Steadily, slowly, it rose to the required pressure. It went slightly beyond and Juba fidgeted. A worried frown spread across his forehead. He shuffled his feet and looked around. Where was the Captain? What if the needle went clean up to the numbers painted in red? Could he dive over the side fast enough if the whole boat exploded?

He looked at the needle again. It had settled down. He sighed. He shoved another stick into the firebox and wiped the sweat from his face.

The Captain appeared. "That's it, boy. Keep her steaming nice and steady. Come on, Laughton. Let's see if we can round up some coffee. About time to wrassle this old river again."

All day, Juba stoked the boiler. The muscles in his back complained. When he swiped at the sweat that ran down his face, it made the raw places on his hands sting. Naked to the waist, he dripped sweat onto the splintery, water-warped floorboards. The placid river turned first one way, then another. Juba lost all track of direction.

Toward evening, they pulled into a landing. Juba helped unload the casks of sorghum and trundled wheelbarrows full of cordwood from the wood yard into the *Silver Lady*'s hold for the next run up the river. The Captain said, "Cook's got a plate of beans for you."

"Thank you, massah."

"By the by—"

"Yes, massah?"

"Where'd you sleep last night?"

Here it came. Might have known he'd get caught. Most likely he'd get a whipping and a tumble overboard.

But the Captain was pointing a finger at him, not waiting for an answer. "Rest of the crew wants you to take the lower bunk. They don't think it's right for you to have the top bunk."

"Yes, massah."

"See that you remember that."

"Yes, massah."

Aching with weariness, Juba ate the beans and found the bunks for the crew. He swung into the lowest bunk and collapsed. No wonder the white men thought they deserved better. With barely eighteen inches between the ceiling and his head, it was airless. And the boards vibrated with the noise of the machinery. But at least his pallet was flat. It seemed to be stuffed with wood chips.

He inspected his hands in the dim light. *Yassah, three blisters on each palm and two more getting a good start.* Another couple of days and his hands would be like leather again. One thing he knew for sure. He wasn't going to spend the rest of his life stoking the firebox. If that man Laughton bought the boat, he'd have to find his own nigger to do that.

What? What was he thinking? Back on the plantation there was no question whether he would or would not work. Slow down a little and the whip cracked over his back. *Freedom.* He was getting the hang of it. Somehow, without realizing it, his mind had made the turn. He was surprised and smiled at the tingling, bubbling elation that welled up in his chest. "Proud of you, Juba," he whispered as his eyes closed.

When they pulled into the landing at St Louis three days later, Juba wondered if he would ever be able to stand up straight again. His bare feet slapped the gangplank back and forth as he shouldered the coiled ropes and dumped them on the wharf. The Captain was standing to one side, pressing Laughton for a sale. Juba made one more trip and let the coil of rope slide off his shoulder onto the pile.

He dodged behind a stack of boxes and zigzagged among the cargoes of several ships tied up at the landing. He tensed for the inevitable "Hey, catch that nigger. He's running away." He heard only the commands echoing from other boats, the jostling, the thump and scrape of cargo, and the grunts of men unloading it. The whistle of a sidewheeler rent the air.

Juba jogged around a cluster of barrels and tripped over a heap of tangled fish net. Three hundred yards beyond, he chanced a look back. Blacks heaved cargo in all directions. Mules pulled loaded wagons. He could not see the Captain or his prospective buyer.

Panting, Juba paused behind a stack of crates. He scratched his neck. A wasp landed on the back of his hand. Juba slapped at it. It stung him. "Nasty little bugger," he said, "sure glad you didn't sting me when I was still stoking wood." He scraped at the damp ground with his toes, knelt, and scooped a little mud onto the sting. His hand began to swell. His fingers stiffened. As he knelt to apply more mud, something shiny caught his eye. He dug into the mud and brought it up. It was a nickel-plated jackknife. He wiped it on his overalls and, smiling, slipped it into his pocket.

The slow plod of horses and creak of wagon wheels caught his attention. He peered around the crates. The wagon would pass near him. A white-haired Negro with a face like weathered leather sat on the driver's seat. Empty crates rattled together in the wagon box. Juba smelled cabbages and saw a few of the large outer leaves clinging to the crates. Juba stepped out into the track. "Hey, brother."

The driver said, "Whoa." The horses stopped, their tails switching at flies. The driver lifted his hat, scratched his scalp, and eyed him with suspicion. "Whatcha want?"

"I need a ride."

The hat settled again on the wooly head. "Where to?"

"Where ya going?"

"Ten miles west of town. Massah's farm."

"You let me off afore you get to massah's farm?"

The driver's face puckered. "Whatcha give me?"

Juba felt of the jackknife in his pocket. He could not give it up. He shrugged. "I ain't got nothing to give."

The old Negro looked him up and down. "Sure don't. You's a ragged brother. You's just off the river?"

Juba nodded. The old man gave him a toothless smile. "Climb on. You kin tell me all about it. I used to live on the river," followed by "Giddap" to the horses. "Now, when I was a boy . . ."

Juba had to scramble to avoid the already turning wheels. An hour later, the man was still talking as Juba nodded and agreed in all the proper places. They turned a corner. A cluster of farm buildings came into view. The white-haired Negro said, "Whoa."

Juba jumped off the wagon. "How far is it to Independence?"

The old man rubbed his face. "Never heard of it. What is it?"

"A town. Where wagon trains are lining up to go to Oregon Territory."

"Wouldn't never want to go there. Now, you take this here river back there . . ." The wagon wheels began to turn. "That's the life for . . ."

Juba waved. He stood beside the road and grinned after the old fellow. Then he darted into the sheltering bushes.

CHAPTER 13

Juba arranged a nest in the loose straw that covered the floor of the boxcar. He had jumped aboard just in time. Pulled by a big Baldwin locomotive, the couplings clanged and bumped through a series of jerks and starts. The wheels screeched in protest as they gradually gained momentum. Sparks and cinders flew past the open doorway of the car. Juba heard a scrabbling. He watched, wide-eyed, as two hoboes scrambled over the edge and flung themselves into the boxcar.

"Hey, Scarface, there's a nigger in here. I ain't riding with no nigger."

"You gonna jump out then? Train's picking up speed."

"Naw, break my neck. Oughta make him get out. We's whites. We got our rights."

"Looks like a mighty strong buck. You shove him out, he's apt to take you with him. I say live and let live."

The shorter one erupted into giggles. "Live and let live, huh? That's a good one."

The two hoboes sprawled at the opposite end of the car. The taller one pulled a bottle from a ragged pocket.

Juba turned so they could not see his face. The monotony of the rumbling wheels clacking over the rails lulled him. His head nodded. Two or three times he roused himself only to find his chin on his chest once more.

Meggie came to his mind. She'd be lighting the gas lamp in Miss Lorinda's room about this time. Maybe turning down the coverlet on Miss Lorinda's bed. And after she'd climbed up and down the stairs a few times, seeing to Miss Lorinda's needs, she would go to her cabin and make sure Granny Em had eaten the hoecake Meggie set out for her. Tomorrow Meggie would rise with the sun and spend the day at the big house again, running, running, to please the whims of Miss Lorinda. Did Meggie ever think of him? Was she sorry she stayed behind? Yearning for Meggie was a bone-deep sadness, a weight on his chest. Tears lingered behind his eyes.

The two whites shared the bottle and talked half the night. Their whooping and raucous laughter merged with the rumble and sway of the train. Once in a while, when Juba opened one eye, he heard the whisper of the skinny man with the jagged scar down his cheek. The other fellow, squat and slack of mouth, giggled. Juba tried to ignore them and stretched out on his back. Exhaustion pulled him into a deep sleep.

It seemed only minutes, but it must have been hours when Juba realized the rising sun of morning was shining through the open door of the freight car onto his closed eyelids. Something tickled him. Juba brushed it away. The tickling persisted, touching his ear, his cheek, his nose. Juba shook his head. Pesky fly. Then he heard it, the hiss of a man's breath pushed from between teeth, ending in a giggle. Close. Too close.

Juba lay still, eyes shut. The scarred man whispered, "When I poke him, you get ready to—"

Lightning quick, Juba scrambled to his feet, hands fisted, face fierce. The slack-mouthed man fell backward, his eyes agog. Clutched in his hand was a piece of straw. Scarface spoke in nasal tones, "Easy, nigger boy. Ain't meaning no harm. Just having a bit of fun, that's all." The blade of a knife glinted in his hand.

Juba stared, "You call it fun, pulling a knife on me?"

Scarface shrugged, "Maybe."

Slackmouth struggled to his feet. "We was just gonna see if you—"

"Shut up." Scarface scowled.

The train began to lurch. The couplings clanged together as it slowed. Scarface stood between Juba and the open door. Juba moved his leg, angling sideways.

Slackmouth whined, "Don't let him get away, Scar. Then we won't ever know—"

"I said shut up."

Suddenly, Scarface rushed at Juba, his knife slashing the air. Juba grabbed the man's wrist and bent it back. Scarface swore. The train jolted and both men fell to the floor. They grappled in the straw.

Slackmouth bent toward them, both arms flailing. He shrilled, "That's it, Scar, get him. Get him." He grasped Juba's leg and held on. Juba tried to kick himself free. Scar took advantage of the momentary distraction to drive the point of his knife into Juba's wrist. Blood spurted.

"See, see," Slackmouth squealed. "He's got real blood. Red blood. Just like you'n'me, Scar. Just like you'n'me."

Scar let go of Juba and struggled to his feet. Bits of straw clung to his clothes. He slapped Slackmouth across the face. "Can't you shut up?"

Slackmouth would not be silenced. "But, we wanted to know, Scar. You said—"

"What's it gonna take, little man, to shut yer mouth?"

Trees and bushes now moved leisurely past the open door of the boxcar. Far ahead, the whistle on the big Baldwin engine sounded. Still berating Slackmouth, Scar temporarily turned his back on Juba. Juba braced his legs and gave Scarface a shove that sent both hoboes sprawling. Their legs and arms tangled in the straw. Juba lunged for the door, crouched, and launched himself onto the embankment.

He rolled down the gravelly slope and landed in tall grass. Panting, he dug the dirt from his eyes as the train whistle shrilled once more, far down the track. He sat up and watched the caboose grow smaller and fade from sight. He became aware of something sticky trickling between his fingers. Blood. His blood.

About fifty feet away, a small stream gurgled over jumbled rocks. Willow trees crowded the bank. Juba shambled over and held his wrist under the water. The coldness of it surprised him. He tore a strip from the hem of his ragged shirt and laid it in the grass. A few inches above his head, in a drooping branch, a spider had woven an intricate web. Careful to avoid the spider, Juba snatched the sticky web from its branch and wadded it up across the wound. Then he peeled a little of the willow bark, pressed it over the cut and bound it around with the cloth.

Juba splashed water on his face and drank from the stream. He sighed, leaned back against one of the trees and thought about the two hoboes. So they wanted to know if blacks had red blood. Guess they found out. White trash, that's what they were. Ignorant white trash. His anger flared momentarily. He should have banged their heads together. What did they think flowed in black's veins? Melted licorice?

Then he saw the humor in it and began to chuckle. Ignorance. He guessed most everybody was ignorant about something. Couldn't know everything there was to know. The chuckle died in his throat. He sobered. His people, kept ignorant on purpose so they could be controlled, kept from learning how to read and write. He studied his knuckles. He wouldn't know his own name if somebody wrote it and handed it to him.

Juba's thoughts turned to Meggie. Her memory was always there, just beneath the surface, like a well-loved melody. He almost wished the cut would hurt more to take his mind off her.

He stood. He was hungry. He was traveling into more open country. It seemed strange, this ability to see far across flat land with no thickets in the way. About a half mile off, there was a large block of green field. Maybe it was ripening corn. He began to walk. He saw no trees to shelter or to hide a runaway slave.

CHAPTER 14

Juba hated to beg, but he was starving. There had been no food since he shucked a few ears of corn from the big field two days ago. They weren't quite ripe, but he ate every kernel and sucked the juice from the cob. Now before him, stood an unpainted shack with a few outbuildings scattered behind it. Juba heard the pleasant early morning cackle of chickens scratching in the dirt on the other side of a mesh fence. He saw a potato patch choked with weeds. A jumble of unsplit wood loomed beside the shack.

Juba tried to smooth his shirt and knocked on the door. The woman who peered out with frightened eyes was thin. A little girl clung to her skirt. She tried to burrow under her mother's dirty apron. The thick aroma of frying bacon wafted through the open door and made Juba's head reel.

"Pardon, ma'am. I'm passing through and wondered, would you like that pile of wood split or the weeds pulled in your potato patch?" Juba tried to smile. His stomach grumbled.

From the dim interior of the shack came a man's gruff tone, "Don't need no bill collectors hangin' round. Tell 'im to scram, Mazie."

Mazie's eyes shifted from just beyond Juba's shoulder to the floor. "No bill collector, Alf. He's a . . ."

Inside, a chair scraped. A florid-faced fellow with a large belly shoved Mazie aside and stared at Juba. His hostile eyes bored into Juba's. "Nigger, huh? Run away down South, didja, boy?"

Juba looked at the porch stoop. He worded his answer carefully. "Just working my way cross country, massah. Thought you might like some help with the splitting or weeding."

The man scratched in his unkempt beard. "Yeah, Mazie's kinda lazy. Don't get much work outta her most times."

Juba did not like this man on sight, but he pressed down the ire that rose in his throat and waited.

The man shrugged. "Sure, sure, go ahead. S'pose you want pay?"

"Yessir—or food, massah."

"Vittles, huh? Guess we could spare a little."

Juba nodded.

"Have at it. Hoe's hanging on the side of the shed. Axe's on the chopping block."

Juba opened his mouth to say thank you and found the door shut in his face. It would take him all day to get the work done. He hoped he could last that long. He inhaled the smell of bacon that lingered in the air, as if it might grant him a little nourishment.

The sun climbed toward noon. Weeds in the potato patch lay wilting in heaps among the blooming plants. Juba now balanced a chunk of wood on the chopping block and raised the axe high above his shoulder. He brought it down squarely in the center of the wood. It split cleanly apart in four pieces. He threw them to one side and reached for another chunk. His back felt like a cellar door with a broken hinge. Sweat shone on the bulging muscles of his arms. It dribbled down his forehead and stung his eyes.

The little girl came out of the house and sat on the door stoop to watch him. She had a kitten in her lap and a thumb in her mouth.

Juba swung into a rhythm: Reach for the wood, lay it on the block, bring the axe down, bend the back to pick up the pieces. Occasionally, he caught a glimpse of the woman. She fed the chickens and picked a bucketful of green beans. Once he looked up to see her pumping water in the yard. And when he next raised the axe, there was a full tin cup on the ground beside the chopping block.

As the sun eased its way across the sky, the cooling breeze of early evening replaced mid-day heat. Wearily, Juba reached for the last chunk of wood. His legs trembled with fatigue. His tongue clung to the roof of his mouth. *Almost through*, he said to himself, *almost through*. Soon he could sit down and eat. He wondered what food this family had to share. The wood cracked and split. He tossed the last pieces on the pile now higher than his head, laid the axe on the chopping block and walked to the door of the shack.

The man answered his knock. "Well?"

Juba tried to stand up straight. "I've finished the work, massah."

The man stared past him. "Wood's not stacked."

From inside the shack, Juba heard the woman's voice. "We only asked him to split it, Alf."

"Quiet, woman." Alf's face twisted into a sneer. "S'pose you want yer pay for only doin' half the job."

Juba's calloused hands clenched. A throbbing vein in his temple picked up its tempo. His scar turned pink. He heard the woman's light step approach the door. "Alf, please. He's worked hard."

As Juba stood there, trying not to stagger, he saw the man turn. He heard a slap and a muffled cry.

Again, the man filled the doorway. "Looks like you just worked for nothing. Yer a fool. I don't give handouts to beggars, 'specially nigger boys."

Hunger made Juba's head swim while rage throbbed through his body. He blinked to clear his vision. He stepped forward, but the door was already closed against him. From inside, he heard the man's harsh bellow. Something, maybe a chair, crashed to the floor. The woman's pitiful wail came faintly through the wall.

Juba eyed the door. His jaw tightened. He ought to break down that door and demand his pay. He ought to— He flexed the cramps out of his knotted fists and tried to still the shaking of his knees. No, he could not break down the door. He could not demand anything. He was a fugitive on the run. He had no rights. And mean-tempered Alf knew it.

With drooping shoulders, he turned away and almost stumbled into the pump. Water. Surely the man would not deny him a drink of water. He levered the handle and watched the cool water rush from the spout into the bucket. As he raised the bucket to his lips and began to drink, he heard a click and felt the barrel of Alf's rifle nudge him in the back.

"Better scram, nigger, before I empty this into yer hide."

Juba glanced at the shack. The thin woman stood in the doorway, twisting her apron with work-reddened hands. Tears blotched her cheeks. Juba bit his tongue. If long years of slavery had taught him anything, he knew better than to show emotion on the outside, even though he was seething on the inside. He shrugged. Forcing his back straight and his weary legs to carry him out of the yard, he started down the road.

Dusk painted shadows in the sheltered places. Blackbirds chirped softly, flitting to their nests high in the trees. Juba's footsteps flushed a covy of quail beside the trail. They rose with a whir and scuttled into the woods. He reflected on the timid woman and the little girl caught in the clutches of the cruel man. Why didn't the woman take the child and run away? Anything was better than living like that.

Then Meggie's face swam before his eyes. Would she have stood the rigors of what he'd gone through to get this far? Women were different. They wanted security, a hearth, and the promise of something to cook for supper. He sighed. He was almost too tired to breathe. Some day, he vowed, letting anger crowd his chest again, some day the bullies of this world would not dare to treat him like that one had.

A sudden flash of color cut across in front of him and paused in the middle of the road. He saw it was the little girl. She stood in the gathering darkness. One bare toe traced circles in the dust. Shyly, she thrust a cloth sack into his hand and skittered away, blending with the shadows in the trees.

Juba opened the sack. A slab of bread, hastily cut, folded over a slice of roast pork. A boiled egg. And at the bottom of the sack was the tin cup with a raw potato in it. He grinned. "Thank you," he whispered. Tears surprised him at the corners of his eyes. The woman took an awful chance sending the girl with the food. That was a mean fella on that farm. He hoped mother and daughter didn't get caught going behind his back.

Juba stuffed some of the sandwich in his mouth and walked on. He willed his feet to put more distance between him and the farm. Somehow he didn't feel quite so tired now. A little kindness sure warmed the heart and gave a body the will to go on.

The road led around a bend and through dense trees. He finished the sandwich and stopped in the middle of the track. The woods seemed as good a place as any to spend the night. He found a broad-beamed oak with a bed of leaves under it and hunkered down against the trunk. He reached into the sack and held the egg in the palm of his hand. "Watch over that little lady, Lawd," he prayed. "She sure needs your protection."

Pieces of eggshell fell into the leaves as he peeled them away. Savoring, holding the food in his mouth, he made himself eat slowly. He would save the raw potato for breakfast.

As darkness enveloped him, doubts gnawed at his mind. What was he doing under a tree in the middle of nowhere? Maybe he should have stayed on the plantation. Maybe this idea of being free was only a dream. Suppose he couldn't make it on his own after all.

Was he a fool, just like the bully said? He rubbed at the tears coursing down his dirty cheeks. Tears. He had cried more these past weeks than the whole rest of his life. Slaves did not dare to cry in front of the overseer. Tears brought more lashes of the whip. Maybe tears were one of the privileges of freedom.

Juba stretched out on the thick bed of leaves and adjusted the cloth sack under his head for a pillow. After a while, a grin tugged at the corners of his mouth. He never had a pillow before. And the leaves were softer than the cracked board that had been his bed on the plantation. *Juba, you're coming up in the world. Got yourself a pillow and a soft bed. Living in luxury already.*

Was freedom worth it? "Yeah," he whispered, and again, "Yeah." A night wind soughed through the woods. It lifted his whisper to the highest branches and tossed it from tree to tree while Juba slept.

CHAPTER 15

Juba skulked in the bushes, ducked under trees, loped across meadows. The ground was firmer now, harder underfoot, the air drier. Alligators never entered his mind. Snakes, seldom. He watched for the North Star and angled west. When he could find haystacks, he slept in them. He dug an occasional turnip or sweet potato from a field, even milked a docile cow that stood under a tree. One day, hiding in roadside brush, he watched a slow-moving wagon piled with sugar beets roll by. He jogged behind it, jumped aboard and rode, undetected, for twenty miles.

A few days later, Juba walked into the tail end of a dust cloud. It covered a wide area. He could not see around it. He heard cattle bawling far ahead, at the same time he stepped into a pile of fresh manure. He cleaned off his foot the best he could on a clump of bunch grass and kept on.

All at once, out of the cloud of dust, a steer ran straight toward him. Juba waved his arms and yelled, "Hiya. Hiya." The steer skidded to a stop and let out a "baaw." It turned with its tail in the air and gamboled away. Juba blinked the dust out of his eyes.

A drover on horseback came into view and galloped toward Juba. His heart lurched. Had he come this far only to betray himself by an innocent gesture? He tried to think of excuses for being there, but his mind was blank.

The drover reined up and yelled, "How come yer afoot?"

That wasn't the question Juba anticipated. He shrugged and automatically shifted his gaze to the ground.

The drover yelled, "Lucky's got an extra horse tied to the grub wagon, I tell ya. He'll let ya have it if you ask him nice."

Through the billowing, churning dust, Juba could barely make out the profile of a horse tied to the back of a wagon bumping along the uneven ground. What did he need with a drover's horse? Beat walking, didn't it? He ran to the wagon.

"Massah say I can have the extra horse."

"Hey?" The driver cupped his ear. The horse that pulled the wagon kept its steady pace.

Juba jogged alongside and repeated, "Massah say I can have the extra horse."

The driver shook his head. "Speak up, sonny. Can't hear yor mumbling."

Juba had never been called "sonny" in his life. He grinned at the grizzled old man and shouted, "Massah say I can have the horse."

"Horse, you say?" The driver spit tobacco over the side.

Juba sidestepped the brown stream and stepped in more manure. "Yassah, the horse."

"You want it?" The driver yelled, almost losing the tobacco tucked under his lip.

"Yassah."

"Well then, take it. Don't hang around here talking like some southerner."

"Thank you, massah."

"Name's Lucky."

The wagon did not slow. Juba trotted beside the towed horse and untied the reins wound around a wagon post. "Whoa there. Easy now." The horse stood still and waited patiently while Juba cinched the saddle. He mounted and rode back to the drover.

The drover asked, "What'd Lucky have to say?"

"He told me not to hang around talking like a southerner, massah."

The drover hooted and gave out a belly laugh. He pointed, "You can watch them dogies over there, I tell ya. They're kinda inclined to wander." He leaned over his horse and stuck out his hand. "Name's Charley. What's yours?"

"Juba." He shook Charley's hand as if it were the most natural thing in the world and wondered, as he rode off to become an instant drover of cattle, at the many different views with which men regarded their fellow humans.

For ten days, Juba breathed trail dust. He ate the cook's beans and biscuits, drank scalding Arbuckle coffee, and herded cattle. Charlie gave him a pair of boots. "I always bring along an extra pair, I tell ya. You ain't got socks neither? Well, try this pair. A few holes, I tell ya, but they still got a couple miles in 'em."

Charlie stood over six feet tall. He could wrestle a young calf to the ground with little effort. His smile came easily and often. He didn't look at Juba as if he were some strange being wandering the countryside without adequate clothes. If he had questions, he kept them to himself. Juba noticed Charlie got along with the other drovers hired to work with him. He treated them well. They respected him and did whatever he asked.

One evening when the cattle were bedded down for the night, Juba and Charley sprawled on the ground not far from the grub wagon. Charley said, "You got yer prayer book?"

Juba was bewildered. "Prayer book?" He shook his head. Charley didn't look like the kind who would use a prayer book.

Charley grinned. "No harm in asking." He hollered to another fellow, "Hey, Grimmet, let me have yer prayer book, I tell ya."

Juba watched, astonished, as Grimmet handed over a packet of cigarette papers.

Charley said, "Thank you kindly, Grimmet." He lifted a pouch from his pocket and with a forefinger tapped a thin line of tobacco along the length of one paper. He ran his tongue along the paper's edge, then rolled the cigarette and settled down with a sigh to enjoy his smoke.

Juba said, "Huh."

Charley said, "I tell ya."

One of the drovers pulled a harmonica from his pocket. As the moon rose, bright and big as a tin plate, the drovers hummed along, song after song. "Hey Lenny, you know 'Cotton-Eyed Joe'?" "Play 'The Arkansas Traveler.'" "Hey Lenny, how about 'Sweet Betsy From Pike'?"

Juba listened and was surprised by the lump in his throat. The camaraderie of the drovers touched a sensitive place. His mind drifted back to the plantation where the slaves had played and sung together. Music was a tie to their heritage. Juba remembered how it soothed their hurts and spoke of their love for one another. He also remembered, with a private grin, that when a hoedown got underway they could dance and sing and laugh and clap for hours.

The moon lifted high and paled. Far off, a coyote yipped. A nighthawk's eerie cry split the silence. And here was Juba, on the open prairie, far away from all he had known. It seemed to him the prairie was too big, almost frightening. He felt a pang for the close, crowded quarters he used to share. Juba wrapped tight in his blanket, another gift from Charlie. The strains of the harmonica died away. Juba heard a drover snore. Then he too fell asleep.

At last, the drovers and cattle arrived at a cluster of buildings surrounded by endless prairie. Never again would Juba wonder at the word. He had experienced it first hand. Here, the rancher waited for his herd. He opened the gate to a large corral and counted as each animal passed through.

"Have any trouble, Charley?" the rancher asked.

"Nope, smooth as butter, I tell ya."

The men lined up for their pay. Juba stood to one side until Charley motioned him over.

"Ain't you gonna collect your pay?"

"Well, I—"

"C'mon now. Saved me a bundle of trouble. Had to ride drag by m'self, till you came along, I tell ya, 'cause nobody wants to breathe the dust. C'mon, now."

Charley pulled Juba into line. Presently, Juba stood in front of the rancher. The man consulted his list without looking up. "Name?"

"Uh . . . Juba, Juba Robinson."

"Don't see your name on the list."

Charley spoke up. "Juba signed on ten days ago, Mr. Wagner. Saved me a bundle of worry, I'll tell ya. Rode drag with me. Kept those dogies hustlin' along, I'll tell ya."

The rancher's head snapped up. "That so?"

Juba looked at the ground and shuffled his feet. "Yassah."

Charley spoke again, "Sure saved me a bundle of worry, I tell ya. Yes, sir, he—"

The rancher's eyes narrowed. "Well, I'll make you a deal, black man. Since I didn't hire you, I wouldn't have to pay you anything. But Charley here knows his drovers. I'll give you two dollars and a mule."

Juba's mouth opened in surprise. "Thank you. Thank you, massah."

The rancher laughed. "Ain't any 'massahs' around here, black man. You're welcome just the same." Then to Charley, "Give him that mule with the blaze."

CHAPTER 16

Meggie stood behind the plantation big house at the clothesline. She folded sheets and laid them in the basket. She unpinned Massah Robinson's stockings from the line. Over by the carriage house, Massah was talking to Pilcher, the overseer. Meggie hurried with her task. Best to be out of Massah's sight as soon as possible. She wished she had asked Sissy to help. But Sissy was working with cook, shucking a washtub full of corn.

Meggie stooped. Into the basket went the handkerchiefs, the white shirts, two of Massah's cravats. It was then she heard Massah say to Pilcher, "You seen Peel lately?"

Pilcher said, "Couple months back. When he came around after hunting for that buck, Juba." Pilcher frowned. "Funny, never knew Peel not to get his boy. Mebbe he's slipping, getting too old."

Robinson said, "Well, Peel stopped in here the other day. We got to talking about that nigger. Said he never did find hide nor hair of him." He slapped his knee.

Meggie jumped. That slap sounded like the crack of a whip.

Robinson said, "You shoulda seen Peel. Nervous as a long-tailed cat in a room full of rocking chairs. Acted like he was running from a spook."

Pilcher laughed, a harsh coughing sound. "Spook, eh? Peel himself's a spook. Surprised he didn't reel the bugger in."

"Naw, that darkie's at the bottom of the Pearl River, like I first told you. Don't matter anyhow. One slave's about as good as another."

Pilcher scowled. "You heard the news about ol' John Brown up in West Virginy?"

Robinson scowled back, "That cussed abolitionist? Crazy man, ain't he? Going at folks, chopping with an axe."

"That's the one. Murdering anybody's got slaves. Trying to get the slaves to rise up against their masters. Slaves afeard of him too, I hear."

"Somebody ought to do him in proper."

"Somebody will, likely. Wouldn't hurt to keep an eye out, though. Slave's grapevine's faster'n ours, you know."

Massah Robinson lowered his voice and pointed at Meggie. "I made it up to mate that one over there under the clothesline with Arlo. Young as they are, ought to get a whole pack of young bucks growing up before those two wear out."

Meggie heard most of what Massah said. Lightning zigzagged through her nerves. Her heart began a dreadful pounding as anger overtook the panic in her chest. She tried to calm herself. *Maybe Massah's just talking, Meggie. He likes to brag. You know that. Maybe he doesn't mean what he said.* It didn't help. It was all she could do to keep from running over there, to scream in his face and scratch his eyes out. She clenched her fingers around the clothesline until it bit into her palms.

But what if Massah did mean to mate her to Arlo? Like she was some kind of cow. She shuddered. Her stomach heaved. She would not abide that. She would kill herself first. Her arm muscles bunched and her fingers formed claws as she yanked towels from the line. She gathered the rest of the clothes, tossed them into the basket, and hurried toward the kitchen door of the big house. Her lips were pinched shut to keep the bad word that scalded her tongue from spewing out at the two men. She could hardly see for the tears streaming down her face. A stick in the path made her stumble and she almost dumped the basket's contents on the ground.

Robinson hitched up his breeches. "Yep, oughta be a good mating there."

Pilcher laughed again. "S'pose the little female'll agree to it?"

The screen door slammed on Massah's reply as Meggie escaped into the house. The roar of laughter from the two men echoed in her ears.

Meggie paused in the dim hallway. Her head reeled. Great sobs began to shake her body. As Reba walked by with a dust mop, Meggie's legs folded and she collapsed on the floor.

"Gracious me, child, you sick?"

"Oh, Reba, Reba. Whatever am I gonna do?"

Meggie felt Reba's strong arms lift her to her feet. Reba's voice came to her through a fog. "Do? Depends, girl. Taking on so ain't gonna help." She led Meggie to a seldom-used back stairway. "Now then, sit down. Nobody gonna come around just now. Tell old Reba all about it."

"It's Massah, oh Reba—" Another onslaught of tears rendered Meggie speechless.

"That don't tell me much, child." Reba pulled Meggie close. "Come on, hon. Reba can't help 'til she knows."

"Wish I'd gone with Juba. Rather die out there than—than—"

Reba patted Meggie's hand and waited. Soon the story, disjointed and jumbled, came tumbling out. Through her tears, Meggie saw Reba nod and heard her mumble, "The old devil, hisself."

Meggie raised red-rimmed eyes. "What'm I gonna do, Reba? I'll kill myself 'fore I'll let that Arlo touch me and if Massah tries to—I'll bite him. I'll kick him. Honest, I will—I don't care how he beats me. I'll—"

"Now now, hon, calm yourself. We got to think straight."

But Meggie heard Reba's sigh. They both knew choices were few and none of them good.

They sat in silence, while Reba clasped and unclasped her hands and Meggie wiped at her tears. Finally, Meggie said, "I'm gonna run away. Don't care if I starve or . . . "

Beside her, Reba cleared her throat. In a strong voice, she said, "Dear Lawd, you see us sitting here. You know Meggie's heart. She's a good girl, Lawd. Make a path for her, please. Show her what to do. We know you're a-watching over all your children. Have pity on our dear Meggie. Thank you, Lawd. Amen."

Meggie laid her head on Reba's shoulder. "Oh, Reba, I shoulda been the one to pray instead of ranting and getting myself all upset."

"That's all right, child. The Lawd won't get tired of hearing the two of us talking about the same problem."

At that moment, Sissy bustled around the corner. "Meggie! There you are! Didn't you hear Miss Lorinda's bell? She's fit to be tied, wondering where you are. Hurry up!"

Meggie scrambled to her feet, Reba right behind her. As Meggie raced for the passage to Miss Lorinda's room, she heard Reba singing, "Nobody knows the trouble I'se carryin'. Oh, my Lawd. Nobody knows why the Lawd's a-tarryin'. Oh, my Lawd."

Meggie took a deep breath, smoothed her skirt, and opened Miss Lorinda's bedroom door. She expected to be scolded for tardiness and was not disappointed.

"Well, Meggie" came the haughty voice. "It's about time you showed up. If you don't want a good whipping, you'd better scuttle yourself around and get my things ready. I'm not going to Jeannie Mae's party looking like a fishwife just because you're so slow!"

It was Earl's job to gather the eggs. But Earl was sick with the fever. Cook asked Meggie to run out and gather a few so she could make an angel food cake.

Meggie took the basket and approached the chicken house. She liked the hens, liked the way they clucked softly, liked to stroke their sleek brown feathers. Maybe they would help to ease her troubled mind.

As she lifted the wooden latch to open the door, her eye caught a movement around the corner. She looked and saw nothing. It might have been a bird flying close. Sometimes they swooped down to snatch the cracked corn the chickens ate.

She went on into the chicken house. The hens crooned and clucked contentedly. "Oh, that's a nice one, biddy," she said as she reached under warm feathers. Sometimes a hen raised up a little to let her take the egg. Once in a while, a hen would hold her body down tightly over the egg, trying to keep it to herself. "Thank you, ma'am," Meggie said and "What a big egg," as she went from nest to nest.

She gathered the last egg and paused to stroke the hen's soft feathers. At that moment, the chicken house door opened. Arlo slipped inside and closed the door.

Meggie's eyes widened. Her heart lurched. "What are you doing here?"

Arlo grinned. "Jus' coming to see you 's all."

"Well, I'm busy, Arlo. Let me pass." She started for the door. He barred the way.

Meggie heard the hens begin to stir uneasily in their nests.

"Don't be in such a hurry, Meggie. Can't a fella be a little friendly?"

Meggie felt the throbbing in her throat as her pulse raced. "I don't have time for that. Now let me out."

"Uh-uh. How about a little sugar, Meggie? Give me a kiss 'n' maybe something more? Nobody's to see us."

A few hens cackled nervously. They flapped their wings and fanned dust into the air. Meggie swallowed hard. She rushed to the door.

Arlo caught her by the arm and swung her around. "Hey, you afraid of me or something?"

Meggie tried to pull away. "Let go of me, Arlo. I don't want nothing to do with you."

The hens, now frantic, fluttered to the roost and set up a chorus of shrill cries. Dust and feathers swirled through the air.

Arlo's grip tightened on Meggie's arm. "You ain't still moping over Juba, is you? He ran off and left you." Arlo's other hand fumbled for her breast. "Looks like if he'd a-wanted you, he'd a—"

Meggie swung the egg basket at Arlo's head. Eggs cracked and ran down his face. He let go of her. "Why you, you little—"

A pitchfork to clean out the chicken house leaned against the wall. Meggie seized it and pointed the tines at Arlo's chest. "Get outta here, Arlo, or I'll run you through. So help me God, I will."

Arlo backed away. "Now, Meggie, I was just having fun." He dug egg yolk out of his eyes. "No harm in a little—"

Meggie shouted, "Out!" She pricked his shirt front and watched a tiny bubble of blood appear. Arlo felt for the door and opened it. "You ain't seen the last of me, Meggie. You ain't seen the last."

She heard his footsteps thumping away on the path. Shaking, she collapsed on the straw-strewn floor. The pitchfork fell with a twang against the wall. There were five unbroken eggs in the basket. They lay among the smear of shells and scrambled whites and yolks. The frightened hens kept up a deafening racket. Meggie cradled the basket in her lap and let her tears fall onto the broken eggs. A single brown feather twirled downward and came to rest on her hand.

CHAPTER 17

Meggie's day was almost done. Wearily, she started up the stairs to bring from Miss Lorinda's room a lemonade pitcher and glass she had carried there earlier. She might have to brush Miss Lorinda's hair while she was in the room. Her foot was on the sixth step when Sissy called to her. "Meggie?"

She turned. "Yeah, Sissy?"

"Massah wants you in the front parlor right away soon's you come down."

Meggie's heart skipped, "Massah? What for?"

"How d' I know? I ain't about to ask him."

Meggie's knees began to tremble. "Uh—thanks, Sissy."

Miss Lorinda was sitting at her writing desk as Meggie entered the room. She picked up the pitcher and glass, and turned. "Anything you want me to do, Miss Lorinda?" Even though she was exhausted, tonight she would welcome duties that kept her safely in that room for hours.

Miss Lorinda frowned without looking at Meggie. "Of course not," she said shortly. "Don't interrupt. I'm concentrating."

"Yessum." Meggie closed the door quietly and stood on the landing. *I know he's just a mean old man*, she reminded herself. *Probably wants to scold me for something I've done. Well, I've been scolded before, haven't I? He don't know you heard what he said to Pilcher this morning. Just stand respectfully and wait. You can do it, Meggie. You can do it.*

She descended the stairs and entered the kitchen. She set the glass beside the sink and put the pitcher in the icebox. The block of ice was about half melted and the drip pan would be almost full by morning. She must remind cook. *Now, go on*, she prodded herself. *Get it over with so you can go to bed*. She walked into the parlor.

Master Robinson was seated on the horsehair sofa. He smiled at her. Meggie studied an ant weaving a trail across the carpet.

Robinson's fingers tattooed a rhythm on the arm of the sofa. "I hear you threatened Arlo with a pitchfork this morning, Meggie. That wasn't a very nice thing to do."

"No, suh." *Never mind what Arlo tried to do to me.*

"You know the penalty for naughtiness is a whipping, don't you?"

"Yassah."

"Pretty thing like you don't want that."

"No, suh"

"Are you trembling? You don't need to be afraid of me, Meggie."

"No, suh."

"I won't ever punish you unless you deserve it."

"No, suh."

"I have the right to whip you."

"Yassah."

"It's my duty to whip you when you disobey."

"Yassah."

"I don't get any pleasure from it."

"No, suh."

"I take good care of you, Meggie."

"Yassah."

"I wouldn't let anything happen to you that isn't good for you."

"No, suh."

Robinson stood. He took a step toward her. Meggie's feet said, "Run!" She made fists of her hands and hid them behind her back as Robinson stepped closer. She kept her gaze on the floor, following the progress of his shoes.

"Look at me, Meggie."

Meggie's chin began to wobble.

"I said, 'Look at me!' "

Meggie raised her eyes to his chest.

"You can do better than that. Look me in the eye." He waited. "Come, come, don't make me lose my patience."

Slowly, ever so slowly, Meggie raised her eyes to his face. He was grinning in triumph. It reminded her of the snake who controls and terrifies the captive rabbit. She felt caught, pinned, as if a spike had been thrust through her chest, impaling her.

Robinson's voice had turned buttery. "Now, that wasn't so bad, was it?"

"N-no, suh."

Robinson extended his hand. She couldn't take her eyes off it. He touched her face. She stiffened. He moved one finger, then another, back and forth under her chin as if fondling a dog.

"You could learn to like me, if you tried, Meggie."

"Y –Yassah."

"We could spend some happy times together."

Oh Lawd, don't let me faint, she implored silently. "Yassah."

"You'd like that, wouldn't you, Meggie?"

Say anything, she told herself. *Just make the right noises and maybe he'll get tired of it and go away.* "Yassah."

With the approach of evening, the room had gradually darkened. The walls of the mansion began to creak as the day cooled. Shapes within the room became indistinct, their outlines blurred. *Would Massah never go?*

"You're a smart nigger, Meggie. I could teach you a lot. How would you like me to name the stars for you? Would you like that?"

"Yassah." A tremendous shudder began at the nape of her neck. She tried to control it.

"Tell you what. I'll come to your cabin tonight, when the time's just right. And we'll stand outside and I'll show you the stars."

In the last of the light, Meggie caught the glitter in his eyes. Could he see her tremble? Could he hear her heart as it crashed dizzily against her chest wall?

Robinson reached out again and touched her cheek. "I'll be there, Meggie. You can count on it."

"Yassah." Surely she would smother, standing there.

"You can count on it," he said again. Moving away from her, he backed toward the parlor door, a dark form framed by solid oak. "Count on it," he whispered, the hiss of his voice barely reaching her across the room. Then he was gone. She heard the tap-tap of his feet in the hallway and the complaint of the stair steps as he ascended to his room.

Meggie heard the soft click as he shut his bedroom door. Still she stood, rigid as a pole. Her knees seemed locked in place. A sob escaped her lips and suddenly her body obeyed and she ran, blindly, through the house and down the back steps. Her feet flew over the churned dirt the slaves trod to their cabins. She fell to her knees in front of Reba's shack and managed to whimper, "Reba. Reba."

Reba's door opened. Backlit by a candle, Reba peered into the darkness. "What on earth? That you, Meggie?" Reba pulled her inside.

"Oh, Reba, he's coming. He's coming at me."

"Who? Who's coming?"

"Massah. He said so. He's after me. I gotta go." Meggie clung to her friend. "Gotta go, Reba. Tonight. Gotta go."

Reba's fleshy arms encircled Meggie. "Poor child. The devil hisself. Poor child." She raised her face to the rafters. "Dear Lawd, you know Meggie's got to go. You watch over her, you hear? 'Cause she's gonna need you real bad. Guide her steps, Lawd. Give her strength. Amen."

"Never forget you, Reba. Love you. If I never see you again— you'll know I love you."

"Yes, child." The tears on Reba's cheeks shone in the candlelight. "You be careful, you hear? Don't know how you're gonna do it. Reckon the Lawd'll show you the way." She pressed a crust of bread into Meggie's hand. "You're gonna need this more'n I do."

Gliding silently from shadow to shadow, Meggie reached her own cabin and darted inside. Granny Em was asleep. Meggie snatched up a ragged sweater and the worn blanket on her bunk. In one corner, behind the reed broom was a little collection of treasures done up in a frayed rag. She spread them on the bunk. There was a comb, a piece of broken mirror, and—her breath caught—a palm-sized flat rock on which water had traced a heart. Juba found it on the riverbank and gave it to her just before he ran away.

"Oh, Juba," she whispered, her throat aching with grief.

Quickly, she retied the little bundle, slipped it inside the folded sweater and rolled the blanket around it. The crust of bread she thrust into a pocket of her dress. She scanned the cabin. Oh yes, on the shelf above her plank bed was a pencil and piece of paper she had found on the road. It might come in handy somewhere. And the stale, dried pancake she had taken from the big house. That too. Massah would have whipped her if he'd known about it. Meggie crammed them in with the bread crust.

At the cabin door, she paused. There was the evening star, shining brightly. A stitch went through her chest. She stood for a moment beside Granny Em's small form. She touched the old lady's hand. "Goodbye, Granny Em," she whispered.

Massah might arrive any minute. Meggie darted around the back of the cabin and ran toward the river. Juba had got away on a mule. She had stood in the dark of night and watched him, hands pressed firmly over her lips to muffle her sobs. She could not steal a mule. Her own sturdy feet would take her away. To where? No time to think. No time to plan. A lonely figure, lost in the shadows, the only sound a faint whisking of the weeds as she passed through.

CHAPTER 18

Juba sat on a wooden-nail keg and leaned against the sun-warmed blacksmith shed. He'd made it to Independence. He took out his jackknife and pared at his thumbnail. Pretty good jackknife. Its nickel-plated surface gleamed in the sunlight. And he had real leather boots, thanks to Charlie, the drover. He didn't like them at first. His toes weren't used to being confined. But the boots did protect his feet from thorns and rocks. He guessed a fella had to get used to new boots like he had to get used to freedom. It was just different, that's all. He smiled to himself. Folks that had freedom all along took it for granted. He didn't think he'd ever feel that way. If it cost a lot in sweat and toil, it was all the more precious. At least, that's the way he saw it.

He was a man with responsibilities as well. Along with the boots and a ten-gauge shotgun, he had his own mule. He named it Jack in honor of the mule the overseer had shot from under him when he first escaped the plantation. Charlie told him the gun was a trader. "Made by the British," Charlie had said. "A percussion muzzle loader.

Folks call 'em traders 'cause they get traded to the Indians often as not." Juba would always think of Charlie with a smile.

The town was a jumble of commotion and noises. Juba stared idly at the settlers who shouted and argued and milled around their canvas-topped wagons. They compared oxen and mules, bargained and swapped goods. The men kicked wagon wheels, spit tobacco juice, and bragged about what crops they would grow in the Willamette Valley of Oregon Territory. Women tried to keep track of children who played hide-and-seek behind voluminous skirts or skittered around ox teams that stamped at flies.

Juba's face gave no indication of his inner turmoil. This was still slave country. If he found someone staring at him or lingering around a corner too long, he moved. He was good now at disappearing into a crowd, at pretending to be with a group, or crouching in a darkened shed. The blacksmith had hired him, no questions asked, because he needed a strong man to help with the settlers' last minute shoeing of animals and making sure wagons were sturdy enough for the trail.

Tomorrow at sunrise, Juba would hitch up Widow Hermstead's mules, keep an eye on all the livestock trailing behind, and join the whole pack of forty families with their noses pointed west.

He was headed to Oregon with the rest of them, although he had no idea where Oregon was. They said it was two thousand miles away. Might as well take a trip to the moon. He'd go along and see what Oregon territory looked like, then decide if he wanted to stay. He was excited and apprehensive at the same time.

Yesterday, the wagon master had looked him over. "Name's Jens Studevant." He fastened a steely gaze on Juba's face. "You willing to share chores with white men?"

Juba willed himself to look Studevant in the eye. The old slave demeanor of staring at the ground was hard to break. "Yassah."

"There's bound to be some who don't want a colored near 'em on this train. What're you gonna do about that?"

Juba did not blink. His chin jutted out. Might as well go whole hog while he was at it. Might as well stand up for himself best he could. "Mebbe they could find another wagon train somewheres else."

For a moment, Studevant stared blank-faced. A chuckle began in his chest and built to a belly laugh. "You got nerve, Robinson," he said. "I like that. Don't make no difference to me what skin the man's wrapped in. I'm looking for what's inside. You'll do." He frowned. "Tell you right now, I got no favorites. And I'm the boss. Agreed?"

Juba nodded. "Yassah."

"You'll be taking your share of night watches. And you'll be helping to hitch up the teams every morning and unhitch at night."

Immediately, Juba was confused. Was he to be a servant on this long trek? He had not come so far just to take up the old life. A flare of indignation burned in his chest. He blurted, "I thought every man hitched his own team."

Studevant's eyes narrowed. "They do. But we got three single ladies to look out for. Two of 'em's widows. Reckon they might like a little assistance."

Shame washed over Juba. He tried to shrug it off. "Sure, I'll help. Thought maybe you was . . ."

Studevant had already turned away. "Early start in the morning. Got lots to see to." As he hurried off, Juba heard him chuckle to himself, " . . . maybe they can find another . . ."

Juba still felt a little ashamed of being so cocky with Studevant. It was hard, this new freedom. Took a little getting used to, that's all. He needed practice.

A horse pulling a hack stopped on the muddy street. He heard the squeak as the wheels came to rest. A voice called to him from out of the past. "Boy! I say there, boy."

Juba's head jerked up, the old reflexes still sharp. His calf muscles quivered, but he did not stand. His eyes met hers in one awful moment of recognition.

"Juba! What are you doing here?" It was Miss Lorinda, Master Robinson's daughter. "Come get my horse, boy." she demanded.

Juba had to swallow twice before he found his voice. The old panic urged him to run. Pride said no. Mindless fear no longer ruled him. "Excuse me, ma'am—"

"My horse slipped a shoe," she said in that imperious tone he would never forget. "And one of my wheels is squeaking horribly. I want it fixed immediately."

Juba rose, leg muscles quivering. He took in her ruffles and lace, the incongruous get-up in this frontier town of coarse linsey-woolsey and stiff calico, of women with hands as calloused as a man's.

Her perfume wafted toward him. "Must I tell you twice, Juba?" Haughty, awful haughty, she was.

Juba breathed deeply. He dared to look directly into her eyes. "I'm my own master now, Miss Lorinda. I'm free." That wasn't quite true, but close enough.

"What! Impudent nigger. I ought to have you whipped right here. Master Robinson would have you shot on the spot."

"Yes, ma'am, I reckon he would."

The next instant he was shocked and baffled as Miss Lorinda began to sob and dab at her eyes with an embroidered handkerchief. "Oh dear, to think I traveled all the way to the civilized part of this bawdy city to shop for new fashions and I'm insulted at every turn. Shameful, absolutely shameful."

"Yes, ma'am." Juba agreed, chewing on the corners of his lips to keep from smiling.

"Is it my fault my horse slips a shoe?" she whined. "Is it my fault I'm directed to this horrible street? Cattle all over the place. Coarse people milling about. I don't want them to touch me. To—" Miss Lorinda abruptly switched gears. "You, Juba. You must help me. Take my horse. Get it shod. Fix the wheel. Surely, there is a gentleman somewhere in this dreadful place who could escort me to the civilized part of town until the work is done."

Juba said softly, "Ma'am, you can leave your horse and hack right here. Smithy'll tend to it. There's a hotel just down the street that-a-way," pointing, "where a lady can set and wait. They call it a tearoom. See? You can make out the roofline of the building from here and—"

Miss Lorinda's brittle tone interrupted him. "Is there no decorum in this awful town at all? I cannot wander the streets unescorted, especially with all these ruffians about."

"Ma'am, I would take you there myself but I'm waiting—"

"You! The likes of you to escort me?"

"No, ma'am, I guess not."

Miss Lorinda gathered her voluminous skirts and climbed down from the hack. As she swished past him, the hem of her dress brushed the tops of his shoes. "You may bring the horse and hack to me immediately when they're ready."

Juba straightened his shoulders. "Beg pardon, ma'am. You can come and get 'em yourself. Likely they'll be ready in about two hours. You'll have to wait your turn." He watched the kaleidoscope of expressions slide over her face. It was hard to keep the laughter down where it bubbled in his chest. He inclined his head in a sort of dignified farewell, turned, and walked down the street.

Now, how was that for a former slave? He was sure getting uppity these days. After he had gone a half block, he pocketed his jackknife and began to whistle. He reckoned he had about ten minutes more before returning to the smithy's to pound iron. Good man, the smithy. Gave a fella time in the middle of the day to get the kinks out of his back.

The sun's rays slanted low in the late afternoon when Miss Lorinda appeared again. She sat in her hack, the top of it surrounding her like a black throne.

Juba was grooming a horse. He saw her approach from the corner of his eye. He knew she would try to find another opportunity to put him "in his place." He could stand it. Did Miss Lorinda have a heart? He longed for news of Meggie. If he asked, would she tell him?

"Well, Juba," she said to his back. "Far be it from me to report you. But you must know if Pilcher ever catches you, he has a right to hang you."

Juba turned, curry comb in hand. "Yes, ma'am."

Miss Lorinda's brows were raised in haughty reproach. "Of course, when I get home, I won't say a word."

Juba licked his lips. His thoughts brushed over her hollow promise and rushed ahead. He leaned forward in his eagerness. "Miss Lorinda—is Meggie—is she . . .?" He let the sentence dangle. Too late, he remembered slaves did not address their superiors unless spoken to.

Miss Lorinda raised her chin and closed her eyes. She said nothing.

Juba waited. He heard his own breath, inhaling and exhaling. At last, he could not stand the suspense. "Miss Lorinda?"

Miss Lorinda opened her eyes and Juba saw how they glittered with malice. Her lips slowly spread into a sneer. "Pa mated Meggie to Arlo right after you disappeared. She'll probably drop a little buck before I get home and another one next summer."

Drop a buck? Rage rose in Juba's throat. Why'd she have to say it like that? Why'd she have to talk so coarse? As if Meggie was no different than a cow having a calf. Or a brood mare. Miss Lorinda's crudeness slapped him like globs of mud thrown in his face.

She appeared not to notice his discomfort. "Pa is most pleased. Meggie's little bucks will make good strong niggers in a few years. That's all Pa cares about."

The scar on Juba's temple turned pink. His fists knotted.

Miss Lorinda twirled her parasol. "Pa was very angry, of course, when you ran away. He made all the slaves work extra hours with no Sunday rest for a month. They blamed you, Juba. Some still are very bitter toward you."

Juba heard her through a haze of hurt. "Miss Lorinda, about Meggie—"

"Well? Speak up, boy. I have no obligation to sit here, you know."

Juba fingered the pocket in his overalls and drew out a small package. Before Miss Lorinda returned that afternoon to claim her horse and hack, he had devised a plan. He would ask her to carry home a button from his shirt to give to Meggie. Meggie would know he had kissed it and sent his love. The blacksmith gave him a piece of brown paper to wrap it in and wax to seal the package.

Now, as he held it out to Miss Lorinda, a lump lodged in his throat. Would she take it? Would she throw it away? His hand shook. He heard himself pleading, "Please, Miss Lorinda, please—could—would you take this to Meggie?"

She stared hard at him, then with a grimace, pinched the folded edge of the paper with thumb and forefinger as if it were dirty, and flung it onto the buggy seat. "What difference does it make? You won't ever see her anyway."

Juba's pain tore at his insides. Miss Lorinda seemed determined to pound his feelings into a pulp.

She shrugged. She lifted the reins and the horse stepped forward. "If it wasn't for visiting Cousin Harriet and taking home new dresses, I would never be in this God-forsaken place. You know you owe Pa a lot for—"

"Owe him?"

"—taking you in and giving you a home."

"A home?"

"Seems to me you ought to be ashamed for running off like that."

"Ashamed? But, Miss Lorinda—"

"I'm very disappointed in you, Juba. After all Pa did for you." She flicked the reins with a flourish. The horse stepped smartly and the hack rolled down the street.

In silent despair, Juba watched her drive away. His eyes stung. He could not swallow. Incredulous, he whispered, "After all her pa did for me?"

From a hundred feet away, he saw something small and brown drop between the hack's wheels to the ground. Was it his package?

Juba bounded forward. Before he could get to the spot, a gust of wind set it cartwheeling under the hooves of four mules pulling a lumber wagon. He watched as the small object tore into muddy shreds and was swept along into a drain. Had Miss Lorinda thrown away his package? He would never know.

CHAPTER 19

Many miles away, wind-driven rain pelted and slashed, sharp as icy needles. Meggie struggled across a muddy field. All at once, her knees folded and she sat down in the mire. She had come to a ten-foot ditch that stretched as far as she could see. There was only one way to cross it: climb down into it and up the other side. Her dress clung to her in dirty folds and wrinkles. Her matted hair was sculpted to her head. She sighed and tried to swallow the lump of despair in her throat. Raindrops trailed in rivulets down her arms and legs.

You gotta keep going, Meg. Get up. You stop, you won't get started again, she scolded herself. She was so tired. She could not remember when she had last eaten. With a sigh, she scooted to the edge of the ditch, curled her lip in distaste and slithered down the steep bank. At the bottom, her feet splashed in the water as she sank to her ankles in the slimy mud. Every step was an effort. The mud sucked at her flesh each time she dragged a foot out of it and struggled forward.

Arms stretched out to balance, she reached for weeds on the opposite bank to pull herself along. She stepped on a sharp rock hidden beneath the water's surface. "Ouch, oh!" Her foot slipped and she fell into the oozing slime. She sat there a moment, panting with weakness. Could she go on? Maybe it was hopeless, this trying to find her way north. How easy it would be to give up. Just give up and die here.

At that moment, the rain beat down with greater intensity. It drummed upon her head and shoulders. A surge of anger flared in Meggie's chest. She raised her face to the sky and cried, "Think you can drown me, do you? Go ahead and pour. Pour harder for all I care. Pour harder, pour harder!"

Shaking with fury, she grabbed hold of a clump of weeds and hoisted herself upright. She dug in her toes and clambered up the bank, grasping at roots and twigs. Her anger propelled her to the top of the ditch where she collapsed onto the grassy field. There she lay, sobbing, skin-soaked and splattered with mud. After a while, too weak to fight anymore, Meggie turned over, opened her mouth and let the cool raindrops fall upon her tongue.

At length, she became aware of bird song, of a breeze that dried her skin. She sat up. The clouds were breaking apart. A watery sun peeked through. Nearby, she spied a stick. She sat up, crawled to it and levered herself a little at a time to her feet. She set her jaw. She would go on. Across the field. Into the foothills on the other side. Step by step.

As she came to the far edge of the field, Meggie heard water running. She plodded through the soggy grass, up a rocky embankment and found the source. Here a stream bubbled over mossy stones, winding and gurgling back toward the ditch she had crossed. Sunlight silvered the branches of aspen trees. They swayed in a gentle breeze and shook the raindrops from their leaves. Their shadows made dappled patterns on boulders strewn about. One huge rock lay like a bulky table in the sun's warmth. As Meggie raised her gaze to the other side of the stream, she saw low bushes. Their branches hung heavily with blueberries.

Meggie splashed through the icy water, frantic with hunger. She reached into the bushes, cupped her dirty palms, and filled her mouth with berries. The juice mingled with the mud and ran down her chin. Had anything ever tasted so good?

Immediately, her stomach rebelled. *Slow down, Meg. Slow down.* She cried out, "I gotta eat. I'm starving. Gotta eat!" *Yes, you can eat. Sit still. Chew a few berries at a time. You can do it.* Shaking, she huddled beside the bushes and listened to the gurgling stream.

As she made herself eat slowly, she watched a leaf caught in an eddy whirl and disappear around a curve. There was peace here. There was a gentle quiet. She needed this balm to her soul as much as she needed food.

Meggie peeled off her dress and, although the sun was warm, she shivered as she stepped into the stream. She sloshed and scrubbed her dress, careful not to further fray the edges of the rips. On the tabletop rock, she spread the dress to dry. After she had bathed and washed the mud from her hair, she examined her many cuts and scrapes. Scratched chigger bites dotted her skin. She climbed onto the boulder and lay beside her dress. The sun-warmed surface soothed and relaxed her tired body and she fell asleep.

When Meggie awoke and slipped into her warm, dried dress, the sun was setting. Still hungry, but refreshed and renewed by the bath and another handful of berries, she picked enough to fill her pocket. She climbed among the rocks and followed the stream.

Eventually, as the light dimmed through the trees, she came to a high meadow where traces of mist, like raveled lace, began to settle in the low places. She decided to walk straight across the meadow, watching out for boggy ground.

She was halfway to the other side when two men on horseback galloped out of the woods. Meggie crouched. But one had already spied her. He pointed and shouted to his companion, "Look there, Josh. Ain't a stray cow. Something more interesting. Let's go!"

Meggie began to run. Her feet tangled in the tall marshy grass and she tumbled to the ground. She struggled up. The horses were upon her. She heard a loop of rope sing through the air. It slid around her neck. Thrashing, twisting, clawing at the rope, she felt it jerk tight and pull her up short. She gasped for air.

"Whoa there, girlie. Take it easy." The man sat tall in the saddle. There was laughter in his voice, "Look what I lassoed, Josh. Why'd you suppose a young thing like her's out here with night coming on?"

"Dunno. Why'd ya catch her? What you gonna do with her? Better let her go." The man named Josh shifted uneasily on his horse and scratched his beard.

"I'll take her home to Sal."

"You crazy, Dan? Sal won't want 'nother woman 'round."

"But this one, she kin help Sal. Tend the garden. Scrub the clothes—"

"Likely belongs to someone, Dan. I don't think—"

"Finders, keepers. Least 'til somebody claims her. Get on up behind me, girl."

Meggie dug in her heels and scowled.

"Lookit that, Josh. Got me a little fighter."

"Still think you're making a mistake. This's free country. You don't need no truck with slaves."

"Aw, don't spoil my fun."

"Fun? She's a girl, Dan. You can't just pack her on home like a— like a wolf pup to play with."

Dan bristled, "Well, what would you do? Leave her out here to—"

"Sure. She was here before we came along. Let her be."

"Bet she's lost. Bet she's a runaway. Betcha. How much you wanna bet?"

"I gotta get on home. Get chores done before full dark. We ain't gonna find any more stray cows tonight." Josh wheeled his horse. "I'll have a few hours to spare tomorrow if you wanna look for any more dogies. Let me know." He spurred his horse and was soon lost in the mist.

Dan frowned down at Meggie. " 'S getting late. Either you climb on up here or I'll hoist you up."

Meggie frowned back. She clawed and strained at the rope that scratched her neck. Dan played it out, then reeled her in again. "Can't win, little gal. Might as well give up." He jumped off his horse and walked toward her.

Terror in her eyes, Meggie shied away from him. He grabbed her by the shoulder. She bit his hand.

"Hey there, you're sure a wild one."

Meggie bit again.

"Ow, that's enough of that." Dan wound the rope around her, pinning her arms to her sides.

Meggie kicked him in the shins. He grabbed her leg and threw her to the ground.

"You wanna play rough, little gal? I'll play rough." As easily as hefting a sack of potatoes, he threw her over the horse behind the saddle, tied her on, and took off at a gallop. He yelled back at her, "Lots easier riding straight up. You wanna trade, let me know."

Meggie's stomach gave up the blueberries. She gagged and gasped and cried. She wished fervently that she had stayed back at the stream. Surely, she would die at the hands of this brute.

CHAPTER 20

The horse finally slowed to a trot. The dim outlines of a cabin and outbuildings came into view. Lamplight spilled from an open doorway.

"'Lo the house, I'm home." Dan called out.

"About time, Dan," a woman's voice answered.

Meggie tried to twist around to see the woman. A pain shot through her for her efforts.

The woman came nearer, "What you got there? A sick calf?" Footsteps scuffed the dirt. "My word, Daniel Crane, it's a girl! Get her down this minute. She's strangling."

Lamplight showed Meggie the silhouette of a woman almost as tall and rangy as Dan. He dismounted. "Now, don't get on your high horse, Sal. I brought her home for you."

"For me? What for?"

"Figured she could work. Ease things up a bit for you. You know—"

As he spoke, Meggie felt the rope loosen. Dan lifted her off the horse and set her on the ground. He left the rope around her neck. She promptly fell into the dirt and sat there, trembling, head down.

The woman's feet came into her line of vision. She wore boots like a man. She hunkered down and with a gentle hand raised Meggie's chin. "I can't believe you did this, Dan. What's your name, honey?" she asked.

Meggie shook her head. The woman's kind words brought tears to her eyes. A sob escaped her lips.

Dan folded his arms over his chest. "Don't reckon she understands what we're saying, Sal."

Sal glanced back at him, "Humph."

Dan said, "Found her in the high meadow yonder. She was running like a scared deer. Had a heck of a fight to get her on the horse."

Sal shook her head at Dan. She touched Meggie's shoulder. "Don't be afraid. I won't hurt you. Don't know where you came from and don't know what Dan was thinking of, but we'll sort it out. Come on in the cabin and we'll clean you up a bit. Bet you'd like something to eat." She began to slip the rope from around Meggie's neck.

Dan sprang forward. "Don't take it off, Sal. She's a wild one. She'll run away."

Sal stood and turned on him. "Well, why wouldn't she be wild? If you tied me up like that and slung me over the horse like a sack of feed, I'd—"

"All right, all right. Supper ready?"

Meggie heard Sal's deep sigh. "Supper's been waiting for almost an hour, Dan."

Dan slapped dust from his chaps. "Can't help it. Josh 'n' me been looking for stray cows all day." He turned the horse toward the barn. "I'll be in soon's I get ol' Prancer t'bed."

Sal bent low and took Meggie by the arms. "Come on, honey. Get up from this damp ground. I ought to take that rope off right now. Suppose I'd better humor Dan a bit though 'til I figure out what he's got in his fool head."

Meggie allowed herself to be lifted and with Sal's help, she stumbled into the cabin.

"Here," Sal said, pointing to a chair. "Sit here."

With no place to hide from the cabin's lamplight, Meggie heard Sal gasp. Under half-closed lids, she sensed Sal's probing eyes traveling from her bare feet to the top of her head. There was an awkward pause, then came Sal's voice, whispering, full of wonder. "Are you a runaway slave? Now that I can see you in the lamplight, I—well, I've never seen a—never seen a—slave before."

Meggie stole a glance at the open cabin door. She tensed, leaned forward as if she might make a run for it. Sal saw her intention and closed the door.

"Don't try to run, honey. Dan'd hunt you down with the horse." She knelt in front of Meggie and touched her hands.

Meggie jerked them away.

Sal pretended to not notice. "Besides it's dark now. Gonna be cold out tonight. I'd feel bad if you were out there trying to find your way in the dark."

Sal stirred something on the stove. "You look like you could use a good meal."

Meggie sat with head bowed. The aroma of Sal's stew made her stomach roil.

Sal went on in her soothing voice, "It's going to be all right, honey. You'll be safe with me. Want something to eat now?"

Meggie opened her mouth. She made a little choking sound.

"Yes?" Sal bent over her, eyes kind, eager to help.

Meggie licked her lips. Did she dare to ask for something? "Uh, wa-water?"

Sal strode across the cabin, poured water into a tin cup from a bucket on a shelf near the stove, and brought it to her. "Here you are."

"Thank you, ma'am," Meggie managed to whisper.

"And I'll get you some warm water to wash your face while I'm at it."

Meggie drank slowly. Never in her life had a white woman brought a cup of water to her. She cast furtive glances about the room. Sal set an enamel wash pan and a soft cloth on the floor beside Meggie's chair. "Wish I knew your name."

Meggie looked respectfully at the floor. She waited until Sal went back to the stove, then wrung out the cloth in the warm water, and washed her face and hands. Feeling a little bolder, she stared at Sal. Sal suddenly turned and caught her at it. Meggie ducked her head. Embarrassed, a smile played at the corners of her mouth.

She frowned, puzzled, when abruptly Sal began to try names in a sing-song fashion. "Let me see, what would your name be? Jane or Emma Lee? How about Liza or Mary or Pansy or—"

Meggie heard herself say, "Ma'am, I'm Meggie." She clapped a hand over her mouth. Underneath the hand was another smile. What was the matter with her? She was playing the fool in front of this strange woman. Must be the hunger weakness.

"Meggie?" Sal repeated. "I'm just plain old Sal and you've got a pretty name like Meggie. Why, that's not fair. Not fair at all." Her laugh was low and bubbly, like the spring where Meggie had paused in the afternoon.

The cabin door opened and banged against the wall. Dan stomped into the room. At once, Meggie stiffened. She looked at the floor with fingers clutched together on her lap.

Dan went to the corner by the stove. "Where's the wash pan?"

Sal said,"Just a minute." She hurried to Meggie's side, retrieved the pan, and poured Meggie's wash water into a bucket on the floor. "Here it is."

Dan glanced at Meggie and shrugged. He dipped water from the bucket on the shelf and sloshed it over his face. Meggie was aware of his stare while he dried on a towel hanging from a nail on the wall. His chair scraped the floor as he sat at the table. "I'm starved."

Sal set a steaming dish of beef stew before him. She cut thick slices of wheat bread and brought a saucer of butter from the cupboard. Back at the stove, Sal poured water into a pan to heat for washing the dishes.

"Ain't you gonna eat?" Dan inquired.

Sal raised her chin a little. "Meggie and I will eat later."

"Meggie? That her name? How'd you know that?"

Sal smiled. "I asked her."

Dan stared at Meggie briefly and shrugged again. "Well, I'll be."

Sal planted both hands on the table and leaned over Dan. "Maybe I'll take her out to the field tomorrow to find some wildflowers."

"Wildflowers? Sal, that gal's somebody's slave. You don't go picking wi—"

Sal held out her arms. "I don't see any slaveholders here. Do you?"

With a piece of bread, Dan sopped up the rest of the stew on his plate and stood. "Now, just a minute here, Sal. I brought her home so you could—"

Sal's hands were on her hips. "So I could work her like a slave?"

"Look here, woman, you don't know nothing about slaves. You might have to take a whip to her to make her mind. They're like savages. They'll turn on you if you don't watch 'em. You gotta keep the upper hand."

An eerie keening interrupted their argument. Meggie had slipped off the chair and crouched near the door. She swayed from side to side. Her hands covered her face as she wailed and huddled there.

"Now, look what you've done." Sal accused.

"What *I've* done, woman? This thing's turning out to be more bother than it's worth. Open the door and shove her out. We'll be shut of her and she can keep on to wherever she was going."

Sal's voice soared an octave. "Shove her out? In the dark and cold? No, I won't. That's one thing I won't do."

Dan slammed his chair into the table. "Then do whatever you want to. I'm going to bed."

His boots clipped the floor as he strode across the room, yanked the curtain that served as a bedroom door and disappeared behind it. His muffled voice came from behind the curtain. "Try to give a woman a present and she kicks harder than a mule."

Sal lifted her shoulders and let out a long sigh. She crouched before Meggie and put her arms around her. She expected the girl to stiffen and pull away, but Meggie still moaned and swayed. Finally, she quieted. She peeked from between her fingers at Sal. And as Sal waited, Meggie said in a small hesitant voice, "Massah don' like me."

"Massah? Dan? He's not— Oh, I'm learning something every minute." For the second time that evening, Meggie felt the tug of Sal's hands as she lifted her to her feet. "Come on. Let's eat while the food's still hot."

Meggie pulled back. "No, ma'am. I mustn't—mustn't eat with you—ma'am."

"And why not?"

Meggie ducked her head and closed her eyes.

Sal said, "You mean—because you—you—"

"Beg pardon, ma'am. Slaves don' eat with white folks."

Sal's cheeks pinked. She frowned. "I don't see any slaves here tonight, Meggie. There's just you and me." Sal slipped the rope from around Meggie's neck and threw it in the corner. "Come," she said.

Meggie stood by the table, head bowed, until Sal was seated. Tentatively, slowly, she sank into a chair and kept her eyes on her plate.

Sal said, "It's beef stew. Tastes pretty good if I do say so."

Meggie stared at the cutlery. She rubbed her fingers together in her lap. Back in Mississippi she had eaten with gourd spoons and sometimes scooped up the food with her hands. Should she—?

Sal startled her and solved the dilemma. "You can use that spoon if you want to. Ever use a fork?"

"No, ma'am. Never had a pretty plate with flowers on it, neither. Just a tin pan is all."

From the corner of her eye, Meggie noted Sal's sad smile. What a tangled mess she had fallen into. How was she to get out of it? Sal didn't know what to do with a slave.

And Dan, was he her massah or not? She certainly did not like him. He was different from Massah Robinson, thank the Lawd for that. But he was like having a speck of sand in your eye or a thorn in your finger. Neither appealed to her as a permanent situation.

Sal fixed Meggie a bed in a leanto room behind the kitchen. She called it the back porch. And Meggie lay down on this strange soft bed, expecting to rise up in the middle of the night and make her escape.

She mulled over her day. It had been full of shocks. The muddy field, the stinging downpour, the warm, flat rock beside the stream, and the blueberries. And then the flight through the meadow. She rubbed her neck. It was still scraped and sore where Massah Dan's scratchy rope had bound around it. And this evening, Sal, a white lady, had brought her water and served her supper. She had never known such a white lady. Sal's kindness filled a hollow place and brought healing to Meggie's bruised soul.

CHAPTER 21

Meggie was surprised when she opened her eyes to a bright morning sky. Sal bent over her. Meggie untangled herself from the blankets and scooted away from Sal. She hung her head and waited for the scolding. Surely, Sal would reprimand her for sleeping so late.

But Sal's voice soothed her as it had the night before. "Don't be afraid, Meggie."

"I—I'se sorry, ma'am. Shoulda been up. Shoulda been at work."

"What? Oh no, Meggie. You were exhausted. I let you sleep on purpose.

"Massah won't like it. I'se sorry."

"Oh, Meggie, you're not our slave. I don't care what Dan said. He's already gone out to fix pasture fence. I saved breakfast for you. Come on to the kitchen now."

Never in Meggie's life had breakfast been "saved" for her, nor had she slept abed longer than Miss Lorinda.

Later, Sal said, "This is my wash day. Dan doesn't help me, but would you like to? Since you're already here?" She gave Meggie a bucket and told her where to find the creek just down the hill from the homestead buildings.

Meggie asked, "Watch out for 'gators?"

"What?"

"'Gators. Uh—alligators."

Sal stared for a moment, open-mouthed. "Oh—no, Meggie. We don't have any alligators here."

Meggie sensed Sal's eyes on her as she trudged away from the cabin. *Was I wrong, asking about 'gators? And how come water's so cold, like it was at the spring yesterday? 'Bout froze my toes off.*

They heated the water on the cook stove and poured it into a galvanized tub. Sal palmed a lump of her homemade lye soap and stood over a bench as she scrubbed the clothes on a washboard propped in the tub. She handed them to Meggie who rinsed them in another tub of water, wrung them out, and snapped them in the air to remove wrinkles before she pinned them to the clothesline.

Sal looked up from the scrub board. "Tell me, Meggie, about life on a plantation. What's it like?"

Haltingly at first, Meggie began to talk about the slaves, her daily routine. She told Sal how she loved Reba, who had been like a mother to her.

Sal's reddened hands stopped scrubbing. "But, how about your own parents, Meggie?"

"My folks? Don't know. As far back as I can remember, I lived with Granny Em. She too old to work in the fields. Sew on buttons and patches and stuff and tell stories to the little kids while they mammas hoeing and picking."

Sal's scrubbing hands paused again. She persisted, "But, surely, someone knows who your family is, where you might find them—"

"No, ma'am. Best not to pay no never mind. No use bringin' the hurt out to look at it. Little babes separated from mammas, husbands and wives sold to different massahs. I was a gift child."

"A gift child? What's that?"

"That's when a youngun's given to someone else to raise if something happens to their mamma. I was Miss Lorinda's slave from the time I was seven years old. Mighty lucky, there. I didn't have to work in the cotton fields."

Sal handed the last dripping article to Meggie, dipped a bucket into the tub, and began to water purple pansies growing near the cabin door. She straightened, bucket in hand. "Meggie—where were you going when Dan—when Dan found you?"

A yearning filled Meggie's chest. She swallowed. "Ain't exactly sure, ma'am. Just going—to Oregon somehow." She turned and gazed over the prairie. Her eyes lingered on the hazy mountains in the distance. "I got a friend. Somebody I—want to find him—so bad—want to—" She dabbed at her eyes. "Coulda gone with him, but I was too scared. And now—"

Sal set down the bucket. Meggie felt a comforting hand on her shoulder. "He's somebody you love, isn't he?"

"Yes, ma'am. All's I know is, he talked about Oregon. I don't know what Oregon is. Don't know where it is. Don't know nothing 'bout it. But I'm gonna keep on until I—"

"Do you know where you are now, Meggie?"

"No, ma'am. I'se just gonna keep on—"

"This ranch is in Nebraska Territory. You've a long ways to go before you get to Oregon. Hasn't anybody told you about the high mountains you have to cross? And the snow?"

"Snow, ma'am?"

"Meggie, winter comes early in the mountains. And sometimes it comes early here. A person can't live on the prairies without shelter or food. Once in a while, the blizzards are so bad the cattle freeze to death."

"Blizzards?"

"Yes, blizzards, when the wind whips the snow into great piles and it's so cold you don't dare go out. Dan tries to keep our herd around the barn so he can feed them. Surely, someone told you—"

"I been staying away from folks. Afraid they send me back to Massah Robinson for a whipping."

"You mean you've been on your own the whole time?"

"Yessum."

Meggie saw the astonishment in Sal's eyes. "And so you came all this way," Sal murmured, as if to herself. "It would have been a lot easier, the two of you."

"But we didn't have time to jump the broom and—"

It was Sal's turn to be puzzled. "Jump the broom? What on earth?"

"Yessum. Lotsa slaves jump the broom together, then folks say they's married. I told Juba I wouldn't go away with him until we was married."

Sal smiled. She tried to put a little levity into the conversation, "Well, couldn't your Juba have found a broom for heaven's sake and—"

"Oh, ma'am, he didn't have time. Massah was taking him to another plantation the next morning, far away. I'd never see him there neither. He'd be gone and I—"

Sal carried the remaining water in the washtub to a willow sapling at the corner of the yard. She splashed the last of the water around its base. "Your mistress, Meggie, did you try to talk your troubles over with her?"

Meggie's eyes were wide with confusion. Had she heard Sal right? "Talk to Miss Lorinda about my troubles, ma'am? Oh no. If she'd a know'd I loved Juba—she'd a made sure we were parted. She'da made sure. Miss Lorinda, she—she thought it was fun to—" Meggie's throat constricted and she turned away.

She heard Sal murmur behind her. "Poor thing—I wonder—do you suppose—what if—?"

"Ma'am?"

Sal hung the tub and washboard on the side of the cabin. She bustled about. "Quick, let's change dresses and hitch up the buggy. I want you to meet somebody."

"I only got this one dress, ma'am."

"Nonsense. You can wear one of my dresses." She stopped and looked at Meggie. "Guess we'll have to pin up the hem a few inches and push up the sleeves. We're calling on Patience Booth."

"Patience?"

"She's my friend, Meggie. And I'm going to miss her dreadfully. But her husband is determined to grow fruit trees in Oregon Territory.

This climate's too cold and dry for them. Next spring, he wants to join a wagon train that always stops over at Fort Bridger for supplies. The wagon trains have been coming through and stopping there the past two years. Next spring, that's where they'll be. And Patience'll be gone for good."

"Yessum."

Sal sighed. "It was a contest between friendship and fruit trees, and the fruit trees won." Sal's voice took on a brittle quality. Her eyes shone with unshed tears. She coughed to hide a cry that begged to escape. "Guess I'll have to get used to hugging corn cobs instead of friends." This last was merely a murmur to herself.

Meggie looked on in pity. Loneliness was not reserved for slaves after all.

CHAPTER 22

For two months, the wagons had rocked and swayed across the open prairie. Juba welcomed the midnight watch. It gave him time to be alone, to think. He climbed onto a shack-sized boulder, held his tin cup of lukewarm coffee in one hand, and his shotgun in the other. He scanned the countryside. Bright moonlight cast deep shadows beside bushes. On the other side of a rocky ridge, a coyote yipped. From far away echoed another's mournful answer. Presently a nighthawk's cry pierced the silence.

Juba poured the dregs of his coffee on the ground and thought about Meggie. He longed to tell her of the dusty trail and the pure cool air of evening. If only he could take her hand and together they would gaze at the snow-crowned mountains. He saw in his mind's eye her surprise at trout that darted and hid under snags in cold dappled water, so different from the sluggish waters of home. Home. Where was home? And who was he? He had become a pilgrim among strangers. Some tolerated him. Some curled their lips, as if he stank, and openly shunned him. Very few, like Studevant, offered friendship.

He was startled by a rustling noise behind him. He jumped off the boulder and hugged the dark side of it, finger ready on the trigger of his gun. Out of the shadows floated the nightgown-clad form of a girl. A gentle breeze played with her long blonde hair, catching golden strands in the moonlight.

Juba frowned as she came close. "What you doing out here?" His voice was not gentle.

She sidled next to him and put out a hand to touch his arm. "Why, I just thought—maybe you'd be lonesome, Mr. Robinson."

Juba jerked his arm away. "Well, I ain't and you better scat." He could see her face clearly. Abbie Townsend, fourteen-year-old daughter of an Ohio farmer trekking his family west to sink a plow into virgin land. A man who made it plain he loathed Juba's black skin.

Abbie's voice was smooth as honey. "I think you're awfully good looking, Mr. Robinson." She stepped closer, her mouth slightly open, the nipples of her young breasts outlined beneath her thin cotton gown.

Juba had a sudden impulse to take her over his knee and spank her. Instead, he leaned into her face and scowled. "Look here, little girl, you trying to make trouble for me? You get back to your wagon quick-like before I tell your papa what you done."

Abbie giggled. "I'm not a little girl. You know how old I am?"

Juba did not answer.

Abbie spread her arms and whirled around, her face upturned toward the moon. "Papa says niggers are more like animals than white folks. That true, Mr. Robinson?"

"Just go, will ya?"

"Not till you tell me."

"Tell you what?"

"Can you see better in the dark than white folks?"

The idea came swiftly. He made his voice a growl. "Sure can. Right now, I see a wolf just beyond those trees over yonder." He pointed. "It's hungry. Probably looking for something easy to pick off. Like a girl with nothing but a nightgown on."

He watched her peer into the gloom. He saw her shudder. "Seeing in the dark ain't all I can do. I can talk to the animals. Tell 'em where the good pickings are. They thank me. They always do."

She cringed away from him. "You're horrible," she cried, her eyes wide with fear. "Horrible." She turned and ran into the shadows between the wagons.

Juba sat down hard next to the boulder. He put a hand over his face and took deep breaths to steady himself. The moon advanced several degrees before the trembling in his body stilled.

The rest of the night passed quietly. Juba stared wide-eyed at the distant mountains, his mind zigzagging from one frightening scenario to another. What if that girl should tell her folks he encouraged her to slip out in the night? What if she told them he made advances toward her? What if—

Life wasn't fair. He found that out long ago. You did the best you could with what you had and kept on trying. Some folks seemed to be favored. But sooner or later, hard times came to them just like everybody else. He certainly did not envy that ignorant Townsend with his silly daughter. Even a jackrabbit had more sense than that.

Just before dawn the temperature dropped and Juba shivered. As he stood and stretched, the sky began to lighten. He heard voices. Somebody lit a lantern. Kettles clattered over the flickering flames of a campfire. The sun would soon break through above the hills. Juba walked among the hobbled horses and caught the bridles of widow Hermstead's mule team. Between the wagons, he saw Abbie Townsend from the corner of his eye. She was watching him. He drew a deep breath and strolled past, intent on the care of the mules.

CHAPTER 23

Mary Waldheim was a pretty woman. With eyes blue as a Nordic sea and flaxen hair, she was what folks called "winsome." Neb, her husband of only a year, doted on her. Whatever Mary wanted, Mary received if it was within his power.

Juba liked Neb Waldheim. He was a strong, angular German with a chiseled chin and an easy smile. Juba had helped him rescue oxen sunk to their bellies in mire. Together, they had fitted scraps of hide from dead oxen onto the sore hooves of live ones, giving the tender spots a few days to heal. And the two of them, out hunting meat for the supper fires, worked well in tandem, understanding each other's unspoken ways.

Juba watched the young couple sometimes, and pictured Neb and Mary in Oregon prospering on their future farm. Completing the picture would be six young tow-headed Waldheims, lean of leg and wide of shoulder, helping to wrest the family dream from the wilderness. It was a fine dream. And Juba was not jealous. He wished only the best for Neb and Mary.

After fighting heat and flies and choking dust on this exhausting fourteenth of July, the settlers searched for a suitable place to make camp for the night. Chimney Rock was far behind them and they had turned south, leaving the shallow Platte. The tired oxen lowed their displeasure but drank the brackish water in a rapidly evaporating mud hole. They seemed to sigh with relief when the yokes were lifted from their shoulders. The settlers slapped sweaty hats against dust encrusted pant legs and sloshed the drinking water in the barrels roped to their wagons, estimating how long it would last until they could find another spring.

Weary and unwashed, cooking fires flickering low, the travelers quickly retired for the night. Surely, the rain would come soon. Surely, the proverbial green pastures were just around the corner if they persevered.

It was an hour before sunrise when Juba heard someone walking around. From his bed roll under Widow Hermstead's supply wagon, he propped himself on an elbow and peered into the darkness. He could barely make out the hulks of other wagons and the humps of oxen bedded within the circle. Then, close by, he heard a woman whimper and moan followed by a man's murmured attempt at consolation. The dry grass whispered under boots and the swish of a long skirt. He could have reached out and touched them. Neb's boots. Mary's skirt.

Wide awake now, Juba clambered out from under the wagon, bumping his head on an axle. He was still on his knees when the couple passed by, walking in the opposite direction. Mary stumbled, doubled over. Neb supported her.

"Neb?" Juba called softly.

"Juba!" Neb whispered, his voice unsteady.

"It's Mary. She's sick. Terrible stomachache. Thought maybe if I walked her a bit we might relieve it."

At that moment, Mary cried out. Her knees gave way and she slumped against Neb's chest. "Mary, Mary dear. Mary, are you—"

Juba rushed to help Neb. Together, they carried Mary to the tarp Neb had spread under his wagon for a bed.

Neb's whispered words tumbled out in a rush of anxiety, "She was all right when we went to bed. She felt fine. Then she lost her supper and she can't—"

Juba worked a match from his pocket and lit Neb's lantern. His dark eyes gleamed in the dim light as he studied Mary's sweat-slick face, her cheeks bleached of color. His heart accelerated. Back in Mississippi, he had seen lots of sick folks like this. Lots of them with bad stomachaches. Most of them died. Cholera had no favorites. He sensed Neb's questioning gaze. How could he tell his friend? Tell him that in a few hours his wife would probably die and there wasn't any way to prevent it.

Juba sat back on his haunches. "Don't know, Neb," he lied. "Maybe she just needs to rest. Maybe it was something she ate." Yeah. Sure. Nobody else had a stomachache like that.

But somebody did. The camp began to stir. Three wagons back, a child cried. Across the circle, a man staggered to his feet. His hands were pressed to his abdomen. He leaned his head against the rough boards of his wagon and alternately moaned and swore as he vomited. Boots pounded the ground as someone ran past, answering a frantic call farther back. "Caleb, Caleb, come quick!"

It was decided by a majority vote that the wagon train would move on. They had to get across the prairie. They had to find fresh water and grass for the animals. They had to get where they weren't so exposed to Indian attack. And so the oxen accepted their yokes. The wheels turned and creaked. The sick lay languidly on their jolting beds. The unspoken word on everybody's lips was cholera.

The tally was seven people death had chosen at random. Three were children: five, eight, and eleven years old. Two were men: husbands and fathers. The other woman, besides Mary, was a scold and complainer who had made her family miserable since they left Independence. She screeched until three in the afternoon, lost consciousness, and died quietly.

Mary clung to life until evening came again and the moon rose, hot yellow, over the endless prairie. Neb Waldheim knelt beside her, whispering his love. Juba paced back and forth, blinking at the tears that streaked his face. A chorus of coyotes yipped and howled nearby until Juba in sudden anger, fired his gun and yelled, "Shut yourselves up, you idiots. Don't you know there's a—" He caught himself and knelt in the dry grass. He was ashamed of his outburst and grief-torn for his friends.

Women prepared the bodies for burial. Men dug the graves. Children gathered stones to cover them. Numbed and hollow-eyed, the settlers paused briefly in reverence and turned again westward. There was no alternative.

Juba didn't mind Neb's being withdrawn for a few days. He expected it. Once in a while in passing, he put a hand on Neb's shoulder or offered to do some chore that Neb found tiresome. Always the two men had shared laughter, poking at the dying coals of the supper fire. Neb was awestruck at Juba's stories of a slave's life. And

Neb shared what he knew of his German ancestors. But, now they sat, often staring at nothing, conversation reduced to a mumble, a nod, or a shrug.

The dam burst one morning, two weeks later. Juba was hitching up widow Hermstead's mules when suddenly he heard a piercing scream. He jumped. The scream continued, echoing over the camp. The mules jerked their harnesses. Juba turned toward the sound. He saw Neb stomp through the camp, kicking over buckets, Dutch ovens, wash tubs. His eyes were red-rimmed. He shoved people aside. His shoulders were hunched, fists clenched hard as he strode straight to Juba.

A hard knot settled in Juba's stomach. He said, "What's the matter, Neb? What—"

Neb seized Juba by the shoulders and shook him. "You! You!" he screamed. His eyes were bloodshot. "Why couldn't it have been you? You don't have anybody. Nobody'd grieve for you. Why, oh why? You're strong. You're alive. Nobody'd miss—Oh, Mary, Mary." One fist drove into Juba's chin. The other connected with his temple. Then Neb, in a frenzy, pummeled Juba's chest. Juba tried to grab Neb's arms. "Easy, Neb, hey. Easy now—uh—Neb, hold on, will you—oh—let off—ow—Neb. Oh what—oh!"

Other hands pulled Neb away. They sat him on a fallen log and held his arms behind his back as he hung his head and sobbed.

Juba stumbled to his feet and brushed himself off. There was a cut on his lip. His nose was bleeding and he could feel his eye begin to swell shut. Something grated in his ribs as he caught his breath. He stared at Neb with overwhelming pity. "It's all right, Neb," he whispered as he wiped his bloody face with a bandana handkerchief.

He felt the stares of the whole camp as he staggered away on trembling legs. What Neb said was true. Why couldn't it have been Juba that died instead of Mary? Nobody would miss him. He didn't belong to anybody. Not since Meggie deserted him. He felt guilty for having been spared, when Neb's Mary had her whole life ahead of her.

Juba wandered into a small stand of trees. He sat on the ground and let his tears course down his face. Behind him, he heard the settlers getting ready to move on. Somebody else finished harnessing Widow Hermstead's mules. The clink of bridle chains, the creak of leather, the squeak of wheels, men talking to their ox teams as they backed them into the traces—all seemed separate, as if he had never been a part of it.

Juba heard somebody tramping in the woods, quick, sharp footfalls. It was the wagon master, Jens Studevant. His voice was iron hard. "Well? You coming or you staying?"

Juba set his jaw at the harsh words. Anger sparked briefly. He rose, took a quick step toward the wagon master, catching him by surprise and rasped, not bothering to wipe his tears away. "I'm coming, Jens. I'm coming." He strode ahead, looked neither right nor left, and took his place in line. He did not hear Jens' murmur, "Thank God," to himself as he hurried to catch up.

CHAPTER 24

Toil and dust, campfires and fiddle tunes, mile after mile rolled slowly by. Then, one early morning, night's gloom lifted from the land. Bushes and rocks came into focus. Soon a rosy glow would signal another day on the trail. Settlers began to roll out from under their wagons. Women coaxed campfires to life and clanged iron skillets. The lookout sleepily sauntered in from his post.

Fwup! The lookout fell into camp with an arrow in his shoulder. Zonk! A flaming arrow buried itself into the canvas of a wagon. Zonk! Another found its mark. Fire crackled. Smoke rose. "Indians!" someone yelled. The settlers scrambled for their posts, guns at the ready. Women doused the wagon fires with water they had saved for breakfast. They herded crying children into the middle of the enclosure and made them lie down. Jens Studevant was everywhere. "Evans, you plug up this hole. McGruder, don't let the animals bolt. Women, on the ground with your children. Men, don't shoot until you have something to shoot at. Pick your target."

Suddenly, the air was alive with piercing screams and whoops as Indians, painted for war, raced down a bluff toward the circled wagons. Arrows flew in all directions. The smoke from discharging guns hung heavily among the settlers. The Indians galloped around and around the wagons, still screaming and whooping ear-splitting cries. Wives, leaving their children with strict orders to stay on the ground, hunched beside their husbands and loaded second guns while men fired the first.

Widow Hermstead crouched beside the man who had lost his wife to cholera and loaded his gun. Suddenly, an Indian leaped from his horse and charged between the wagons almost on top of her. She looked into his eyes. The hatchet she had been using ten minutes earlier to split kindling lay beside her. The Indian raised his knife. She grabbed the hatchet. The slice of the knife went into her arm as she brought the hatchet down on his head. The Indian let out a shrill cry and tumbled, dead, into the dirt beside her.

Calmly, Mrs. Hermstead called to a friend, "Emma, come drag this thing out of the way, please." Modesty was not needed in this situation. Mrs. Hermstead lifted her dress and ripped off the hem of her petticoat. Holding the end of the cloth in her teeth, she tightly wound it around the wound in her arm. Then, pale with pain, she turned to her partner. "Sorry for the delay. Here's your other gun." Stunned, he stared at her and accepted the loaded gun. "Many thanks," he mumbled, sighted on one of the enemy and shot him off his horse.

Juba felt a nudge as someone crawled close to him. He looked up. It was Neb Waldheim. Juba raised his eyebrows. Neb nodded slightly. In that instant, an arrow sang past Juba, nicking the skin of his ear. Neb shoved him sideways, stuck his own head in the line of fire, and squeezed off a shot. The adversary tumbled to the ground and lay still.

Juba dabbed at his wound. Blood dribbled down his collar and the front of his shirt.

"Thanks," he said.

"Been wanting to tell you," Neb said through clenched teeth, "how sorry I am for the way I acted after Mary died. Went out of my head, I guess. You ought to hate me." He aimed again and shot.

Juba raised his gun and sighted past the wagons. "Hate you? Never." His finger slowly squeezed the trigger. "Losing Mary musta ripped your heart out." He stared at the young Indian he had toppled off his horse. He felt sick. Some pretty Indian princess would mourn her lover tonight. Juba put the gun down, looked at the ground, and shook his head. "Senseless," he muttered. "Senseless, man killing man."

All at once, the Indians were loading their injured and dead onto their horses. Without a backward glance, they rode away. Sudden quiet descended on the camp.

Lester Townsend, several wagons down the line, sighted on a young brave's back. His finger teased the trigger of his gun. Studevant knocked the gun out of his hands. "No, Townsend!" His whisper was ferocious. "Don't shoot a man in the back when he's running away."

"Whatdaya mean 'man'? Them's ignorant savages. Ain't men a'toll."

Studevant didn't answer. He walked the circle, asked about ammunition supplies, inspected wounds, commented on strategy. He faced the settlers. "Good job, folks," he said in his strong voice. For the most part," his gaze slid past Townsend, "you held to how we practiced if we needed to defend ourselves. I'm proud of you. Now, get your things together. We're moving out. We'll eat later where it's more peaceful."

CHAPTER 25

The settlers squinted into a brassy sun as it slowly sank behind the hills. They had trekked through mile after mile of sagebrush, aiming for the distant mountains that seemed no closer than when they had begun at daybreak. About all they had to show for it was the gradual slowing of the exhausted animals and now the lowered level in the water barrels as each man rationed out his share.

Behind them, a tail of dust hung in the air and stretched as far as they could see. The settlers seemed to collectively sigh with relief as they viewed the river that swirled and eddied near by.

Juba looked forward to the minute he could plunge into its cool depths and wash away his frustration and irritation along with the soil. Twice, he had caught young boys attempting to spoon dirt into his water skin. And both times, biting his tongue, he had said nothing. A frown was sufficient to send them scampering away. But his clenched fists ached to snatch them by the shoulders and give them a good shaking.

Not wanting to camp on the rattlesnake-infested sage plain, the settlers prodded their animals up a slope into the cooler air of some low hills. Juba found a fallen tree a couple hundred feet from camp and sat down to unlace his boots. He looked up to see Jens Studevant standing before him, scowling.

"What do you have to say for yourself, Juba?" Jens' voice was not friendly.

Juba wrinkled his forehead in surprise. "Suh? Haven't I been doing my share of the work?"

Jens leaned a shoulder against a scrubby pine and, with a calloused thumb, began to peel the bark from it. "I'm not talking about work."

Juba stared at his boots. A premonition of trouble began to gnaw at his empty stomach. "What then, Mass—uh, Jens?"

Jens went on as if Juba hadn't spoken, "I'm so disappointed I could spit. Thought I had you pegged right. Guess I was wrong."

The old familiar sinking tightened Juba's chest. He couldn't stop it, this lifelong reflex. Was blame about to be heaped upon him again because of the color of his skin? He set his boots aside and stood barefooted before Jens. "Don't know what you're talking about."

Jens' laugh was a bitter grunt. "Everybody in camp knows what it is. How come you don't?"

"Sorry, Jens, this don't make sense to me." Tension was building in his muscles. He lifted his gaze to Jens' glare.

Jens' chest rose and fell with a sigh. "What did you do it for? Didn't you know that girl would tell the whole almighty camp?"

Panic stabbed him. "G-girl, suh?"

"Aw, come on, don't play dumb. Sneaking out nights. Taking advantage of her innocence—"

Juba's emotions exploded. He could barely keep his voice down. "What, suh? What you talking about?"

Jens rounded on him, eyes flashing. He hissed between his teeth. "The Townsend girl, that's what! As if you didn't know."

Juba's mouth fell open. His pulse thudded in his throat. He tried to form words and failed. The Townsend girl. That little snipe who approached him the night he stood guard. "She-she . . . ?"

Jens was staring at the ground and shaking his head. "Says she's in the family way and you—"

"Me?" Juba's voice came out in a squeak. His knees trembled.

"They want to lynch you, Juba. I held 'em back until I could talk to you." There were tears in Jens' eyes.

"Who?" Juba's neck hair prickled.

"The whole camp."

CHAPTER 26

Juba stared at Jens. The words jumbled together in his mind as he tried to make sense of them. Lynch him! Hurt knifed through him as anger coursed along his veins. He snatched up a brittle pine branch, broke it over his knee, and threw it as far as he could. He was hungry and tired and cooking aromas from camp were wafting his way. But all he wanted, right this moment, was to ram his feet back into his boots, grab his mule, circle the camp to kick up as much dust as possible, then run away. Far from these miserable, hateful people. White-hot fury was about to choke him while the hurt tore him apart. "You believed 'em," he said brokenly. "Even before you came to me, you believed 'em."

Jens bowed his head. He let pieces of bark dribble from his fingers. "Some—sometimes a man, even a good man, gets tempted and I—"

Juba pounded his knotted fists together. He wanted to lean into Jens' face. He wanted to shout, "If you never believe another thing in your life, Jens, believe this: I did not touch that girl. You hear me? I did not touch her." Instead, he shoved into his boots and stomped away stiff-legged.

Jens called from behind him, "Where you going?"

"Guess there's only one thing I can do. Saddle up and light out. I'm gonna go down and get my mule."

"You can't go down there."

"Why not?"

"Because, because Townsend already said he'd shoot you if you came near and—"

Juba muttered under his breath, "Well then, Townsend'll just have to dig a hole and bury me." Tears of frustration pricked his eyes. He thrashed through weeds, kicked at a bucket in his way, and came face to face with Neb Waldheim.

Juba pushed past. In his hurt and shame, Neb was the last person he wanted to talk to.

Neb grabbed him by the front of his shirt. He said, "Whoa."

"Please, Neb, let go. I got business I gotta tend to." He heard Studevant trying to catch up. What were both men going to do? Escort him into an angry mob?

Neb said, "I heard, Juba. Heard what they're saying. I don't believe it. Never will."

"Good of you, Neb. Now let me pass. Gotta get my mule. Hurts so bad I can't stand to be around here."

Jens had caught up. "You have to face it, Juba. Can't run away."

Juba skidded to a stop. He dared to look Studevant straight in the eye. "You never been a slave, Jens. Slaves don't have a chance. They's guilty. That's all."

Neb said, "I'll tell 'em, Juba. They'll believe me."

"No they won't." Juba plodded on. He had to pass Townsend's wagon to get where his mule was tethered.

As the three approached the circled wagons, Townsend emerged from his, a rifle in his hand. "There's the low-down scum," Townsend yelled. "See, everybody? Told ya niggers was worse than Injuns. Told ya he'd—"

Juba felt a swift displacement of air erupt by his side. He saw Neb kick the rifle from Townsend's grasp and grab him by the front of his shirt. "I don't like the lies you're circulating about my friend, Townsend."

Townsend's body seemed to slither under Neb's grip. His eyes, like murky marbles, reflected his contempt. "Ain't no lies. This here nigger ruined my little girl. He dirtied her. You nigger-lover, sticking up for him?"

As if by reflex, Neb's left hand came up and connected with Townsend's jaw. Townsend's knees sagged. His head tilted to the side.

Juba's shoulders slumped. "Let him go, Neb. Ain't no use."

Neb said, "No!" His face was blotched red with anger. He called over his shoulder, "Jens, you gonna help me?"

Jens' voice was muffled. "Now, Neb, we gotta take this calm-like. No use getting so worked up."

Neb yelled, "Worked up!" He tightened the twist of Townsend's shirt. "Your girl hiding in the wagon? Get her out here. Make her tell the truth."

Juba became aware of the other settlers crowding around. Some were yelling and pointing accusing fingers at him. Others nodded and called out in hostile agreement. He smelled their sweaty bodies and glimpsed the mixture of fear and loathing in their eyes. Over the turmoil, Studevant's voice boomed. "Let go of him, Waldheim. You can't get anywhere that way."

Waldheim ignored him. "Call your girl, Townsend. Let's see her tell her lies to Juba's face." He shook Townsend and the man went to his knees. Two settlers stepped forward and helped Townsend to his feet. One of them spat at Juba's face. The spittle dribbled down his cheek.

From the corner of his eye, Juba saw Studevant shoulder his way between the settlers. He stood beside Juba and fired into the air. "Calm down," he shouted to the crowd. "We'll handle this in an orderly manner." He turned to Juba and whispered, "I'm warning you. These folks'll—"

The settlers drowned him out. "Let's fetch a rope. Necktie party's the only way to see justice."

Juba raised his gaze from studying his boots and searched the faces of the men and women surrounding him. There was not one friendly eye in the mob that pressed him against the side of Townsend's wagon. He pulled on Studevant's sleeve. "Get the girl to tell the truth."

Studevant scowled at Juba. "Since when you givin' the orders around here?"

Juba blinked. Was this the same Studevant who had been his friend? He looked at the ground and murmured, "It's my neck that'll be doing the stretching."

Studevant hesitated. The crowd surged closer. A voice rang out. "Lookie here, we got the rope. And that tall pine over yonder'll do just fine. Let's get to it. Whatcha waiting for, Studevant?"

Studevant held up his arms for attention. He bellowed, "Quiet down! I'm the wagon master of this train. We'll give the girl a chance to tell her story before there's any hanging."

Waldheim said, "What about Juba's chance?"

Studevant rasped in his ear, "He doesn't get one." Again, his voice rose, "Townsend, get your daughter out here."

Townsend whimpered, "You can't do that to my little girl. Why should she have to—"

Studevant's jaw was set. "I said, get her out here, Townsend."

Townsend stared hard at Juba. "I'll see you roast in hell." He turned and climbed into his wagon.

Moments later, Abbie Townsend emerged, her hair disheveled, face pale. In the sudden silence, every settler leaned forward to catch her words. She perched on the wagon seat. Studevant touched her arm. "Now Abbie, don't be afraid. Take your time. But we got to know the truth."

Abbie stared at her lap. Her hands twisted a handkerchief. "He—he'd wake me up in the night."

Studevant asked, "Who woke you up, Abbie?"

Without looking up, Abbie pointed at Juba. "Him, that nigger."

Studevant prompted, "Go on, Abbie."

Abbie's feet swung forward and back, kicking the side of the wagon. "Ma and Pa was allas asleep."

Studevant said, "Always? Did this happen more than once?"

Abbie nodded. "Lots of times. Maybe six or seven. I don't remember."

Studevant grimaced. "Go on."

"He—took me—into the trees where it was nice and quiet and—"

Juba's anguished cry echoed over the camp. "No! No!"

Studevant turned on him. "Shut up."

Shouts pelted the air. "Let the girl talk. Poor little thing. That nigger—"

Juba shuddered in revulsion as Studevant patted Abbie's writhing hands. "Now Abbie, we're almost done. You must be brave. When he took you into the trees, what did he do then?"

Abbie cast a quick glance at Juba. Her face reddened and she suddenly bit a fingernail to hide a smirk. The settlers held a collective breath. Then Abbie's voice rang out for all to hear. "He forced himself on me. Like—like a—"

The maddened settlers crowded closer. Their clawed fingers raked Juba's clothes. They shouted in his face. "Where's the rope? He'll pay for this."

A dozen grasping hands reached for him. In a blinding blur, Juba heard Studevant call for order. Others shouted him down. "You heard 'er, Studevant." "Don't need more proof." "Ain't no need for order a-tall." "We know how to mete out justice."

Spitting epithets, the crowd surged forward. Waldheim lashed out with his fists. Four settlers attacked him and threw him to the ground. Others punched and shoved Juba. He felt the repeated sting of a willow stick against his face. Somebody kicked him behind the knees. He stumbled. They pinned his arms behind his back and dragged him along.

Juba tried to struggle, but there were too many against him. They pummeled and struck him and mercilessly twisted his arms.

At last, panting, he felt his strength dissipate into trembling futility. He stood beneath the chosen tree, quivering, his face shining with sweat. He heard the rope slide over a branch high above him. A pine cone tumbled to the ground at his feet. With savage efficiency, they ground a wire into the skin of his wrists and secured his hands behind his back. He bit his lip as the rope's scratchy loop was shoved over his head and tightened around his neck. Four men grasped the end of the rope and backed away from the tree, holding it taut, waiting for the signal.

A sudden silence descended over the mob. It was so quiet Juba heard their synchronized, rhythmic exhalations, their chests rising and falling in unison. Juba searched for Waldheim and saw two burley men pinning his arms behind his back. They had gagged him with a ragged piece of cloth. Tears streamed down his cheeks.

Juba gazed over the heads of the mob toward the distant mountains, silent witnesses to all the world's agonies. He held a picture of Meggie in his mind and whispered her name.

"What's he saying? That nigger ain't whispering a curse on us, is he?"

Somebody yelled, "Studevant, get over here and do your duty."

Studevant shuffled forward. The crowd parted as he approached. He could not quite meet Juba's eyes. "I'm sorry it came to this, Juba. You got any last words?"

Juba stared beyond him. Strange, when life was about end, all that really mattered was what was in a man's own heart. He raised his face to the sky and said, "Lawd, God."

The rope jerked and choked him. He opened his mouth, desperate for air. A dizzying roar crescendoed in his head as the world turned dark. Dimly, barely penetrating the deafening rumble in his ears, he heard a woman scream, "No, no. Let him down. Let him down. Please, please, let him down!"

Somebody clawed at his body and yanked at his shirt. The screaming seemed to go on forever as Juba felt himself dumped to the ground. The rope loosened. Blood pounded in his temples. On his knees, he pulled air into his lungs with shuddering gasps.

Juba struggled to sit up. As his sight began to clear, he saw Townsend's iron grip whipping his wife back and forth like a rag doll. The settlers stood back, their boots scuffing the dirt in uncertainty. Juba shook his head and Mrs. Townsend's billowing skirt came into focus. Painfully, he raised his head and stared at her face.

She was sobbing, "I—I couldn't let them do it. I couldn't let them do it."

Townsend bellowed, "What're you stammering about, woman? You interrupted a hanging." He gave her a shove and she fell to the ground.

Mrs. Townsend knelt there, her shoulders heaving. "She—Abbie— told me—"

Her husband grabbed her arm again and jerked her upright. "Quit yer caterwalling. Shoulda stayed in the wagon. Meddling where you ain't—"

"I couldn't let them—Lester. Abbie told me—"

Townsend twisted her arm behind her back and pushed her. "Get to the wagon, woman. You're talking nonsense."

Mrs. Townsend clamped her hand over her eyes and sucked in air as if to inhale courage. No longer sobbing, she straightened her back and jutted her chin. She found an authoritative tone her husband had never heard. "You're hurting me, Lester."

The crowd began to murmur. Mrs. Townsend wrenched free of her husband's grip. The people stilled and leaned forward to catch every word. She stared at her husband with narrowed eyes and spoke in a loud voice. "Abbie told me, Lester, that you'd do anything to get rid of this black man. That disgusting story she told—you put her up to it. She thought he'd run away. She didn't think they'd hang him."

Lester Townsend stood gape-mouthed, his hand raised to slap his wife. "Why you—why you—"

The crowd moved restlessly. Their mutterings came in waves to Juba's ears. "You mean it ain't even true?" "I thought sure he done it." "The girl said—"

Juba felt somebody lift the slackened rope from his neck. The wire no longer pinched his wrists. The settlers moved away, two or three at a time, like little knots unraveling. Not one faced him to say they were sorry they had believed the lie. Their whisperings faded into the surrounding sounds of bird trill and wind soughing in the trees.

Finally, a lone pair of boots came into Juba's line of vision. He looked up. Jens Studevant stood there.

"Jens?" Juba said, his voice a mere croak.

Studevant toed the earth. Little spurts of dust rose around his feet. "Guess—anything I might say would sound . . . Well, I'm sorry I doubted you. Puts me to shame, that's all."

Juba nodded. Part of him wanted to reach out, shake Studevant's hand and say, 'We all make mistakes, Jens.' But his throat still hurt, and worse, the pain of knowing Jens had doubted him, had not even tried to defend him, was like a knife twisting his insides.

He tried to stand up and fell back to the ground. Studevant reached out a hand to steady him, but Juba pushed him away. "No," he said, without making eye contact. Once more, he willed his legs to support him and held on to the tree, swaying a little. He looked up into its branches. "Strong tree," he mumbled and saw from the corner of his eye a flicker of shame pass across Studevant's face. "Guess I'll get a drink and get my stuff together."

He knew Studevant watched him as he limped toward camp. There was a canyon yawning between them now. A rent so big no amount of talking would ever fill it up.

Busy with evening chores, the settlers tended their cooking fires and saw to their livestock. Among the wagons, a baby cried. Nobody came to bid him goodbye. Not even Widow Hermstead, who was already negotiating with another man to help with her mules.

Juba caught his mule and tied his bundle on behind his saddle. A figure emerged from the trees. It was Neb Waldheim. He walked with a limp and held a handkerchief to a bleeding cut on his cheek.

"Juba?"

Juba's arm went around his shoulder. "Thanks for trying to help, Neb. Sorry you got beat up."

"Beat up? I was so mad I felt like telling them to string me up too."

" 'Preciate that. You take care, ya hear?"

"You too. Where you headed?"

"Don't rightly know. Guess I need to think on it first."

"Never forget you, Juba. All you did for me, and I . . ."

Juba gave him a soft punch on the arm. "You get to Oregon, think of me once in a while."

The two men shook hands. A separate sadness assailed Juba as he watched Neb walk away; the parting of friends who would never meet again. Full dark now hung over the camp. Juba took one last look around. Most of the settlers were bedding down for the night. He could barely make out the guard for the first watch perched on a nearby knoll. Something else caught his eye. A flash of white emerged from a wagon. Another figure, slightly taller moved alongside. Juba watched the two approach a thick stand of pine. As they disappeared into the shadows, a giggle floated on the breeze. Abbie Townsend's giggle. Abbie Townsend's tryst she had not told her father about.

Juba's mouth was a grim line. He settled his hat, mounted his mule, and rode away.

CHAPTER 27

Juba wandered aimlessly. The moon gave him barely enough light to follow a deer trail that climbed a rocky escarpment. The hooves of his mule clattered on the loose stones and occasionally sent one tumbling over the edge into a shallow valley. He didn't know where he was going and he didn't care. It was enough for now to just put distance between himself and the wagon train. He paused at a fork in the trail and drank from his water pouch. A coyote on a faraway bluff wailed a mournful howl. "You and me both, brother," he said.

The wind gusted and blew fine sand in his face. He spat and rubbed his eyes. He was sick of sagebrush, burning sun, stale water, and people. "So, my plans have changed, Jack," he said. "I ain't going to Oregon after all. So, where am I going?"

Jack's ears flicked back and forth.

"Looks to me nobody's hankering to know whether I'm alive or dead. That don't make it important that I get some place in a hurry. I could just sit here and not budge for a couple hundred years. Turn to stone. By and by, somebody might come along and sit on me and say, "Hum, mighty interesting shape to this here rock.""

Juba dismounted. Jack nuzzled his elbow. Juba scratched the mule's ears and rubbed the blaze on his nose. The shame heaped upon him by the folks in the wagon train rose to goad him. He gritted his teeth. "Guess they see me just like you, Jack. Animal, black all over. 'Cept you got that white streak down the middle of your face. I ain't got that. Sure look funny if I did, wouldn't it? Matched pair, that's what we'd be."

He paused to clear the catch in his throat. "A matched pair. Mule and a jackass." He kicked a piece of shale with the toe of his boot. "Only, I'm not a jackass. I'm a man. No matter what some might call me. God made me a man and I'm proud of it." He lifted his head and shouted into the wind, "I'm a man, you hear?" His echo wavered faintly back to him.

Juba coaxed the mule off the trail, down the slope, and into the valley. After weaving around several large boulders, he found a rock overhang with plenty of grass close by for the mule. With a lighted match, he searched for snakes in the recesses of the rock. He took the mule's saddle off and tied him to a nearby pine. "Don't you go wandering off now. Might need you come morning."

Juba spread the saddle blanket and tried to get comfortable. No use trying to sleep. He was too heart sore. The humiliation back there at the camp rankled deep. It'd take a month of Sundays for it to taper off. And what was Meggie doing on a night like this? Snuggling up to Arlo? He curled his hands into fists and dug his fingernails into his palms at the thought. "Lawd," he cried out, "is there no letup?" A tormented man could rest, but he wouldn't sleep. You couldn't expect a man to sleep with such pain tearing at his guts. If he could just relax for a while, he'd . . .

The smoke and aroma of cooking meat awakened him. Juba opened his eyes and squinted at bright sunlight. "What the—!"

He sat up. He saw two Indians sitting on a rock watching him. Something was roasting on a spit over a campfire. *My mule! They're cooking my mule!* He scrambled to his feet and cracked his head on the overhang. His fists balled. "What did ya do with my—" He stopped. Jack was cropping grass, tethered where he had left him. "Oh." Juba looked back at the campfire. He saw now it was a rabbit roasting on the spit. A small rabbit. "But, I thought—"

Juba stared as one of the Indians sauntered over to the fire and turned the rabbit on the spit. He beckoned to Juba and rubbed his stomach. Juba eyed the Indian's muscular frame. "Yassah," he said tentatively. "Yassah—I'm hungry. You, uh—thank you."

The Indian nodded. His companion came silently across the grass on moccasined feet. His dark eyes shone as he stood close and peered into Juba's face. Juba backed up a step. The Indian stepped forward. He pinched Juba's cheek.

"See here, now—," Juba began. He swallowed down a sliver of fear.

The Indian pointed to his own bare brown arm and pushed up the sleeve of Juba's shirt. With a long tapered finger, he rubbed the skin on Juba's arm, then examined his finger. He said something to the other Indian and shrugged.

The cook took the rabbit from the spit and pulled it apart. He motioned for Juba to sit on the ground. Juba sat gingerly and tried to keep his eyes on both Indians at once. The cook handed him a steaming, smoking piece of the meat. It seared his fingers as he juggled it from hand to hand. Both the Indians laughed at him. He noticed their fingers didn't burn as they quickly devoured their portions. He wondered why.

"Good, very good," Juba said. "Thank you." He licked his fingers.

The two Indians sat quietly, studying him. Both wore bear-tooth necklaces and the cook had bits of turquoise fastened to his ears. Juba wished he could read their minds. Were they waiting for him to offer something in return? They wouldn't want his mule, would they? Please Lawd, not his mule.

The wagon train gossip had been thick with tales of marauding Indians stealing cattle and horses. But these friendly Indians could have stolen his mule while he slept. They could have scalped him too. He worried the thought around and around like a marble in a tin can, and became more nervous with each passing minute.

If only he had . . . and then he remembered the bright blue bandana handkerchief. He had found it half hidden in the mud near a spring where somebody had dropped it. It was good as new after he washed it. But there were two of them, these friendly Indians. He could not tear the handkerchief in half. He must have a present for each of them. Another worry began to needle him. What if they were only playing with him, giving him a final meal before they . . .

He swallowed the last of the rabbit, along with the nervous lump in his throat. He stood. From his back pocket, he drew out the clean blue handkerchief. The Indian's faces revealed no emotion as he walked toward them.

"Thank you for a nice meal," he said. "Yassah, a fine meal." He nodded his head and tried to smile, keeping his lips from quivering. He held the handkerchief out to the one who had cooked the rabbit. "For you," he bowed.

The Indian grinned. He opened the handkerchief and waved it like a flag. He said something that sounded like "eeya."

Juba sighed with relief. Well, at least one of them was pleased. Now, how about the other one? The second Indian sat like a stoic, staring into the distance. Juba's hand went to his pocket. He fingered the jackknife. No, he could not give that up.

Then, he remembered. In his saddlebag was a brass buckle. He had carried it all the way from Independence. Like the handkerchief, he had found the buckle on the street, cast down by some careless person. All at once, he realized these two fellows might have gone through his possessions while he slept. They probably knew exactly what he had.

Juba reached into the saddlebag and brought out the buckle. He presented it to the second Indian. The Indian accepted it shyly. Then he held it in his palm and moved it so that it gleamed in the sunlight. He did a little jig, laid his finger on Juba's arm and said, "Um."

The cook strolled to the campfire, broke the spit into pieces, and flung them into the coals. He poured dirt over the feeble flames. A thin spiral of smoke rose and dissipated in the cool morning air.

Juba saddled his mule while the other Indian brought two pinto ponies from their hiding place in a copse of aspen trees. The cook stirred the fire with a stick and sprinkled more dirt on it. Then the two Indians mounted their ponies. They sat bareback, waiting for Juba to ready his mule. As they kicked their ponies into a trot, they waved to him and rode on down the valley from the direction Juba had come.

Juba turned his face toward the escarpment above and picked his way up the slope to the faint trail he had followed the night before. He found himself grinning. The morning's encounter seemed like a dream. But he still had the smell of rabbit grease on his fingers. His belly was not rumbling with hunger. The blue handkerchief was gone from his back pocket. He turned in the saddle. He saw only trees and bushes, rocks and scrub brush. The Indians had disappeared as if they never were.

For the next few miles, the Indians were on Juba's mind. He'd heard somewhere they could sense things others would miss. Maybe, just maybe, these two brown friends had said, "Here's a man who needs cheering up. Let's cook him some breakfast."

CHAPTER 28

Juba loped along for hours over rocky terrain. Jack's hooves stirred up dust that coated them both with a gritty film. The noisy twisting river rushed far below between vertical walls. As the sun began to set, the cut of the riverbanks became shallow, the slope more gradual. The river widened.

"Whoa, Jack." Juba studied the water. He had to cross it sometime if he intended to continue north. And he certainly wasn't going to hang west and chance meeting the wagon train again.

Three small islands somewhat equally situated jutted up like stepping stones. "Let's go for a swim, Jack." Juba held his gun and poke high, and kneed the mule into the water. "We're wanting a bath anyhow."

Jack clambered onto the first island and cropped at the grass. Juba urged him across and down its slippery side into the water again. "Ain't stopping yet. Two more to cross." Twice more they took the icy plunge and finally scrambled onto dry ground on the far side. "Whew, glad that's over. You did good, Jack. Just fine." Juba dismounted and wrung out his wet clothes while the mule grazed.

"Night's coming on." Juba looked around. He wondered how many Indians might be close by. How many out of a hundred would be friendly? He'd heard of the Choctaws, the Kiowas, and the Chinooks. And what was that tribe farther north? The Nez Perce, that's what they called 'em. Had he drifted into their territory?

It would be nice to have a fire to dry his clothes and maybe find a rabbit to cook. But an uncomfortable sensation, as if hidden eyes watched his every move, made a shudder not caused by cold water rippling down his spine. He checked his ammunition and whispered to Jack, "Come on, I think we'd better make tracks." He mounted and rode until well after dark when his neck muscles relaxed, and his back no longer tensed as if any minute an arrow might pierce his flesh.

Couldn't blame the Indians for feeling hostile. All these wagon trains invading their territory. Couldn't expect them all to be kind like those he saw this morning. Besides, the more he thought about those two, the more he wondered if they were real. Maybe he had imagined them. And yet . . .

He and Jack were sheltered by trees again, wide-girthed giants. Juba heard the wind soughing high in the branches. The tang of pine and spruce needles was everywhere. Jack's ears pricked forward and his steps quickened. Soon they came to a field of tumbled boulders that outlined a stream cascading down the mountain. Moonlight flashed on the foaming, splashing water. Juba drank deeply and filled his water pouch.

He moved away from the stream and found a grassy open space to tether Jack. "Hate to mention it," he said, "but I'm powerful hungry. Ain't used to your kind of diet. Grass just don't hit the spot somehow. And water makes a fella more hungry. About to make my stomach seasick, sloshes around so. No use to build a fire without meat to cook." He looked up into the branches of the trees. "Wish I could knock down a squirrel or two, but can't even see that high. 'Sides, it's too dark."

Juba spread the saddle blanket on the ground and used his poke for a pillow. As he adjusted it under his head, he thought back to the night, many months and miles away now, when he slept under the trees after splitting wood for that mean fellow and his timid wife. Wonder if she ran away yet. Not likely, some folks just accepted their lot in life and stuck it out. Drew the short straw and knuckled down.

Hadn't he drawn the short straw too? Born to it. He'd thrown away that one, got handed another, threw it away too. "I ain't quitting 'til I gets the long straw and that's that. Know what I want now. A place to call my own. Where I can put my boots under the bed and have a . . ." The soft wind in the trees lulled him and he drifted into sleep.

The scolding of magpies woke him. He sat up and threw a pine cone at two that sassed and tormented Jack. Squirrels chattered among the trees. He reached for his shot gun, took aim, and fired. "Ah, something to chew besides water."

They climbed with the sun and presently heard a sound that did not belong in the virgin forest. "That's a engine, Jack." The sound grew louder. A whiff of exhaust carried on the breeze. Juba came upon a field of stumps. Nearby was the source of the exhaust. Juba watched while a cable, winched to a donkey engine, dragged a huge log to a pile of other logs just as big. Up the hill, two men on springboards wrestled a crosscut saw back and forth as it cut into a giant spruce. A voice bellowed, "Hey, you down there, get out of the way. Timber!"

CHAPTER 29

Juba stood before Clem Fordyce, the three-hundred-pound foreman of the logging crew. "Bull of the woods," they called him. Juba figured the man had earned the title.

Fordyce scowled, "You? You're asking for a job? Bet you never did nothing more than scratch between the cotton rows in your bare feet down south."

"I'm willing to learn, mas—uh suh," Juba said. *This time*, he thought, *if I say master, he'll think of me as a slave. I'd better not look him in the eye too much, though. There's fire in those eyes. No use me being the match to kindle it.*

"I'm short a bull puncher," Fordyce was saying. "Last one broke a leg dancing with the oxen."

Juba said, "I like animals."

Fordyce countered, "You haven't seen these brutes yet."

"Like to try."

Fordyce snorted, "Pay's not much."

"Don't mind."

There was a long pause. Juba felt Fordyce's eyes on him, studying him. "Work starts at four in the morning. You gotta feed and water the oxen before breakfast. Make sure the skidder timbers are solid. Quitting time is sundown."

"Yessuh."

"Skid greaser goes with you. That's him over there. Will Conant. Just a kid."

"Yes, sir." Juba knew he had the job. He was feeling rather pleased with himself.

Fordyce brought him back to earth. "Kid like Will don't mind working with a darkie." Fordyce walked away. Juba heard him yell, "Hey, Will, show this darkie around."

When Juba first signed on at the logging camp, he heard stories that the cook, Martha Mattocks, went to bed with a butcher knife and a rolling pin under her pillow. It was probably true. The loggers respected Martha. She had drawn an invisible line they dared not cross.

It was five o'clock in the morning. The men had already rousted from their bunks to feed the horses, check ropes and chains, kick the skids for loose timbers, and inspect the condition of their saws.

Now, amid the scraping of benches at the long tables and occasional guffaws, they hunkered over stacks of pancakes and bacon. Their mouths, like insatiable maws, accepted the fried potatoes and eggs shoveled into them.

Juba sat by himself at the far end of a table. Once in a while, he caught the eye of a logger who immediately shifted his gaze elsewhere. *Might as well have leprosy.*

Martha came by with the gray granite coffeepot. "How's it going this morning, Juba?" She smelled of bacon and fried potatoes.

Juba shrugged, "Can't complain, ma'am."

Martha poured his coffee. She set the pot on the table and leaned close to his ear. "Grapevine says somebody's fixing to set you up."

"Nothing I can do about it, ma'am."

"Keep your eyes peeled." Martha turned away, filling cups as she greeted the other loggers. "Morning, Joe." "How's the stiff back, Lem?"

Juba watched Martha wind a stray lock of her auburn tresses into the bun atop her head. She secured it with a tortoise shell comb. The ample flesh of her stomach jiggled as she shared a joke with the men.

"What you looking at, darkie?"

The sharp tone brought Juba's head around. Clem Fordyce, bull of the woods, scowled down at him. Juba breathed deeply and tried a shrug.

"I asked you a question, darkie."

"Same thing you're looking at, I reckon," Juba said. He started to rise from the table.

Clem blocked his way. The man's lip curled into a sneer. "Take a little advice from me, darkie. Keep yer eyes on yer food."

Juba nodded to his plate. He half expected to feel Clem's meaty hand on the back of his neck. Instead, the floor vibrated under his boots as Clem swaggered to the other end of the table and elbowed a sizable place to sit.

Three weeks to the day, that's how long Juba had been at the camp. If he could stick it out one more week and draw his pay, he'd have a wad to see him through. Farther north, farther west, he'd heard tales of cool, clear springs that flowed right out of hillsides. Of places not overrun with chiggers or fire ants. Of territory that had never felt the imprint of a slavemaster's foot.

Juba took his tin plate to the pass-through that separated the main room from the kitchen. "Thanks, ma'am."

Martha turned from the dishpan, suds glistening on her hands. Suddenly, the room quieted. Juba felt the eyes of the men boring into his back.

In the silence, Martha murmured, "You're welcome." Her eyes held a message and Juba read it: *Be careful.*

He nodded slightly and went out. As he closed the door, the volume of noise rose again.

The dawn turned from pearl to rose. Juba hitched up Salt and Pepper, Mike and Mack. They were gentle oxen. Patient and slow, they enjoyed having Juba scratch under the yokes they wore. He ran his hand over their backs.

Will said, "How come yer spiling them oxes?"

Juba grinned at Will. "I ain't spoiling 'em. They like me. I like them. They work harder that way."

Will shrugged. "Last bull whacker kept 'em moving with the prod an' the whip."

It was Juba's turn to shrug. "I like doing it my way."

Will wouldn't let it alone. "Don't see much difference. They're still pulling the load."

"Sure they are. But, if it was you, wouldn't you rather somebody treat you nice instead of whipping you?"

Will stared at Juba. "I reckon."

Juba figured it was no use telling Will he remembered the lash of the whip and had scars to prove it. Somehow, he had an aversion to whips. Just the sight of one set his back muscles to quivering.

CHAPTER 30

Juba unhitched the oxen and waited while they drank their fill, then strolled to the cook shack for dinner. It was still a long time until supper after sunset.

Will went off to sit with some of his friends. Scarcely older than Will, they had more important jobs and he dreamed of the day when he could join them. Juba sat alone. He was too tired for conversation anyway, even if one of the men had wanted to talk to him.

He noticed a couple of the buckers whispering and stealing glances at him. That was nothing new. He'd watched these older men, who no longer vied for the most dangerous jobs in the woods, trimming off branches and sawing the logs into more manageable lengths. He scraped his plate clean, thanked Martha, and went outside.

Some of the men sat smoking on a bench outside the cook shack. When they were through, the butts had to be thrown into a bucket of water kept there for that purpose. There were no exceptions, else Fordyce fired the man on the spot.

Juba sauntered past and started up the hill where the oxen and the skid waited. He did not see the shadowy figure behind a log. He did not see the log begin to move and gain momentum. Too late, he looked up as it crashed over rocks and saplings, a behemoth coming straight toward him. He tried to run, to dodge. Someone yelled. The jagged end of the log caught him, spun him, crushed him, and rolling away, rammed into a couple of giant trees and lay still.

For a few moments, Juba's whole body was numb. He lay on the ground in a stupor. The log had knocked the breath out of him. Struggling to fill his lungs, the pain in his ribs began—sharp, relentless. He moaned and tried to turn over. His right leg would not move. Was it on fire?

He heard shouts, boots pounding the earth, curses.

"It's a wonder he's alive."

"Take it easy, Juba."

"Somebody send for Doc Sims."

"Hand me your belt, Oscar. Let's use this stick. Gotta make a tourniquet."

As Juba wavered on the edge of consciousness, their voices faded in and out.

"Musta hit his head too. See the gash?"

"How'd you suppose it happened?"

"I ain't speculating."

"Bernie's supposed to look after them logs. Wonder—"

"Don't wonder too hard, Arnie. Here, help me."

Doc Sims did what he could and pronounced, "He'll either live or die."

They carried him to Martha. "You're a better nurse than we are, ya know. We gotta get back to work, ya know. Woman's got the touch, ya know. Figure you can work it in somehow, ya know."

Martha nodded and waited until they had exhausted all their excuses. "Put him in this spot by the pantry and the stove, so I can look in on him." Then she shut the door on the loggers.

"Woman's touch, huh? It's a wonder they can pull out their own slivers." She gazed sadly at Juba. Logging camps were notorious for fatal accidents. But, somehow—the thought gnawed at her mind: This was no accident.

She washed the blood from his face and spread a blanket over him. He did not open his eyes. "You're going to live, Juba," she whispered fiercely. "You're too ornery to die." She angrily swiped at a tear coursing down her cheek and left him alone. There was dough for six apple pies waiting to be rolled out.

As Juba began to heal and was able to sit up, Martha said, "Here's your opportunity, Juba. Since you can't work in the woods, you might as well let me teach you to read and write. I can spare a few minutes now and then to get you started."

One particular morning, Martha bunched up the pillows behind Juba's back. She straightened the blanket on the cot, laid a board across his legs, and centered a slate on it. "Here," she said, handing him the stylus. "Let's see how much you remember today."

"Don't remember nothing today."

"Yes, you do. How about starting with the alphabet?"

Juba shook his head and closed his eyes. He let the stylus fall to the floor.

"Juba!"

"Aw, can't you leave me alone? I ain't gonna ever—"

Martha leaned over him, her eyes blazing. "Look here, I've a mind to tell Clem you're getting too uppity. Maybe he'd better throw you out of the camp."

Juba raised up in the bed with a roar. "I ain't letting no Clem work me over. Not now, not never. I'll run away first. Even if I got only one leg. I'll—"

Martha turned her back and clamped her hand over her mouth, but the chuckle slipped out anyway. "Gotcha, didn't I?" She picked up the stylus. "Here, you dropped something."

Juba settled back against the pillows with a groan. "You tricked me, Martha." He grimaced against the pain.

"Had to do something. I'm not going to watch you lay here, withering on the vine." She laid a comforting hand on his brow. "You work hard on your slate this morning and I'll make you some chicken soup for dinner. If you don't work hard, all you'll get is half a cold potato."

Juba said, "Worse than a plantation overseer."

Martha said, "They learned their tricks from me. Now you print out the alphabet nice and pretty, and we'll go on to numbers." She turned away. "Takes me about ten minutes to fill the woodbox and another ten to mix the biscuit dough. See if you can be done by then."

"Log poked a hole in my head, remember? All my brains leaked out."

Martha wagged a finger. "You've got plenty left."

Juba watched her go. He let a grin play across his lips. Here he was with seven broken ribs, a concussion, and a smashed leg that Doc said was broken in three places. And every day, he was learning things he had only dreamed of a month ago. "Cold potato," he said to the quiet room. How about c-o-l-d? There. He'd show her.

CHAPTER 31

Martha was a patient teacher and once Juba got over being self-conscious, he was a good student. But he loved to argue her logic. Martha would pose a problem. "If one hen lays twenty eggs and another lays fourteen and a half, how many eggs are there?"

Juba saw his chance. "What kind of a problem is that, Martha? No hen's gonna lay that many eggs and I never heard of one shelling out a half a egg."

Martha sighed, "Juba, I never said the hens laid the eggs all in one day. It doesn't matter if—"

Juba glared at her, "Eggs'd be half rotten by the time you—"

Martha glared back at him and pointed a finger. "What's the answer, Juba. That's all I'm interested in."

Juba continued to mutter. "Chicken'd be about worn out . . ."

Martha's skirts caught at the splinters in the floorboards as she crossed the room. Before she slammed the door, she yelled, "I must have been crazy to let Doc Sims talk me into letting you stay here till you could get around again."

Juba wrote on his slate: *34 ½*. "That what you want, Martha?" he mumbled to himself.

Most evenings, after the last dish was dried and put away, Martha spent an hour teaching Juba. He learned the multiplication tables and recited them as he began to hobble about the room. The succession of American presidents slipped off his tongue with ease. His eyes shone as he learned to draw a rough map of all the states and territories.

As one particular day drew to a close and dusk cloaked the lumber camp with a gray fuzzy mist, Martha sat by lamplight, darning a hole in Juba's sock. She said, "I've noticed you're more determined about being able to draw a map of the territories than anything else I've taught you. Why?"

Juba massaged his leg and worked his toes. "'Cause I'm moving on as quick as I can and I need to know how to get there."

Martha paused with the sock in her lap. "And just where are you headed?"

"Don't know for sure. Just know when I get there, it'll feel right."

"A feeling?"

"Yes, ma'am, like I've found home."

He watched Martha's needle slip in and out of the sock, closing the hole. The lamp's glow highlighted copper strands in her hair and the faint blush on her cheeks. "You're a good-looking woman, Martha."

He hadn't meant to say it. His mouth just blurted it out. He began to stammer to cover his confusion. "Guess I shouldn'ta—"

Martha looked him straight in the eye. "Don't spoil it, Juba. I thank you for the compliment." She grinned. "And besides, it's true."

Juba said, "You sitting there, darning my sock, the lamp shining on your hair. Whole thing looks kinda domestic, like we—some folks might think—"

Martha tied off the thread and snipped the end of it. "Now, you are getting into deep water." She threw the sock at him. "Let me tell you something. Folks can see whatever they want to see in any situation. That doesn't make it true, does it?"

"No, ma'am."

"Well then, all that matters is how you and I look at it."

Juba tried to maneuver his foot into his boot. He bit back a gasp. The pain seemed to travel clear to his elbows.

Martha hadn't glanced up. "Not ready, huh?"

"Guess not."

"Anxious?"

"Yes, ma'am. Thanks for darning the sock."

"You're welcome."

"How come you gave up teaching? Lot easier than cooking for a lumber camp."

"You want an answer that'll do or the truth?"

"The truth."

"I was afraid you'd say that. Well, you asked. Guess I owe it to you." She got up and paced the floor, pausing to run her fingers over the windowsill. She stood there, hands on hips, looking out at the darkened landscape and seeing only her reflection in the glass. "It was three years ago. I had a good little school up the draw at Hunters Grove. Fifteen of the nicest scholars you could want."

She turned and faced Juba. For the first time, he saw heartache mirrored in her eyes.

"One of the little girls had a widowed daddy. He and I kind of . . ." She examined her fingernails. "Well, I fell in love . . ." She moved to the table and fussed with the lamp wick. "Thought he did too . . ." She smoothed the oilcloth on top of the table. "Anyway, there was a picnic. All the children went. Down to the river. Played games. Ate fried chicken. Little Molly . . . wandered off. She fell in the water and . . . before anybody knew . . . she drowned." Martha folded her arms across her chest as if to hold in the hurt.

"Her—daddy blamed me. He . . . said some terrible things and, well, anyway, I had to leave. A few months later, I heard he'd married somebody else. That's about it."

Martha sat at the table, shoulders hunched forward. She traced the flowered pattern in the oilcloth with a forefinger. The room was silent except for the crackling of the fire. Juba watched her. After a long while, he said, "I'm sorry, Martha. Real sorry."

"Thanks." Martha sat a moment longer and sighed. She went to the door, lifted her shoulders, and took a deep breath. Her face changed. "Now then, tomorrow I figure you can sit at the table and peel potatoes, then we'll start in on fractions. Good night, Juba."

"Good night, Martha." Juba waited until she closed the door, then limped to the table and blew out the lamp. He felt his way to his cot and sat there in the dark. "You hear that, Meggie? Somebody else got their heart broke too. Hurts real bad."

He lay down and pulled the quilt over him. Martha's hurt had been three years into the healing and it wasn't done yet. 'Course, the little girl drowning, that was a tough one. "How are you, Meggie?" he whispered. "Wish I could know. Wish I could . . ."

CHAPTER 32

He was moving on. Clem Fordyce had grudgingly paid him for three weeks of work, subtracting for the meals he ate in the kitchen while he healed enough to travel. Martha, without consulting Clem, packed enough food to last him several days.

She stood now in front of the cook shack, watching him as he mounted the mule. "Where do you think you'll end up, Juba?"

"Don't know, ma'am. Just like I said, wherever it feels like home."

"Got your slate?"

"Yes, ma'am."

"Got your gun?"

"Yes, ma'am."

"Got your food?"

"Yes, ma'am, right here." He patted his poke.

"Got that little tin cup they gave you back along the trail?"

"Yes, ma'am."

"Got those matches I gave you?"

"Yes, ma'am."

She stepped forward and squeezed his arm. Her eyes misted. "Be careful, Juba. Goodbye."

"Goodbye, Martha. Thanks for everything." He kneed the mule.

He was a hundred feet down the trail when she hollered, "If a speckled hen lays an egg every other day and a red one lays an egg once a week, what do you have?"

Juba turned in the saddle and waved. He hollered back, "Chicken dumplings, ma'am. Bye, Martha."

He had a lump in his throat big enough to choke a horse. That Martha, she was a good woman. Bet if she and Meggie ever met they'd be good friends. Meggie—she hadn't haunted his thinking every minute like she used to. A little easing of the pain.

"Git on down the road, Jack." They turned a corner and left the lumber camp behind.

Days later, after many miles of steady riding, Juba came to a huge lake and skirted around it, noting the buildings clustered along one side. He saw houses, a blacksmith shop, a mercantile, and a tall building on a bluff that looked like a hotel. In the open doorway of a shed, somebody sawed a butchered beef in two. Juba stared at the fancy boats on the lake. From one came the faint sound of music. Along the road, he saw a sign that said: "Welcome to Rock Lake City." Thanks to Martha, he could read it. "You taught me good," he whispered and rode on.

Soon he came to a spring that flowed right out of the hillside. "Would ya look at that, mule? Ever see anything like it?" He dismounted, knelt, and drank. "Cold 'nuff to hurt yer teeth." The branches of a pine tree swayed beside him in the breeze. Across a meadow, he spied fawns rollicking while their mother grazed. "Pretty," he murmured. "Wonder . . . feels kinda like—like home."

Juba walked through an open field. "Trees over yonder make me a cabin and firewood." He hunkered down and pulled up a clump of bunch grass. "Pretty good pasture. Get me a cow . . . Better nose around that town back there. See if somebody has claim to it."

Juba felt the stares of the white people like pebbles on the back of his neck. He ducked into the livery stable. "Pardon me, suh." He scrubbed the straw underfoot with the toe of his boot. "Anybody claim the property few miles out of town that way?" He gestured and described it as best he could.

The stable hand looked startled by the appearance of a Negro in Rock Lake City, then his mouth twitched as a chuckle escaped his lips. "Ya mean the other side of Duvetts?"

"Don't know Duvetts, suh."

"You thinkin' of locatin' here, you will."

"Yassah."

"The answer to your question's no. Right good piece too. But s'long ol' Henry Duvett lives this side, nobody's gonna touch it."

"Thank you, suh. Thank you." He didn't understand the stable hand's remark about Duvett and it slipped from his mind.

Later, Juba stood in the twilight and studied where he would build his barn and cabin. "Get me a cow. Sell to the creamery I saw in that town. Use the spring to cool the cream. Mebbe some chickens . . ." He was surprised at the tears that streamed down his face. "Oh, Meggie, if only you were standing here with me."

CHAPTER 33

The empty cream can rattled in the wagon as Juba drove home from Rock Lake City. He saw his neighbor, Hank Duvett, standing beside a wagon in his field. He had been chopping thistles and paused, hoe in hand, to stare. Juba waved. Hank stood stiff-legged and stern. Hank's dog gamboled around his legs, hoping for a pat on the head. The horses stomped in their traces. Their tails swished at flies.

Juba spoke to his mule and eased the wagon onto the lane leading to his shack. He smiled. Well, it wasn't a mansion, but it belonged to him. He got down and unhitched the mule. "Good boy, Jack. Know the way to town now 'bout as well as I do."

A strident yelp from Hank's dog startled Juba. He turned. He saw Hank chasing the dog with a hoe. His voice carried over the field. "I'll teach you to get under my feet, you worthless cur."

Juba's hands knotted into fists. He couldn't take his eyes off the dog. Like a jagged sliver, bloody images scratched through his mind:

Pilcher, Master Robinson's overseer, making a slave run inside a circle, a tight fence of slave bodies to hold him in. The thwack of whip striking flesh, the screams of the slave, the blood running down . . . Hank's dog fell down. Juba saw the upraised hoe. He gritted his teeth and burrowed his face in Jack's side. "Nothing I can do about it," he muttered. Jack snorted and began to crop grass.

Juba tried to shut out the dog's piteous cries. *Leave 'em alone. Ain't your dog. Don't look. Don't look.* But he had to. He couldn't help it. He turned again and saw Hank holding the dog by the scruff of the neck, beating it with the hoe handle.

Before his mind registered the impulse, Juba was running toward Hank's field. "Hey!" he yelled. "Don't! Your dog—" He froze. Too late, he realized what he had done.

Hank swore and dropped the dog. He shook his fist at Juba. "You interfering with my business, nigger?"

Juba's shoulders sagged. He kicked a dirt clod. "No, suh," he mumbled. He kept his gaze on the ground.

Hank's voice cut through the buzzing in Juba's ears. "Better watch yer big mouth, nigger."

"Yassah."

Juba heard Hank climb into his wagon and urge his horses forward. The squeak of leather and clatter of the wagon faded away. Juba looked up with shame-filled eyes. Had he forgotten so soon? Hank had a right to treat his dog however he pleased. Slaves were beaten all the time and nobody said a word. He shook his head. Cruelty was cruelty, be it applied to man or beast. He laid his hand on Jack's broad back and watched his fingers tremble. Trouble was, he thought escaping legalized slavery would make things different. He had forgotten that the heart of man was the same no matter where he lived.

The dog was standing, shaking all over, tail tucked between his legs. Juba watched as it limped slowly out of sight into a stand of trees. Hank's wagon stopped farther down the field. The thunk, thunk of Hank's hoe echoed as he chopped at another patch of thistles.

Early morning, Juba was not quite awake. Something moved the gunnysacks that served as a door to his shack. He felt the rush of cool air on his face. He opened his eyes. The dog whined.

"Well, I'll be—what you doing here?"

The dog's tail wagged tentatively. Juba rubbed the sleep from his eyes and sat up. "What'd you come to me for? I can't—"

The dog moved stiffly. Juba saw how he dragged one hind leg. "Here, fella." Juba held out his hand. The dog came to him and licked his fingers. Juba ran his hands over the dog's body. Plenty of bruises, especially on that hip. He looked into the dog's soulful eyes. "What'm I gonna do with you? Your massah will whip us both."

The dog sank to the floor and lay his head on Juba's bare feet. He'd be in real trouble with Hank now. Hank would think he stole the dog. He wasn't ashamed the dog came to him. The shame was in his reply to Hank. He had hung his head and said, "No, suh." That was slave talk. In his anxiety for the dog, he had reverted to slave talk.

"I'm not a slave no more," he said to the dog. "Up north here, folks don't talk like that. No more 'yassah' and 'no, suh.' " He reached down and scratched the dog behind the ears. "Gotta learn to talk northern talk, dog," he said. "Gotta say 'yes, sir.' " He said "yes, sir" again. It felt funny on his tongue. The dog liked it. Maybe he'd name the dog "Yessir."

CHAPTER 34

Hank Duvett had a burr in his boot. He'd always intended to lay claim to that land between his place and Toby Sandberg's. But with one thing and another, he never got around to it. He knew why, if he wanted to admit it. No use buying when you can pasture for free. His cows and horses grazed over there every summer and nobody said anything. He'd made sure when he first settled by Rock Lake that nobody stepped on Hank Duvett's toes. Folks pretty well left him alone. He liked it that way.

Now that nigger from the South was squatting on that 80-acre piece. A nigger, contaminating the land! The injustice of it rankled something awful. Sitting on his door stoop, he could look across and see the man working on the property. He cornered Toby one day in his hay field and vented his gripes. Toby listened politely for a while to Hank's tirade about "that damned nigger buttin' in." After a while, he grew increasingly irritated with Hank's slurs and insinuations.

At last, Toby said, "Aw, Hank let the man be."

"Whaddya mean, man? He ain't no man, he's a nigger. He stole my dog. No telling what else he'll—"

"He didn't steal your dog, Hank. Your dog ran away. If I was your dog, I'da run away a long time ago."

Toby noted Hank's open-mouthed stare. He stepped back as Hank spat at the ground and twisted his lip into a sneer. "Damned if you ain't a nigger lover, Toby. A damned nigger lover." Hank wiped the spittle from his chin and turned, mumbling to himself as he marched away on stiff legs.

Toby watched him go. He smelled trouble. You didn't argue with Hank. Few people could match him for hard-headedness. Few people wanted to. It was easier to stay out of the way, to turn a blind eye, to let Hank have his way. But something in Hank's manner—something in his face told Toby that Hank wasn't about to let that black man have his farm in peace.

Toby sighed. He ought to warn the man. He took off his hat and scratched in his hair. He pulled his handkerchief from his back pocket and mopped his face. You couldn't just go up to a fellow and say, "You being a black man and all—your neighbor over yonder don't like—that is—the rest of us kind of let him do whatever—"

Toby rammed his pitchfork into a windrow and spoke out loud, "We let Hank do whatever he wants because we're a bunch of sissies and don't want to stir up trouble." There, he'd admitted it. They were like a bunch of school kids letting the bully have his way. Maybe it was past time they all stood up for what was right instead.

Toby jammed the pitchfork into the hay again, working off his frustration. He wondered what that black man planned to feed his livestock come winter. He'd seen the man had a cow and a mule. Pasture wouldn't last past frost.

He was on his last windrow. Maybe he'd have time this afternoon to—well, it wouldn't hurt, would it? Just say he was passing by. He gazed over his field. Extra good crop this year. Didn't hurt a body to share a little now and then.

An hour later, Toby followed the track to Juba's place. He reined in his horse and looked around. The black man had a little late garden started. Might get something out of it. Too late for corn or spuds. He heard the whack and ring of a hammer and followed the sound past a makeshift leanto. Hank's dog came out of the leanto, his tail wagging his whole body in greeting.

The black man had hung his shirt over a rail of the corral he was building. His skin glistened with sweat as he nailed the notched end of a pole to an upright. Toby strode over, grasped the far end of the pole and held it in place. The black man looked up, startled.

Toby said, "Afternoon, neighbor."

The black man said, "Afternoon." He went right on hammering until the pole was secure, then looked questioningly at Toby.

Toby noted the crescent-shaped scar on the man's temple, the bulging muscles of his upper body. He wouldn't want to tangle with this one. "I was just passing by," he began. "Thought I might stop in and say howdy, you being a new neighbor and all. Folks call me Toby. Toby Sandberg."

Hank's dog trotted to the black man and licked his fingers. The black man caressed the dog's ears. "Juba," he said in return. "Juba— uh, Robinson."

Toby said, "That's a good dog you got there, Juba." He saw a smile flicker over the man's face.

"Guess he kinda got attached to me."

Toby looked at the ground and toed a fist-sized rock out of the way. "Hank called him a lazy cur."

The black man's eyes narrowed. His jaw tightened. Toby saw the expression and a pang of apprehension hit him in the chest. "Don't— don't get me wrong. Dog's better off with you."

Juba reached down and picked up another pole. He looked at Toby from the corner of his eye. "I didn't steal him. Yessir came to me."

"Yessir? That what you call him?"

Juba grinned. He flashed white teeth. "Yessir," he said.

Toby laughed. "Yessir, son of a gun," and scratched the back of his neck. The dog bounded playfully between the two men. "Don't suppose you'd tell me why you called him that?"

Juba flashed another grin. "No, sir."

Once more, Toby lifted the far end of a pole. The two men worked together for an hour, saying little. At last, Juba laid down his hammer. "If you'd like a drink, I got good water." He led the way down a path to where the spring gurgled out of the side of a knoll. Farther downstream, Toby saw a tethered Jersey cow and a blaze mule.

Juba reached for a tin cup hanging by a leather strap from the branch of a nearby pine tree. He dipped it into the stream. "Cold enough to make your teeth ache," he said and handed the brimming cup to Toby.

Toby hunkered down beside the spring. He squinted up at Juba. "What you gonna use for fodder to keep your cow and mule through the winter?"

"Been wondering about that. Don't have much money for hay. Winter's get pretty cold here?"

"Sometimes it's bad, real bad. Seen several feet of snow on the level. When it's like that, don't go off till March."

"Never figured—"

Toby grinned. "Guess where you come from you never saw such a winter, eh?" As soon as it was out of his mouth, he wondered if the man might take offense. "Well, shucks, what I mean is—" Now that his foot was in his mouth, he might as well go whole hog. "You one of those slaves brave enough to come all the way north?" He saw Juba flinch.

"You mean, am I a runaway?"

Time stopped for a heartbeat. Toby stood and stuck out his hand. "Yeah, that's what I mean and I'd like to shake your hand because, man, you had a heap of courage to do it."

He saw Juba's shoulders relax. Their hands met. "Tell you what, I usually have some hay to spare. Good crop this year for sure. I'll have plenty left over and—"

Juba was shaking his head. "Mighty short on money. I couldn't—"

"Don't expect you to pay. Fella getting started needs help sometimes, that's all. I'm figuring on some corral building myself next spring. Maybe you could help me." He watched Juba rub a callus on his palm.

"Why'd you want to help me? Don't know nothing 'bout me."

Toby held his gaze. "No, but I can guess. You risked your neck to break free down south. No telling what you went through to get here. Right?" He handed back the cup. "That's sure good water. Come on over to Sunday supper sometime. Wife makes a tolerable chicken fricassee."

Riding away, Toby reflected on his visit with Juba. Black man and white man sharing the same cup. As far as he was concerned, that kind of sealed a friendship. By gum, let ol' Hank chew on that for a while. As long as he had cantankerous neighbors in mind, if there was trouble in the days ahead, his being a justice of the peace might come in handy if Juba should need some help that way.

CHAPTER 35

Juba ambled toward the door stoop of Toby Sandberg's cabin. He nervously clenched and unclenched his fists. Had he scrubbed his neck and ears enough? Had he checked his fingernails? What would Toby's wife think of a runaway slave sitting at her table? Naw, he shouldn't have come. He ought to tiptoe away. Tell Toby he forgot next time he saw him. Anyway, Toby probably meant for Juba to have a tin plate outside somewhere while the white folks—

The cabin door opened. "There you are, Juba." Toby Sandberg reached out to shake his hand and draw him inside. "Isabel, Isabel, come meet our neighbor."

Toby's wife turned from the stove. She was short and round. A few gray hairs had escaped the bun atop her head and curled at her cheeks. "Welcome, Juba. Glad Toby invited you over."

"Th—thank you, ma'am." He felt all thumbs and feet. He jumped as Toby pulled out a chair. "Here, sit down. Isabel's got supper about ready."

Juba hesitated. *Sit down? At the table?* Already Toby was hitching his own chair forward. Juba glanced at Isabel. She had wrapped her apron around a hot bowl and approached the table with a limp. Juba couldn't see her feet; only the wide column of her long dress dipping as she stepped, like a dinghy riding gentle waves. He clasped his hands in his lap and tried to still their trembling.

Toby bowed his head. "Heavenly Father, thank you for the company of our guest this evening and for the bounty of this food. Amen."

For the second time, Juba jumped. *Guest? Toby talking about him?* He looked around. There were only the three of them at the table and Isabel was passing him the bowl.

He tried to keep his eyes on his plate. Tried not to spill anything. Tried hard to be a guest. He flicked occasional glances at Isabel and the time she caught him at it, she held his gaze with her own. Her eyes were smiling behind her spectacles and her voice was filled with warmth. "Are you wondering why we invited you to supper, Juba? Fact is, we like to get acquainted with all our neighbors. Not very many hereabouts. Not like in Rock Lake City where houses are close together. I'm just talking about farmers like yourself. Folks who live off the land."

Toby said, "Have another helping of spuds. Yep, there's the Tillys and the Degerstroms and ol' John Callum and—"

Isabel said, "Don't forget Sol and Mary Adams and their six little cuties." She turned to Juba. "I helped bring every one of them into the world."

Toby said, "Yep, and the Finnerts over on the Waverly place. Anyhow, we've made friends with every one of them except—well—guess Hank Duvett's a different kind of—" He looked at Isabel.

A funny squeak of a laugh escaped Isabel's lips. She cleared her throat and murmured, "Juba needs to know."

Toby slapped the table. "Well, sounds like we're spreading gossip. But that isn't it. Think you should be warned, that's all. Folks around here kind of walk way around the other way when they see Hank coming. You know what I mean?"

Juba shrugged, his eyes full of bewilderment.

Isabel whispered across the table. "In other words, leave him alone."

Toby nodded. "Yeah, no use tethering your calf out in the woods just to see if the wolf will take a bite out of it."

Juba debated whether to speak or not and decided to go ahead. "Sounds like I already got myself in trouble."

"Oh? You mean about the dog? That was the dog's fault, not yours. Smart dog, I'd say." Toby grinned. "Don't mean this for an insult, Juba, but the dog was kinda like you. Saw where he could live better than what he had and ran for it."

And Juba, who had tried to be so carefully proper this evening, burst into laughter. He heard Isabel chime in and Toby's deep chuckle boomed the bass.

"Now then, Juba." Isabel bent over the table and replenished the coffee cups. "Tell me some of your experiences. Toby says it's quite a story how you got your mule."

Later, walking home under the stars, Juba pondered what he had heard. ". . . a guest . . . a farmer like yourself . . . a neighbor . . ." Juba raised his eyes to the sky, "Oh Lawd, bless these good people." And then, in a whisper, "Meggie, wish you'd been there with me. Wish you . . ."

CHAPTER 36

Juba grinned and jingled the coins in his pocket as Jack turned the wagon into his lane. "My lane," he said aloud, "my farm." The Rock Lake City restaurant was pleased with the cream he brought twice a week and the mercantile gladly exchanged eggs for groceries. He had established a small business and he was proud of it.

Jack stopped abruptly, throwing Juba forward. "What—?"

One of the pine trees that bordered his lane now lay across the road, its jagged stump a testimony to hurried chopping. A piece of paper anchored with a rock fluttered from the stump. Juba climbed down from the wagon. "Whoa, Jack. Who coulda—?"

He read the note: "Nigger go home." He sent another silent thank you to Martha for teaching him to read. A thought presented itself. Maybe he'd be better off if he couldn't read. No, that wasn't true. *Best to know as much about your enemy as you could.* Enemy? Who was his enemy?

Juba whirled around. Hank Duvett, toting an axe over his shoulder, was walking nonchalantly across his field. Juba opened his mouth to call to Hank. *No, calm down. Don't go flying off the handle.* He raised his hands in a futile gesture, stuffed the paper in his pocket, and bent to drag the tree out of the way.

He knew Hank was sore about the dog. But that hadn't been his fault. The dog chose him. He didn't really know Hank. Hank never gave him an opportunity to be neighborly. Juba climbed back into the wagon and as Jack plodded along, he thought. *Hank didn't want to be neighborly. Hank hated him because he was a black man. It was that simple.* Juba frowned and shook his head. If he lived to be a hundred, he'd never understand it. And if Hank lived to be a hundred, he'd never change.

Look on the bright side, Juba told himself as he unhitched Jack. *Hank had done me a favor by felling a tree. Now, all I have to do is cut it up to warm my cabin next winter.* He couldn't help the grin that crossed his face. Hank would be twice as mad if he thought Juba saw it that way.

CHAPTER 37

Early morning, still dark, Juba rolled over and tucked the blanket around his shoulders. He closed his eyes . . .

. . . the ground was covered with frost. Juba stood on his door stoop, milk bucket in hand. He reached back into the cabin and pulled a wool jacket from a nail beside the door. "No wonder folks in this country need heavy coats in the winter," he said to Yessir. "Brrr, and this is just the first taste of it. I see you've got a heavier coat too, dog. Didn't notice when you started to grow it, but looks like it fits you good."

Yessir waited for his morning pat on the head, wagged his tail, and went down the path to the barn ahead of Juba.

Juba entered the warm barn. Its mingled smells of hay and peeled logs and steaming manure were somehow reassuring to him. "Now, Bess," he said as he laid a hand on the cow's back and stroked her side, "that restaurant in Rock Lake City's waiting for some rich cream."

He straddled the three-legged stool beside the cow and positioned the bucket under her udder. With his head resting against Bess's warm flank, he settled into a rhythm, filling the bucket with foaming milk. He hummed a tune as he sorted a mental list of things to do during the day.

Yessir's growl alerted him. Bess pulled back in her stanchion and rolled her eyes. "Easy, Bess, easy now." Juba held onto the bucket and started to turn around. Yessir growled again. And then came the sound of a leather boot striking the dog's ribs. Yessir yelped.

"Don't bother to turn around, Juba," said a voice he had put out of mind. The barrel of a rifle dug into his back. "Just set there, nice and easy. Don't want to get the cow excited."

Juba's stomach lurched. "Hezekiah Peel," he said.

"Ah, you remember me, Juba." Peel gloated. "Thought maybe in your high and mighty state you would've forgotten me."

"Some people are hard to disremember," Juba muttered.

Yessir, who wasn't allowed in the barn while Juba milked, peered inside. His lip curled over his teeth in a snarl. He growled intermittently.

"Better shut yer dog up. Makes my trigger finger nervous."

"My dog's a good judge of character." Inwardly Juba prayed, *Please don't let Peel shoot my dog. Please, Lawd.*

"You sure led me on a chase, boy. Wore out my shoes lookin' fer you. Wore out my patience too."

"Sorry to disappoint you, Peel, but I'm a free man. This's my farm you're trespassing on."

Peel's gutteral laugh scraped Juba's nerves. "Got it wrong, boy. Fugitive's a fugitive 'til the day he dies. You're a runaway slave in the eyes of the law and the law's on my side."

Somehow the frosty morning had turned hot. Sweat trickled down Juba's sides. The cow shifted uneasily as his fingers trembled on her udder. "Whoa, Bess, easy now."

If he tried to get up, Peel would probably shoot him before he was on his feet. Even if he could somehow get out the barn door, he couldn't outrun Peel's gun. With his back turned like this, Peel had all the advantage. Peel had him. Or did he?

Juba said, "If you're gonna shoot me, Peel, the least you can do is come around where I can see you."

"My pleasure," Peel said. He moved until he was directly behind the cow. His face was as Juba remembered it—shifty eyes, hard cheeks, cruel mouth curved in a sneer. He leaned forward and aimed the rifle at Juba's chest. "This is better anyhow. I'd rather watch your face while you die."

"I ain't gonna die, Peel," Juba said.

Peel laughed, his eyes boring into Juba's. "No? You think I'm here for a tea party?"

Yessir took one step inside the barn door. He growled again.

"Told you to shut that dog up." Peel glanced toward the dog.

At that moment, Juba reached high on Bess's udder. He pinched hard. Bess kicked. Her hoof whacked Peel's knee. He swore and toppled backwards. "Cussed cow!" The gun discharged. Bess's hooves sent the bucket banging across the floor. Milk sloshed in all directions.

Juba grabbed for the gun, but Peel's grip was sure. "Uh-uh, you ain't ruining my rifle like you did last time. I told you I'd get you." Peel struggled up. In his lunge for Juba, he passed too close to Bess who was plunging and pacing in her stanchion. Lightning quick, she struck out again. Peel roared in pain as Bess's kick landed once more on his bruised knee and then his stomach. He slipped in the spilled milk and fell on his backside. The rifle slithered across the floor.

Juba scooped it up and pointed it at Peel. His fingers were slick. Milk dripped from the rifle barrel and the stock. "Get up, Peel," he said quietly, as if his sides weren't shaking, as if he were perfectly calm. "I'll give you ten seconds to find your horse and ride away."

Peel moaned. "I can't hardly move. Help me up."

"You don't need help."

"Your cow—she—"

"Cow and dog are friends. She's a good judge of character too. Five seconds, Peel." Juba pressed his lips together to still their trembling. He watched Hezekiah Peel stagger out the barn door, holding his stomach. Yessir nipped at his ankles and ripped his pant leg. "Call yer dog off, you cussed nigger," he managed on a strangled breath.

"Three seconds," Juba warned.

"Give me back my rifle."

"Two seconds."

"Can't get on my horse that fa—"

Juba aimed the gun at Peel's stomach. "One second."

Peel's horse was tied to the hog pen corner post. He kept glancing back at Juba as his frantic fingers worked to pull the reins loose. He hoisted himself into the saddle. Juba fired once into the air. The horse took off at a full gallop with Peel weaving from side to side. They disappeared in a cloud of dust.

Juba let the air out of his chest. He leaned the rifle against the side of the barn and hunkered down beside Yessir. "Good dog, good dog," He laid his cheek along the side of Yessir's face. He walked back into the barn, a little unsteady, and picked up the dented, dirty milk bucket. Bess's hind feet were still dancing on the milk-slicked floor. Her muscles twitched under her skin when Juba touched her. He undid the stanchion and set her free. "Only milk I'd get outta you now would be buttermilk, old gal. Right proud of you." He watched her run into the pasture, switch her tail a few times, and begin to graze . . .

. . . at that moment, Juba woke up. "Huh!?" His blanket was half on the floor. A cold sweat covered his body. He felt the edge of his bed and shivered. He dug his fingers into the corners of his eyes and blinked.

What a nightmare. Parts of it were so real he couldn't get it out of his mind. He shook his head. He looked at the floor, expecting to see it covered with dirty milk. The imprint of Peel's rifle still seemed to press against his palms.

He groaned and lay back on his bed, trying to erase the images that lingered like cobwebs in the recesses of his mind. Had he seen the last of Peel? Only God knew. He hadn't thought about him for over a year. Runaway slaves were supposed to be safe once they arrived in free territories. But Peel had never been one to go by the rules.

God sends guardian angels, doesn't He? Sometimes, I reckon, they might take the forms of dogs and cows. It was a thought anyway. He hoped, in his case, it would never be necessary, not like that nightmare.

CHAPTER 38

Juba could see the pond from his door stoop. Toby told him it seeped underground from the big lake and sometimes the Canada geese hung around until the pond had a skim of ice on it. Those geese would be mighty good eating. Juba's mouth watered at the telling. He had been so busy plowing, seeding, building, getting ready for winter. Now, for today, he had other plans. He would go goose hunting.

It was freezing inside the shack. Sometime in the night, the fire had gone out. Juba pulled the blanket closer around his shoulders. The move uncovered his feet. He looked at the door. Good thing he had set those hinges in place last week. Not a day too soon. White frost glittered here and there on the frame. He'd better use what was left of the gunnysack to chink the cracks.

Gingerly, his bare toes touched the cold floor. He opened the stove's firebox and stuffed in wadded paper and kindling. Two dry sticks went on top of the kindling. He struck a match. The fire roared up the chimney. He jammed another stick into the firebox and turned the damper in the stovepipe to choke it down and send warmth into the room.

As he pulled his shirt and overalls on over his long underwear, he heard Yessir scratch at the outside of the door. He let the dog in.

"So you don't like the cold, huh, Yessir? Gotta get used to it. Counting on you sleeping in the shed to keep the cougars away from old Jack and Bess."

Yessir banged his tail against Juba's leg and licked his hand. Juba scraped last night's leftover fried potatoes from the iron skillet into a tin pan and placed it on the floor. "There's your breakfast. I'll top it off with warm milk soon's I get the chores done. We're going goose hunting this morning. Birds're hunkered down on that pond out there."

Yessir's tail swished back and forth over the dirt floor. He watched Juba's face eagerly.

"—and lately it's been frozen over ever' night. I been watching those geese. Just sitting there waiting for you'n'me to come get 'em. We'll take ol' Jack with us. He's gettin' fat what with no plowing to do. Needs the exercise."

Near the pond, Yessir nosed through the grass, exploring old scents. Jack snuffled air through his nostrils and looked back longingly at his shed a quarter of a mile away.

"You're all right, you ol' mule," Juba said. He pulled his cap flaps more firmly over his ears. "Cold enough to freeze the tail off a monkey, though." He turned to Yessir. "Now, you stay quiet. Not many more chances to get a goose before they all takes off for warmer country."

The words were hardly out of his mouth when the old familiar pain began. *Warmer country, where there was Meggie and her little boy and that good-for-nothing Arlo.* Juba filled his lungs and throat with the frosty air. His nose hairs froze. His lungs ached. *Let 'em ache. It'll help numb the other pain.*

Juba crawled quietly through the weeds and settled down where somebody had once built a goose blind. Moldy straw bales, warped boards, and broken tree branches littered the area. Thirty feet out from shore, a flock of geese began to stir on the thin ice. A reddish sun inched above the horizon and showered diamonds over the grass.

Juba crouched. He kept his hand on Yessir's head, willing him to be still. He figured the geese would take off when the morning warmed a little. They would head for the wheat stubble fields behind him. If he waited to shoot until they were almost over his head, angled into the sky, he'd be sure to get one.

He opened his powder pouch and poured out a pinch. He'd put his "spit patch" in his mouth before leaving the cabin. Now he took it out and wrapped it around the ball. He shoved the ball against the powder with the rod and tamped it down. The cap went on the end of the hammer tube. Now, he was ready.

The geese began to talk. A honk here and another over there, a few more, back and forth. They reminded Juba of people having a group discussion. Or was it an argument? Juba quietly parted the weeds. A lone goose stretched its wings and flapped them a couple of times as if warming up for the take off. Then others stretched and flapped, until the whole flock began to honk and lift their wings in unison. The sight of it made Juba catch his breath. His hands trembled and he gripped the gunstock hard, willing his fingers to steady. *Easy now, easy. Don't shoot too soon.*

Obeying a silent signal, the flock suddenly lifted from the ice and angled toward the sky. Their choreographed ballet brought them circling low over his head. He heard the swoosh and beat of their wings, saw their white underbellies, their necks stretched forward. Juba chose his goose. He caught him in his sights and fired. He saw the goose hesitate, then fall away from the flock. Broken winged, it spiraled against the coral sky, each turn taking it closer to the pond.

Juba muttered, "No, no." He held his breath, willing the goose to veer toward land. Its body tumbled over and over. "No, no, too far. Not that way." It plunged downward and fell with a thump on the ice. A handful of loose feathers floated briefly in the air, then settled over the dead bird.

"Now, what'll I—"

Yessir nudged his arm and pushed past him. Startled, Juba stared with open mouth. The dog crashed through the brittle weeds and headed straight toward the pond.

Juba flung down his shotgun and yelled, "No, Yessir, no! Come back, come back." He stumbled along behind the dog, arms outstretched, imploring, "Come back, Yessir, come back."

Yessir plowed into the cattails at the edge of the water and trotted onto the ice. Juba watched helplessly as the ice began to snap. "Yessir!" Water seeped through cracks and splashed over Yessir's paws. Far away, the flock of geese became no more than pepper specks above the distant trees.

"Oh Lawd, oh Lawd. Yessir!" The dog was almost to the fallen goose. Juba saw the widening rifts in the ice. One of Yessir's legs slipped into the water. A pool opened up. Yessir disappeared beneath the surface.

"Yessir!" Juba's agonized cry ricocheted off the bluffs surrounding the pond. He turned this way and that, searching frantically. "Gotta find something—something to help." He spied an abandoned fence post lying in the weeds. *Too heavy.* A piece of thick cardboard was frozen to the ground. He tried to pull it up and it tore in two. "Oh Lawd, help me."

In his desperate search, Juba began to run. He tripped and fell into a weathered rowboat hidden among the cattails. There was no oar. He snatched a stick protruding from a pile of brush, yanked the boat free of the weeds that clung to it, and pushed it into the water.

"Yessir! Yessir!"

Juba dug the shaft of the stick into the pond's muddy bottom. Broken ice crackled and curled around the bow of the boat as he clumsily propelled it to the spot he had last seen Yessir. Or was it? In his confusion and fear, it all looked the same. He leaned far over the side of the boat and scanned the water. He glimpsed a small black knob a few feet away, seeming to float on the surface. Black knob? That was the tip of Yessir's nose! As he watched, it disappeared. Juba swung the stick wildly, jabbing it into the mud, cursing the snail's pace. The knob surfaced again, closer. He could see Yessir's head now, arched back, the paws paddling weakly, sinking.

Juba shifted his weight and as he scraped his feet against the bottom of the boat, he looked down. Water swirled around his ankles. He drove the stick into the mud with one hand and plunged his other arm into the icy water. He grabbed Yessir by the scruff of his neck and held on. The dog broke the surface, hanging limp in Juba's grasp. *Mustn't let go. Mustn't let go.* Juba leaned far back and heaved the dog into the boat. "Yessir, Yessir," he cried.

Water was over Juba's boot tops. Shaking violently, he cradled the dog on his lap. The boat wallowed and sloshed more water over his legs as slowly, slowly, he steered it toward shore.

Almost to the cattails that lined the shore, the boat tipped and settled in the water. With hands that could no longer feel, Juba clung to the dog. He stumbled from the boat and thrashed toward the marshy bank. His waterlogged clothes dragged like weights. He shambled into the slick grass and fell face down with the dog beneath him.

"Jack, Jack," he called, his voice wavering with fear. The mule had been pulling at dry tufts of grass and now ambled over to stand just out of reach. Juba raised his head. His lungs were on fire. He strained to reach Jack's dangling reins. After several failed attempts, he finally hooked one club-like hand onto a rein and drew Jack closer.

Juba's clothes were frozen as stiff as his arms and legs. A thin coating of ice was forming on Yessir's body. Juba stumbled to his feet. He swayed and almost fell with Yessir in his arms. "Whoa, Jack. Whoa, there. Stand still."

Juba tried to heave the dog high enough to balance him onto the mule's back, but his strength gave out mid-way. "Hold on. Gotta make it—somehow. Gotta—keep trying."

His icy pant legs crackled as he bent his knees. He forced air into his lungs and, straining, hoisted the dog again. Yessir plopped across Jack's back like a half empty sack. His body convulsed. Water gushed from his mouth.

Hurry! Juba's mind shouted. But his feet could only shuffle like sticks as he led Jack to a stump. He used the last of his strength to climb aboard. "Home, Jack," he mumbled.

Jack plodded along. *Would he ever reach the cabin?* "Move, you old mule, move!" Juba tried to shout, but the words came out in a hoarse whisper.

Jack stopped abruptly by the cabin door, almost throwing Juba off. He tried to climb down. His legs would not cooperate and he tumbled from the mule and landed by the door. He staggered to his feet, forced his arms to reach up and drag Yessir off Jack's back.

Juba's mind was as numb as his body. *Open the door,* he told himself. *Hurry, hurry!* He wrestled with the door latch. Just before he stumbled into the shack, he saw Jack turn toward his own warm shed.

Juba laid Yessir in front of the stove and tugged repeatedly at his gloves to get them off. With fingers that refused to bend, his body encased in frozen clothes, Juba upended an open gunnysack of potatoes, scattering them over the floor. He massaged Yessir with the rough sack. Kneading, rubbing, pressing gently, he bent over the dog. He talked softly all the while of adventures they had shared. "You'n'me, Yessir, remember the time we . . ." As the circulation returned to his own legs and feet, excruciating needles of pain made him wince.

Yessir began to shake. His rib cage expanded beneath Juba's hands. He coughed. Juba felt another breath fill Yessir's lungs. "That's it, Yessir. Come on, come on." Yessir's tail thumped the floor once, twice. Juba stroked his head and was rewarded with a licked hand. Juba sat back and peeled out of his clothes, now dripping on the floor. He sighed. "We made it, dog. You and me, we made it." He scratched Yessir between the ears. "Sure surprised me, ol' fella. Bet Hank never knew your granddaddy was a retriever neither."

Later, while his clothes steamed before the fire, Juba rested his feet on the fender of the stove and sipped a cup of strong coffee. Yessir, racked with occasional tremors, dozed beside him. He could have lost the dog. Might have frozen to death himself if Jack hadn't carried them home. He could not have lugged Yessir and his shotgun and—

The shotgun! It was still out there lying in the tall weeds. Juba leaned forward with his elbows on his knees and his head in his hands. There was only one way to bring the gun in: fetch it himself.

CHAPTER 39

On the same winter day, Meggie stood at the stove stirring corn meal mush in Sal and Dan Crane's cabin on the Nebraska prairie. She watched the storm through the kitchen window. She shivered. It was a good thing Sal had made a loft bed for Meggie over the kitchen. The back porch now was a frigid place to store things until spring.

Sal was right when she first told Meggie about blizzards. Last summer, she had begged Meggie to stay on until spring. Meggie glanced out the window again. The snow pelting against the glass had almost completely hidden the view.

Sal often sat by the fire these days, sewing little garments for her expected baby. Meggie kept the woodbox full, swept the hearth, cooked the meals, and kept busy with many other daily chores. Sal told her over and over, "What would I do without you, Meggie? You came just when I needed you most."

"Yes, ma'am."

On Christmas Eve, Dan wrestled a scrub pine into the cabin. He had found it on a windswept knoll. He hammered together a stand for it and asked Sal, "How about it, Sal? Pretty good Christmas tree, huh?"

"Yes, Dan. It's the best we can find around here, I'm sure. Let's push the dresser over and put the tree in the corner so it won't be so near the fire."

That evening, the three of them popped corn to string on the tree. Meggie tried to sit respectfully behind Dan and Sal, but Sal said, "No, Meggie, you sit here with us." She moved the bench so they could all feel the fire's warmth. The popcorn kept breaking as the needle and thread passed through each kernel, and they laughed over their feast of the broken parts.

Sal reached into the bottom of her trunk in the bedroom and brought out a small box. Inside, wrapped in cotton, were twelve tiny candles attached to clips. She snapped them onto the tree branches, struck a match and lighted them. "Now, blow out the lamp, Meggie. There. Oh look, isn't the tree pretty? Merry Christmas, Dan. Merry Christmas, Meggie."

January 3rd, the wind howled and snuffled around the cabin like a wild animal trying to force its way in. Meggie tucked papers over the two windows and poked rags into the cracks around the door. Dan, covered with snow, stomped inside. "It's a bad one out there. I'll wait a while, then throw some hay to the cattle. They're all trying to shelter on the lee side of the barn."

Sparks flew up as Meggie threw another stick of wood on the fire. Dan dipped into the water bucket for a drink. Neither saw Sal grimace, suddenly still, as she hung onto the back of a chair.

The moment passed. Dan took off his boots and heavy coat, and dozed beside the fire. Meggie peeled potatoes and sliced a slab of bacon to fry. Sal retired behind the curtain into the bedroom. Time ticked by. Dan roused himself. Meggie put the dinner on the table.

Dan called out, "Ain't you eating, Sal?"

"Maybe later. I just need to lie down for a while."

The cabin grew dim and Meggie lit the lamp. Dan bundled up. As he opened the door, the wind whipped wet snow into the cabin. "Gotta get those cattle fed. Give 'em energy to make body heat so's they won't freeze."

Dan slammed the door shut, and Meggie tucked the rags into the cracks again. She heard a moan from the bedroom. "Meggie?"

"Yes, ma'am?"

"I need you, Meggie."

Meggie shyly pushed the curtain aside. She had never before been in the Crane's bedroom.

Sal lay, tense and pale, on the cornshuck mattress. She held out her hand. As Meggie approached her, she bit her lip and raised her knees under the quilt. "My baby's coming, Meggie. You'll have to help me."

Meggie took a step back. She clenched her hands under her chin. "I—I ain't never helped with a birthing before."

Sal tried to smile. It became a pursed-lip groan. "I never had a baby before, either. But my Aunt Sadie was a midwife. She taught me—" Sal paused, scrunched up her face, and pressed her hands over her tightened abdomen. "Guess we'll—"

Meggie turned toward the curtain. "I'll go get Massah Dan. He—"

"No, Meggie. Stay with me. Dan'll be back when he gets the cattle fed."

Sal told Meggie to boil water, to sterilize the scissors and some string, to gather all the clean towels and sheets she could find. And then she said, "In my trunk—you'll find—a little blanket and a kimono—and—"

Meggie waited, fingernails marking half moons in her palms as Sal stiffened and cried out.

"Ma'am? Sal?"

Sal let out a pent up breath. "Go. Go quick!"

Shaking with nervousness, Meggie hurried. When all was in readiness in the kitchen, Sal told her, "Put a flannel blanket under me and wash me where the baby will come out."

Meggie hesitated.

"Don't be afraid. You won't hurt me. I—oohh, Meggie."

Meggie jerked back, her eyes wide with fear. "I'se sorry, ma'am. I'se sorry."

"Oh no, Meggie. It wasn't you. It was—" She stopped and bit her lip.

Meggie approached the bed again. "I reckon that was the baby knocking on the door, wanting out."

Sal managed a wan smile. "Yes, Meggie. That's exactly what it was."

From that moment, Meggie was so busy she had no time to be afraid. An hour flew by while the wind shook the cabin and pummeled it with snow. Meggie kept the water hot, mopped Sal's face with a soft cloth, and let Sal squeeze her hand until she thought her knuckles would break. She laid out the sterilized scissors and string on a towel and gathered papers to wrap the placenta in. Then, mopping her own brow, she peeked and saw the crown of the baby's head. "It's a-coming, it's a-coming, ma'am."

Meggie waited, hands outstretched, as Sal labored. The baby's head slipped out. A shoulder showed itself. Then laughing and crying,

Meggie caught the baby in her hands. "We gots him, ma'am. We gots your little boy."

The baby filled his lungs and wailed. "That's all right, little feller. You jist go ahead and beller."

Groggily, Sal told Meggie how to tie the umbilical cord and cut it. Meggie cleaned the baby, wrapped him in his soft blanket, and laid him in Sal's arms. "He's a right pretty one, ma'am. You done good." She tidied the bedroom, then went to the kitchen and stoked the fire. Tea, that's what Sal would need after all that work. Meggie propped her up a bit and cuddled the baby while Sal savored the tea. "Ooh, what a nice baby you is. What's your mamma gonna call you?"

"His name is Edgar. Edgar Benton Crane. Edgar was my father's name." Sal set down the cup and reached for the baby. "Thanks, Meggie. You've been wonderful help."

Wearily, Meggie ducked around the curtain and sighed as she sank into a kitchen chair to drink her own tea.

Sal's voice, on the edge of sleep, reached her. "Where's Dan?"

Oh Lawdy, in all the hurry and bustle and excitement, I forgot Dan. How long has he been outside? Too long. Meggie's brow wrinkled, but she kept her voice steady. She poked her head around the edge of the curtain. "Don't you worry none. I'll go see what's keeping him."

Sal drifted off, a slight smile on her lips. Meggie tiptoed through the kitchen. She found boots, mittens, and the knitted cap Sal had given her for Christmas. She lit a kerosene lantern. Wrapped in Dan's deer hide coat, she pushed open the door and stepped into a drift almost to her waist. "Dan, Massah Dan," she called. The wind tore the words from her mouth. "Massah Dan!" she screamed. "Massah Dan!"

The only answer was the howling, buffeting wind that would have thrown her off balance but for the snow that held her legs.

Hours earlier, Dan had plunged into the storm. He held tightly to the rope stretched from cabin to barn as he lifted his feet high through the drifts. "Better string a rope," his old neighbor cautioned the first winter he and Sal settled here. "Sometimes a feller gets lost in a whiteout and don't know which way's t'other."

Dan's heavy boots plowed a trail to the barn. The cattle crowded around him as he threw forkful after forkful of hay into the trampled area. Sometimes, the wind threw the hay leaves back in his face. He tried to aim some of the hay to a couple of timid cows that hung behind the rest of the herd. Once he turned and came face to face with the shorthorn bull. "Move on," Dan said gruffly. "Get out of the way." The bull lowered his head and bunted a cow out of his path.

Dan turned to lift another forkful of hay. The bull butted him in the back with the force of a battering ram. He dropped the fork and fell to his knees, the breath knocked out of him. The bull butted again. It pushed Dan into a snowdrift and rolled him over, its hoof grazing the side of Dan's head. It then backed a step or two and picked at the hay that clung to Dan's blanket-lined coat.

Dan struggled to breathe. Stars swam before his eyes. When the bull's hoof scraped his head, he felt a momentary sharp pain, then a soft blanket of unconsciousness pulled him down, down into a fuzzy cocoon. Two cows near the barn fought over the abandoned forkful of hay. One hooked, with her head, the lantern Dan had hung on a nail. Crazily, she tossed her head to be rid of it and smashed it to the ground. The wind gusted and, little by little, covered Dan with a blanket of snow.

Meggie clung to the rope, stumbling and swaying as she trudged toward the barn. By the time she reached it, she was sweating underneath her heavy clothes. She swung her lantern in a wide circle and called again, "Massah Dan, Massah Dan." The wind made her eyes tear. She swiped at them with her mittens and called once more. "Massah Dan." Only the wind answered her.

Most of the cattle had bedded down for the night. Their breath blew small steamy spurts of moisture into the swirling snow. Meggie stood very still and listened. Dan's broken lantern crunched under her boots. She looked down, puzzled. A few feet away, she saw the bull as he sat chewing his cud. He rested beside a rounded drift. Meggie took another step and stumbled over the handle of the hayfork. She pulled it out of the snow and propped it against the barn wall. *Why had Dan been so careless with it?*

The barn door was partly open. *Now, Dan would never have left it like that. The cattle might push their way inside and ruin the stack of loose hay.* Meggie quickly slipped through the door. "Massah Dan?" The eerie silence inside the barn made her shiver.

Her lantern light traced a giant shadow moving on the rough timbered walls. Meggie's heart skipped. She whirled around and squealed in fright. Something touched her legs. She jumped. The barn cat had left its hollowed out nest in the hay and came to rub against her. Meggie knelt and petted its back with a mittened hand. "You scared me, Tiger. Looked like a boogey man 'bout to get me."

Hearing her own voice, touching the cat—small proofs of life in this whitened, howling world—helped her to summon her courage. She stepped outside, latched the barn door, and swung the lantern again over the herd. She smelled their gassy breath. They stared at her, their wide, stupid gaze catching the light.

Just to make sure the bull had not moved, she aimed the lantern at him once more. Her eye spied a bit of color in the drift beside him. *Color? In a snowdrift?* Wary of getting too close, she plodded a few steps, leaned toward him and peered. Tiny tendrils of steam rose from his side and wafted away in the wind. The warmth from his hide had melted the snow beside him. Meggie took another shaky step. Her eyes grew round. She gasped, "Massah Dan!"

A bolt of fear went through Meggie. She felt so small and inadequate compared to the bull's massive strength. Massah Dan was lying there in the snow. She was sure of it. She had to help him. What if he was already dead? She shuddered.

Meggie inched closer, set the lantern down, and pawed at the snow. The rest of Dan's coat, then his cap came into view. Meggie kept glancing at the bull and murmuring softly, "Masssah Dan, Massah Dan." As she cleared more snow away, images of Dan over the months flashed through her mind. He no longer saw her as a nameless, untamed servant, but a helpful companion to Sal. He had roared with laughter when she and Sal sang "Ol' Susannah." And the times he joined in with his tuneless baritone, they had to stifle their own laughter.

Now, he lay helpless and she alone knew of it. She alone must rescue him somehow, some way.

The bull snorted and rose, shaking a broadside of snow over her. Terrified, Meggie stumbled backward. But the bull had had enough of this creature with the glowing yellow eye. He lumbered away into the swirling shadows.

From the imprint in the snow, Meggie saw where the bull had lain, leaning slightly against Dan. The bull's body warmth must have kept Dan from freezing. Meggie gently shook Dan's shoulder. "Massah Dan*?" Oh please, don't let him be dead. Not when he's just had a baby boy born.* Meggie heard a faint moan. Yes, yes, he was alive!

She must get him to the cabin. She must get him to where there was warmth and comfort. *But how?* Dan was a big man. She could not lift him. She thought of the sled. She and Sal had used it to haul split wood when the snow began to pile up.

The sled was hanging on the wall inside the barn. Meggie tramped back to the barn and hauled the sled out, now to maneuver Dan onto it and pull it to the cabin. She strained to turn Dan over and caught her breath when she saw the blood on the side of his head and in the snow. Sweat ran down Meggie's face. It trickled down her spine and slicked her hands inside her mittens. Finally, she pushed the sled as close as she could to Dan's body, tucked her hands under his armpits, and heaved. As she lifted, his shoulders touched the sled and the sled slid away from under him. Meggie began to wail. *It's no use.* There was nobody to help. Dan would die and she was standing right there and—

In the barn, stacked against the inside wall, were some fence rails left over from the new corral built last summer. Beyond weariness, Meggie stumbled back to the barn and dragged out a couple of rails. With all her strength, she rammed them into the snow next to the sled. *Now.* She took a deep breath and gritted her teeth. She gripped Dan's coat under his arms again and pulled with all her might. The sled moved slightly, but she had lifted Dan's upper body onto it. She stood there panting, chest heaving. She was so hot she wanted to rip off her coat and cap. "Don't you dare," she said out loud. "You wanna catch your death?"

It was then she realized the wind had stilled. The storm had lessened to a few flakes drifting lazily to earth. Meggie could see stars and a crescent moon. Dan moaned again. Meggie shook her head. "You's too tall to get all of you onto the sled, Massah Dan." His legs and feet would have to drag in the snow.

Pushing, shoving, she positioned him as best she could. *I better get a rope and tie him on.* "Don't want you falling off," she said to his silent face. It meant another trip to the barn. *Well, if that's what I have to do . . .*

The rope had a big knot in it. Meggie could not work it free without taking her mittens off. Fingers numbing, growing more frantic by the minute, Meggie tugged and twisted and finally untangled it. She wound the rope around Dan's chest, pushed it under the sled, and brought it up and over again. "Now I got you trussed, Massah Dan, so you can't fall off." She propped the lantern on top of him and began the pull toward the house. He had not opened his eyes nor moaned again.

Every few feet, Meggie stopped to catch her breath and make sure Dan was still on the sled. It bogged down in the deep snow. She spent considerable time breaking a trail with her boots. At last, she reached the door stoop. The snow had filled in the step and made a ramp. Meggie reached for the latch, swung the door open, and with determination in every quavering muscle, she tugged Dan—sled and all—inside the cabin.

The baby cried, a newborn's insistent call for attention. Dan's mouth opened. "Whassat?" he slurred, his eyes still closed.

Meggie knelt beside him, almost too tired to hold her head up. "That, Massah Dan, is your baby son. That's what it is." She grinned. Dan's head turned to the side again. His chest rose and fell as he breathed. Meggie sat back on her heels and sobbed with exhaustion and relief.

She bustled about, made a pallet by the stove for Dan, and eased him from the sled onto it. She tugged off his boots and coat, and piled blankets on him. She hurried into the bedroom and spooned soup into the new mother's mouth and tended the baby. Back in the kitchen, she washed Dan's head wound. In a corner of a cupboard, she found, saved in a jar, a mixture of shepherd's purse and thistle down combined with tallow. Ever so carefully, she spread it over the wound and bound his head with a strip from a sheet.

Sal's voice called from the bedroom, "Where's Dan? Isn't he back yet?"

Meggie poked her head around the curtain and whispered, "Dan's all tuckered out, ma'am. He fell asleep with his coat on." Back on the other side of the curtain, she whispered, "Dear Lawd, please forgive my lie."

Meggie chafed Dan's hands. She shook him gently and kept whispering, "You gotta wake up, Massah Dan. You gotta wake up."

At last, he stirred. His eyes opened. He looked around the kitchen. "Where—what? Oh-h . . ." He tried to sit up and groaned. "Busted— a couple ribs. The bull—" He felt of the bandage on his head. "You—?"

Meggie nodded. She filled a foot tub with hot water, helped Dan into a chair, and eased his feet into the water. "Too hot, Meggie. Too hot."

"No, Massah Dan. Just right. You keep your feet in there now. Get yourself thawed out real good."

He felt the bandage on his head again. "Don't remember how I— you bring me to the cabin?"

"Yassah, Massah Dan, me and the sled. Sure glad to see you waking up. Here, have some soup. You gonna need it."

The baby cried. Dan looked bewildered. "I hear a baby? Where's Sal?"

Meggie's giggle filled the kitchen. "Yassah, right in there." She pointed at the bedroom.

It was midnight before Meggie had a moment to herself. Before she climbed to her own loft bed, she set the sled outside against the cabin wall. She looked up at the stars and murmured, "Thank you, Lawd, for giving me strength. Thank you for helping me save Massah Dan. Guess you been directing my path all along and I just didn't know it. Keeping me here to help Sal with the birthing. Giving me a roof over my head when I woulda died out there in that wilderness."

CHAPTER 40

Spring brought budding trees, lush prairie grass, and just as Sal said—the Booth's wagon ready to roll toward Fort Bridger. Meggie would go along as mother's helper and companion to Patience Booth's two little girls. Sal gave Meggie a bonnet and two dresses she had made. Dan patted Meggie on the shoulder. He wished her luck. Meggie thanked him and hugged Sal in a tearful goodbye. She kissed little Edgar. "You be a good little boy for your mamma now." Then Meggie turned her face toward the western mountains.

Even while her tears in parting were still wet on her cheeks, an excitement built within her. She was headed toward Oregon Territory, toward Juba. As she walked beside the wagon, a film of dust gradually settled on her clothes and skin. She didn't mind. Every speck of dust brought her closer to Juba.

Five-year-old Lucy Booth held her hand and skipped beside her. Sometimes, Lucy spied a clump of arrow leaf balsam that had not been trampled by the animals and she ran to pick the blossoms.

"Got yourself a nice bouquet, Lucy," Meggie said.

"Mamma says we'll have lots of flowers in Oregon. Rooms and rooms of flowers." Lucy spread her arms wide. "Will you live there with us, Meggie?"

"No, honey, I'm not sure where I'm gonna live."

Lucy whirled around and gave a little skip. "Mamma says everybody should have a goal. Do you have a goal?"

"Yeah, Lucy, I got a goal. Gotta find my man. That's my goal."

Lucy laughed. "I'm gonna raise goats. Lots and lots of goats. Mamma says I can."

"That's fine, Lucy. That's a fine goal."

"You know what Mamma's goal is?"

"Well, I kinda heard your mamma talking—"

"Mamma wants to have a big—" arms spread wide, "—big boarding house. And Papa will sell apples and peaches and cherries and—" Lucy stopped for breath. "What's a cherry, Meggie?"

Meggie smiled. "A cherry is a little round red thing about as big as the end of my thumb and when you bite into it, it squirts sweet juice in your mouth."

Lucy did a little dance in the dust. "Oh-h, I'm gonna have lots of cherries then."

The child talked on. Meggie encouraged her. It kept her from wondering how she would ever find Juba. This country was so huge, the mountains with their majestic peaks overwhelming. She felt about as significant as an ant in this vast wilderness.

The wagon train nooned at Soda Springs. It was a favorite spot for all the wagons that came through. Elard Booth pointed out the trampled earth and the tracks sunk into the prairie soil.

Meggie took a water bucket from the Booths' wagon and followed the path to the river. A breeze whispered in the willows on the bank and cooled her sweaty brow. She knelt to dip into the water and, at the same instant, smelled tobacco smoke and heard men's voices.

"Making better time than we did last year." Meggie recognized the wagon master's voice.

"Yeah, well, you ain't got the Thompsons holding you back this time."

"Lord have mercy, Neb, if I ever run into another troublemaker like that one."

"Awful, just awful what he did to Juba. Ya know, Juba was my friend. I'da trusted him with my life."

Meggie paused. *Juba?* The water sluiced over her skirt. Her heart began to thump. She peered through the willow branches. The men were sitting under the trees a few feet away.

The wagon master spoke again. "Looking back, I know I handled that one all wrong. Couldn't believe it myself, but—hope Juba can forgive me some day."

Meggie bit her lip. *Forgive? What was Juba to forgive?*

"Just up yonder in them pines, wasn't it?"

"Never forget it. Wonder where he lit out to. Man alone on a mule's back got a lonesome ride."

Meggie shifted her feet.

"He couldn'ta stayed with us. His pride was hurt too deep."

"Yeah, you're right, Neb. And it was my fault. Know what he said when I signed him on at Independence. I asked him what he'd do if some on the train didn't like riding with a black man. Know what he told me?" The wagon master chuckled, "Said maybe they'd have to wait for another wagon train. He was determined to take this one."

"Brave man, that Juba. We don't know the half it it, never been slaves ourselves."

Meggie tried to rise with the full bucket of water. Her knees turned to jelly.

The men continued. "Sure glad you stayed on to guide for me, Neb."

"Well, wasn't nothing in Oregon for me after Mary died. Decided maybe I could help somebody else since my own dreams got smashed."

With all her being, Meggie wanted to ask the men about Juba. Was it her Juba? Could there be another runaway named Juba on his way to Oregon? Something had happened, something bad that made him leave the wagon train. She put a hand over her mouth. Tears of frustration coursed down her cheeks. She swayed on the path. A black runaway woman could not approach two white men. What would they think of her? The worst, of course.

She stumbled and fell. The bucket spilled its contents and clanged down the incline. She looked up. There stood the wagon master and the fellow named Neb. They were helping her to her feet, filling the bucket, asking her if she was all right.

"You sick, ma'am?" They were talking to her, calling a runaway "ma'am." The wagon master said, "Looks like you're kinda shaky. Let me carry this back to your wagon. You with the Booths, ain't you?"

Meggie nodded. "Thank you, massah, thank you. I'se all right now, massah."

Jens Studevant carried the bucket while Neb Waldheim held on to Meggie's arm. They grinned at each other over her head. "Get that? I had the durndest time breaking Juba of saying 'massah' every time he turned around. Even when I got him to call me Jens, felt like he was saying 'massah' under his breath. Doggone, miss that fella yet."

And right there, Meggie's knees folded and she fainted.

All through the hot afternoon, Lucy patted Meggie's hand and leaned on her arm as they trudged westward. She kept saying, "Don't cry, Meggie. Don't cry, Meggie." Lucy's mother, Patience Booth, occasionally offered a cold wet cloth for Meggie's forehead and murmured, "Oh my."

Eventually, the sun slipped behind the mountain peaks. Meggie watched the horizon fade from rose to violet and dissolve into the purple velvet of night. She slowly shook her head. Now, she knew, Juba had traveled this same trail last year with the wagon master. Juba had been a friend of Neb Waldheim. Then something went wrong and Juba left the train. The knowledge of it was an iron weight setting on her chest. Every step took her farther away from the last anyone had seen of Juba.

She wanted to ask these men a hundred questions. *Had Juba been well? Was he happy? Had he mentioned my name?* But she dared not. She longed to touch a sleeve he might have brushed past, to hold a tin cup he might have drank from. *Had he seen the same morning star that greets me each fresh new day?*

Meggie plodded along. All the spirit and joy had gone out of the journey. At the end of the trail, there would be no Juba to meet her. She was going to Oregon Territory and he was not there.

CHAPTER 41

On a Tuesday, they reached the eastern boundary of Oregon Territory. The whole wagon train pulled into a cluster of buildings beside the trail. Jens Studevant explained to the travelers: "Place's called Varney. Ira Varney decided several years ago to put down roots here. He knew any trains coming through would be pretty worn out by the time they got this far. He runs the smithy. He'll shod your animals for the last pull over the mountains. See to any wagon repairs. Every few months, a supply train comes by. His old lady runs the mercantile. Stocks up on sides of bacon and flour and the like. Prices are outrageous, but you can't get 'em nowhere else around here. Coyotes 'n' lizards don't deal in merchandise." He turned. "Oh, by the way, any of you expecting folks back home to send letters—might inquire here. Post office's inside the mercantile."

They were close to a deep, quiet river. Not like the Snake with its tumultuous rapids and inaccessible rocky banks. Elard Booth had carefully wrapped the roots of his apple and peach seedlings in burlap before leaving home. Now he hauled them down to the water to soak. Patience Booth pulled bedding out of the wagon and shook it. The girls played tag and found a few wildflowers to pick.

Meggie looked around. Varney was a regular little town of perhaps 150 people. Besides the smithy and mercantile, she saw a saloon with a dance hall attached. A second story apparently held apartments as she glimpsed curtains at windows. A towel, hung out to dry, flapped from an open window. The outer walls of a leather shop, not yet weathered, appeared to be the newest building erected. A sign on its front said: "Get your harness repaired here. Boots made to order. Satisfaction guaranteed." A few shacks with rusty stovepipes shoved through their roofs lined the dusty street, and more shacks were perched on the sloping ground behind. Meggie glimpsed a cemetery on a knoll.

Since the wagon train would pause for several days, the Booths bought a canvas tent at the mercantile and set it up beside their wagon. Patience Booth said, "We'll use it again on our new property before we get our boarding house built."

The girls were excited. "Meggie, Meggie." Lucy pulled on Meggie's sleeve. "We get to sleep in the tent."

The following afternoon when the girls were napping in the tent, Patience said, "Meggie, I'm afraid we've been so busy we've neglected you. While the girls are asleep, why don't you go ahead and spend some time looking around town."

"Tha's all right, ma'am. I don't mind—"

"No, Meggie, I insist. You've hardly been out of this tent except to wash clothes at the river since we've arrived. Now, go on."

"Yes, ma'am." Meggie ducked through the tent flap. She paused. "You're sure, ma'am . . . ?"

"Yes, Meggie. Now, go on and enjoy yourself."

"Yes, ma'am." Self-conscious at first, Meggie tried to assume an air as she strolled the boardwalk of a black lady accustomed to going where she pleased. *Strange, this new freedom. Imagine, walking around like a white lady, holding my head up like I owned something. Well, I own me. Guess that's what I own, myself.* She grinned. "Hafta get used to that," she muttered under her breath, "not being owned by nobody else but myself."

Along the boardwalk, there were plenty of stares and whispers among the ladies and ogling by the gents. All the way on the westward travel, it had been like that. She was used to it by now and with a half smile on her lips, she peered into shop windows and watched the reflection of wagons and people on horseback along the rutted street. They hadn't the faintest idea what she was thinking. They didn't need to know.

Meggie passed the saloon. Its door constantly swung back and forth as patrons came and went. A sensation, a crawly feeling at the back of her neck, caused her to look at the apartments upstairs. A man lounged in an upper window. He coolly met her gaze as he smoked a cigar. The sleeves of his white shirt were rolled up. His black hair was parted in the middle and slicked with pomade. And as she paused, startled, the man raised an eyebrow and nodded.

Meggie immediately broke eye contact and hurried away. *Mercy! What had I done? Sent some kind of silent signal to this man?* She quickly crossed to the other side of the street and pretended to be engrossed in the merchandise of the mercantile store. Soon, curiosity got the better of her and she shot another glance toward the window. The man was still there. A woman with heavily rouged cheeks had joined him. The woman pointed at her. A sliver of panic pierced Meggie's chest. She bowed her head and ran all the way back to the tent.

Out of breath, she slipped through the door flap and stood shaking while her eyes adjusted to the dim interior. Her cheeks burned with shame.

Patience Booth looked up from some measurement calculations for her intended boarding house. "My goodness, Meggie. What's wrong? Here, sit down."

Meggie collapsed onto a pillow at the corner of the tent. She hid her face in her hands. "Oh, ma'am, I ain't never going there again."

"Where, Meggie? Where did you go?"

Tears cascaded down Meggie's cheeks. "I was—was just walking down the boardwalk and a man—a man and a—" she swallowed, "—a p-painted woman pointed at me. Like they was—was picking me out to—oh, ma'am, I dunno, I dunno."

Patience Booth laid a calming hand on Meggie's shoulder. "Well, you're safe now, Meggie. Don't think of it."

"Yessum." Meggie swallowed and dried her tears. *But how can I not think of it?*

The girls woke up, demanding Meggie's attention. And soon it was time to see to the family's supper.

Meggie lay on her cot that night and listened to the hoot of an owl. Freedom was so new. Yes, and frightening too. It was wonderful not to go around staring at the ground like a slave. But looking up had got her into some kind of trouble. She hadn't meant any harm. It was hard to understand people in this place so far from home. She wished she could ask Miz Booth to explain it to her. But a runaway slave did not bother a white lady with her troubles. If only Juba . . .

CHAPTER 42

On Thursday, Patience Booth told Meggie, "We'll be packing up and traveling west again tomorrow. Wish I'd thought of this earlier. I need you to go to the mercantile and get me a package of needles. Get the ones with large eyes so I can see to thread them. These tiny-eyed needles are nothing but an aggravation any more. Oh yes, and a thimble. I seem to have lost mine. Let's see, is that all? No, I need six yards of buckram. Be sure the clerk gives you full measure."

"Yessum."

Patience pressed some coins into Meggie's palm. "This should cover it."

"Yessum." Meggie felt the beginning of a trembling in her knees. She would have to go back, across the street from that saloon. Miz Booth must have forgotten how frightened she was the first time. She could not say, "Miz Booth, I don't want to go." Her lips quivered.

Patience raised an eyebrow. "Did you have a question, Meggie?"

"N-no, ma'am. I'll go right away."

Patience turned from her and began to brush Lucy's hair. "Well, do hurry. We need to spend some time packing the wagon this afternoon."

"Yessum." Meggie ducked under the tent flap. She repeated to herself with each step, "I am not afraid. I am not afraid." *But I am afraid, heart-thumping, shallow-breathing afraid.* She kept her gaze on the boardwalk and looked neither to the left nor right.

That was why she did not see the man who darted out from the alley between the mercantile and the weather-warped boards of a shack. He grabbed her from behind, encircled her neck, and pressed his hand over her mouth. Other hands thrust her arms behind her back and bent them upward toward her shoulder blades. "Cry out and I'll break yer arms," rasped the owner of this rough treatment. He smelled of whisky and sweat.

Stumbling, rigid with fear, she was pulled into the alley where someone blindfolded her with a filthy rag and shoved another rag of coarse fabric over her mouth, entangling her hair in a knot at the back of her head. They tied her hands behind her back with twine. "There," said a female voice. "Now, we've got her. Let's go." Between them, they whirled her around and around until she was completely disoriented.

They pushed her forward. "Come on, my sweet," the woman said. But Meggie was so tottery from dizziness and fright she weaved and staggered and would have fallen. "Oh, for pity sakes, get your feet under you," the woman said crossly. She took hold of Meggie's arm, pinching the flesh. They walked her through another alley, Meggie knew, because she felt the change from the sun's heat to the abrupt coolness of shade. They paused. A door squeaked. They pushed her up a flight of steps and along an echoing hallway. "In here," the woman said. "It's good as any and the lock's on the outside of the door."

"Now, you listen to me," the woman went right on as they elbowed her into a musty-smelling room. "We don't aim to hurt you if you play along. We'll take that gag off when we're sure you won't raise all kinds of hell. The blindfold stays. Make yourself to home." The door dragged on the wood floor and clicked shut. Meggie heard the key turn in the lock. She was alone.

She stood uncertainly for a few minutes as her racing pulse hammered in her ears. Then she began to sidle along the wall. *Got to get out of here, got to get out of here.* She bumped into a washstand. A pitcher on top of it jiggled. A few more steps and she stumbled into a bed. She lost her balance and sagged down onto its lumpy surface. The smell of stale urine accosted her nostrils. She had to get out of here. *Miz Booth will wonder what's keeping me so long.* A catch in Meggie's throat turned into a sob. *She'll think I ran away. She'll think I . . .*

In the next few minutes, she puzzled over and over the events leading up to this moment: *The duck through Miz Booth's tent flap, my purposeful stride to the mercantile store, the sudden arm choking me, the shove up the stairs and into this room. Who are my captors? Are they the same man and woman I saw in the upstairs window of the dance hall? What do they want with me? What does the woman mean when she told me to "play along"? Oh, Juba, Juba, where are you? Need you so bad. I'se so alone. Wish you could . . . Oh, Juba— I miss you so.*

She scolded herself. *Ain't I ever gonna keep from getting into scrapes? Such a fool, walking right into traps. Letting others take advantage of me. 'Course when Dan Crane caught me out in that meadow, caught me like a scared rabbit, lassoing me with his scratchy rope—it turned out good, him taking me home to Sal. Sal was nice. Never thought I'd have two dresses and a bonnet and traveling with a family to get to Oregon. Only, I wouldn't have needed to come after all. 'Cause you ain't here, Juba. You ain't here.*

Meggie bowed her head. Fresh tears ran down her face into the gag that chafed her mouth. Her cry, through the cloth, sounded like the mewing of a lost kitten.

She sat motionless, shoulders drooping, too dispirited to explore the rest of the room. She supposed there was a window somewhere. But even if she could kick the pane out, no one would hear her call for help. If someone happened to see her standing at a window, they'd probably think she belonged there. Head bowed, her whole body slumped in despair.

At length, a knock on the door made her jump. She uttered a pleading sound behind the gag. Her heart raced.

The door opened and as it closed, Meggie heard the same grating sound on the floor.

A soft feminine voice said, "I've brought you some lunch." Ever so carefully, the gag was untangled from her hair and pulled away from her mouth. "Goodness me, that nasty cloth made your lips sore."

Meggie sat up straight. Whoever this girl was, no matter the soft voice, she'd be on her guard.

"I'm just one of the girls," the soft voice said again. "Name's Pansy. What's yours?"

"I—" *Should I tell my name? Maybe this's part of the trap.* Meggie shook her head and clamped her lips shut.

"Hey, you can talk to me. I won't hurt you. We're friends here, all us girls. Except for a couple of us, that is. You know how some folks think they're so high and mighty. They—whoops, goodness me, you got me rambling." The girl's tone changed to wheedling. "Please, pretty please, won't you tell me your name? Besides, your lunch's getting cold."

Meggie licked her lips. She sighed in resignation. "Meggie. I'm Meggie—ma'am."

"Goodness me, I never had a body call me ma'am in all my born days. Wait 'til the other girls hear about this. There's six of us and you make seven."

Sudden anger raced through Meggie and made her bold. She raised her chin. "Don't reckon I make seven of anything. I want you to send me back to Miz Booth right this minute!"

"Goodness me," Pansy said again. "You've got spirit, I'll say. No wonder Raoul and Germaine wanted you. Here, have a bite. Lunch looks pretty good today. This is chicken and some of Charlie's gravy and—"

Meggie drew a long breath. No fist had pounded or slapped her for her first outburst. *All right, I'll dare to speak out again.* "I don't want your food. I just want out of here. Take this blindfold off and I'll find my own way out. Miz Booth must be frantic. She won't know how come I ain't home yet." She rose from the bed and bumped into the raised spoon that Pansy held. It clattered to the floor.

"Goodness me. Now, look what you've done. Who's Miz Booth?"

"I ain't answering your questions. I want outta here." With hands still tied behind her, Meggie took a step and fell over Pansy.

Pansy said yet again, "Goodness me. Whoa there." She steadied Meggie and held on to her. "How come you don't like Raoul and Germaine? They're good to us girls. And you should see the pretty dresses we get to wear."

Meggie's anger now surpassed any fear that remained. She twisted her body and freed herself from Pansy's grip. She shouted, "I don't want your fancy dresses. I don't want your food. Just turn me loose!"

Footsteps thumped along the hallway. The door opened abruptly. A male voice said, "What's going on here, Pansy? I can hear this vixen clear downstairs."

"I don't know, Raoul. She won't let me—"

Meggie cut in. "You the same man what tied me up and put me in here?" Meggie knew she was in for a severe whipping. She no longer cared. Let the white man whip her, she'd show him how brave she was. Let him whip her to death. Then she'd be out of her misery. Juba was lost to her anyway and nobody else cared.

At that moment, a firm but soft hand led her back to the bed. She caught the scent of pomade and something else, sickening-sweet and smoky. She couldn't define it. The man's voice became gentle. "I'm sorry you're so angry with us, little lady. We don't mean you any harm." He had an accent she'd never heard before. His voice was almost musical. "Now then," he said, stroking her arm, "let Pansy feed you your lunch. You'll feel so much better. And I'll raise the top sash of the window. It's stuffy in here."

Meggie jerked away from the soothing touch, the musical voice. Her lips quivered. Her former bluster had evaporated. Her whole body trembled and tears gathered in her eyes. "Please, sir," she said, "please let me go back to Miz Booth."

She heard the window sash settle on its pegs. The man crossed the room. The bed squeaked as he sat so close his hip touched hers. Meggie, acutely aware of his presence, moved aside.

The soothing voice was near her ear again. "We have wonderful plans for you, little lady. Plans that will make you rich with pretty clothes and places to see and—"

Meggie gathered her courage again and tried to stand. "You can whip me if you want. But I already told this here girl in front of me, whoever she is, I don't care about your pretty clothes. I don't care about your—"

The man's voice turned silky. "Wouldn't you like to bring nice things back to your Miz Booth? Wouldn't you like to help her build her boarding house? And how about the little girls? They'd like pretty dresses too."

Meggie flared, "What you know about Miz Booth? How come you know about the girls? You been spying on us?"

"Oh no, little lady, spying isn't nice. We have other ways of finding out things. But I do wish you'd tell me your name. It's awkward to keep saying 'little'—"

"Don't know why you want to know my name so bad. Once I get out of here, I ain't gonna see you never again."

"But we can't let you go, don't you see?" he said. "It wouldn't be nice of you to interrupt our plans." The whispery voice in her ear reminded her of a snake slithering near. She shuddered.

Pansy said, "Her name is Meggie, Raoul. She told me."

"Why, thank you, Pansy." The soft, crawly voice repeated, "Meggie. Meggie, it is."

Meggie felt his hand patting her wrist. She tensed her arm muscles and turned sideways. It was awkward with her hands still tied behind her back.

"You'll learn to like me, Meggie, I promise. All the girls do. They like the things I do for them. Isn't that right, Pansy?"

"Oh yes, Raoul. We all do."

Meggie thought Pansy's remark sounded like rote, like when you memorized something and repeated it word for word. But she kept quiet.

"Now, Meggie," Raoul's slippery voice went on, "you eat your lunch and don't make a fuss, then we'll take the blindfold off and I'll show you a nice surprise."

Meggie felt the mattress tip as he rose from the bed and crossed the room. If she could see him, she was sure he would slither and leave a slimy trail rather than walk to the door. "Germaine will be in soon," he said. "Do the best you can, Pansy." The door scraped across the floor. The latch clicked.

Pansy laid a hand on Meggie's knee and began to entreat. "Please, Meggie. It ain't so bad. Raoul's a soft one. But you don't want to make Germaine mad. Come on, let me feed you. Do what they want, huh? Ain't so bad."

Meggie slumped. The sting of a whip hadn't been laid on her. But she felt like a dishrag wrung out once too often. The fight had all been squeezed out of her. She sighed and opened her mouth.

"That's a girl," Pansy said.

Meggie heard Pansy scraping the last bite from the bowl as the door opened again. A woman's authoritative voice filled the room. "What's keeping you so long, Pansy?"

Pansy said, "We're just done, Germaine."

"Well, it's about time. And how is our new girl?"

Meggie sensed the woman standing close, the eyes inspecting every minute detail of her. She jumped as the woman said, "Take the blindfold off, Pansy. I want to see if our efforts were worth it."

Meggie blinked in the sudden light as the rag was drawn away from her face. The woman said, "Humm, well, Raoul was right. Yes."

Meggie implored, "Please, ma'am. All I want is to go back to Miz Booth. She'll be worried—"

The woman interrupted, "Now, I don't want to hear any of that. You have lots of potential. Lots. You hang with us. You'll be rich. Rich, you hear? You'll never amount to anything sticking with that couple and their two little brats—"

Meggie mumbled, "They's sweet little girls."

"Well, whatever."

"They'll be worried about me."

"Don't kid yourself. Servants are easier to find than ticks on a dog. They'll get another, easy. And you'll be moving up. Moving up, you hear? Now, I have to talk to Raoul. You just sit tight and don't make a ruckus." Then, as if to allay any potential trouble, she said, "Pansy, you stay with her until I get back."

"Yes, Germaine."

The door dragged across the floor. The latch clicked shut. Pansy said, "See? She ain't so bad. She's really the boss, you know. Raoul's just the gofer."

"Gofer?"

"Yeah, you know, he goes fer whatever she wants and fetches it, like that."

And in her mind, Meggie said, "Musta been me he fetched for that woman."

From beyond a thin wall, Meggie heard Germaine's impatient tones overriding Raoul's soft comments. "Tell them this one's exotic. They'll love her. Bill her as an exotic."

Raoul's answer was mumbled.

Germaine again, "We'll cash in on this one. Call her— " There was a pause, then Germaine's voice exploded. "No! Absolutely not. We will not call her Meggie!"

They were talking about her. Meggie glanced at Pansy, who was listening intently as well.

"What they—?" she began.

Pansy shushed her and leaned closer to the wall.

Germaine's no-nonsense tone sounded through the thin partition. "We'll call her Exotic Erlina. That's it. That's it, Raoul. Exotic Erlina. Oh, they'll love it. What a find!"

Meggie shuddered. "But—but I just want to go back to Miz Booth. What are they—?" She heard a door slam. Footsteps descended the stairs and faded away.

Pansy squeezed her shoulder. "You'll be famous, Meggie. What'd I tell you? Oh, the other girls'll be jealous. You'll have to watch out for them." Pansy tittered and hid her mouth behind her fingers. She sat quietly for a few moments. "Oh, goodness me, you're hands are still tied behind you. Germaine must have forgotten. Don't see any harm in—you wouldn't sock me, would you?"

Meggie frowned, puzzled. "Sock you?"

"You know—hit me—if I untie you."

"No, ma'am." But the idea made Meggie wonder if she could overpower the girl and escape.

As if hearing her thoughts, Pansy dashed all hopes. "We're both locked in here, you know. Germaine don't take chances. I don't see no harm in untying you though. Bet your hands're about numb by now."

Pansy untied her. Meggie winced at the prickles that ran up her arms as circulation was restored. She stirred and hung her head in embarrassment as Pansy continued to stare at her.

Finally, Pansy said, "You a runaway or something? I never seen hardly any darkie girls before."

Meggie whispered, "Yessum." Now, she was caught. Pansy would tell that Germaine woman and Germaine would tell the sheriff and—*oh, I done it again, fallen right into a trap. Will I never learn?*

She jumped as Pansy's trilling laugh filled the room. "Germaine'll love it. Putting one over on the gov'ment. Showing you for a exotic and—" She slapped her knee and doubled over with laughter. "Germaine'll love it."

Meggie looked up, brow furrowed. "She won't turn me in?"

Pansy stopped laughing. "What? You crazy? 'Course not. She'll make more money offa you than all the rest of us." Then, as something came to mind, she got up and pounded on the door. "I gotta get out of here. Got to get ready for tonight. Don't look to me like you're gonna make trouble. No use me sitting around all day."

Presently, the door opened a few inches. Pansy said to the person on the other side, "Tell Germaine I gotta get ready for tonight. Meggie ain't gonna make no trouble. 'Sides, we can lock her in." She turned back to Meggie. "You stay quiet now and you'll be all right. I gotta go."

Meggie's heart leaped. "No, no, no!" She jumped up and ran across the room. She grabbed the side of the door and braced her feet. "Please, please, let me—" She barely missed having her fingers pinched as the door slammed shut. The lock clicked into place.

Meggie stared at the door for a moment. This must be a nightmare. Surely, she would awaken and find herself back with the Booths. She grabbed the flesh of her arm and dug her fingernails in until it hurt. No, this was not a bad dream; it was real. And she was trapped.

She shuffled dispiritedly to the window and peered out. She saw one deserted shack with its roof caved in. Tall weeds and scrub sage surrounded it. This room must be at the rear of the building. She sat on the bed and wrinkled her nose. After a while, she noticed shadows forming in the corners of the room. "Evening's coming," she said aloud. "Evening's coming and Miz Booth don't know where I am. She'll think I ran away for sure. What'm I gonna do? Miz Booth, Miz Booth, I want to come back to you. Truly, I do."

CHAPTER 43

A fly buzzed at the windowpane. Presently, Meggie heard music from below. Someone sawed on a fiddle. A banjo twanged to life. Heavy hands began to pound on an out-of-tune piano. She went back to the window and tried to raise the bottom sash. It would not budge. She tried to see more of the landscape outside. Now that she had her hands free, she could break the window and crawl through it. She glanced at the bed. Didn't she hear one time of somebody escaping by tying the bed sheets in a knot and dangling them down the side of a building? If she could tie them tight enough, she wasn't afraid to jump.

Meggie yanked the sheets off the bed. She was trying to tie a knot that would hold when the door burst open. Startled, she dropped the sheets and stepped back.

The woman named Germaine rushed at her. "Quick, tie her up. Raoul, hurry up with that twine. Get the blindfold on."

Abruptly, it seemed a crowd of people surrounded Meggie, prodding and grasping at her. Through the confusion, she heard bumps and thumps in the hallway. Footsteps pounded down the stairs. The building was alive with shouts and squeals from all directions. The blindfold cut off her vision. Rough hands grabbed her.

"Get a move on," Germaine ordered. "Who'd have thought! Who'd have thought! Those cussed self-righteous—who do they think they are? Do the same if they were in my shoes."

Raoul's soft voice intervened, "Now, now, Germaine. We'll make it."

She cut him off. "Easy for you to say. If we don't get out of here, I'm ruined. Take her to the wagon. Hustle!"

Somewhere, down in the street, a gun boomed, followed by shrill cries. Meggie was half dragged down the stairs and out the door. Uncaring hands bruised her flesh as they lifted her and threw her into a wagon. She landed on hands and knees. Brittle straw scraped across her skin. "Get over," a cross feminine voice said. Its owner gave her a shove. "You're taking my space."

"Sorry, ma'am," Meggie said. She tried to scramble away only to bump into another body. "Look where you're going," this one said, just as cross, and followed it with a slap. There was a moment's silence, then, "Oh—how come you're blindfolded? Didn't know you couldn't see." Another whined, "It's so dark in here. How can anybody see? This canvas is about to smother me. Germaine's gonna have a dead body on her hands if I can't get some air."

Meggie recognized Germaine's voice outside the wagon. "Get those horses moving."

The wagon jerked and began to roll forward. From all sides, came the rhythm of clattering hooves, the shouts and curses of angry men, another blast from a rifle. Above the racket, Meggie heard Germaine bellowing orders. "Whip them up, whip them up. Don't tell me you can't go faster. Do it!"

Meggie trembled. Her pulse pounded in her dry throat. There was a rustle in the straw beside her and Pansy spoke. "Don't be afraid, Meggie. We're just moving on, that's all. Once in a while, we have to. Folks get—uh—get tired of us and we—"

"Why don't you tell her the truth?" another girl said. "They run us out of town, that's all." A plaintive voice said, "Wish I coulda tole Dooby goodbye. Wish I coulda." Almost at Meggie's feet came a sarcastic reply. "Oh, Dooby, li'l Carla miss you so. Poor ole Dooby."

Meggie heard bodies wrestling in the straw. The wagon rocked. Bits of straw pelted her. There was a grunt and a well-placed punch. The girl named Carla said, "You take that back Miss Priss with the wart on yer nose or I'll bean ya. Honest, I will. Dooby said he loved me. So there."

At Meggie's elbow, a dry laugh cackled, "That's what they all say, Carla. Ain't you caught on yet?"

So close that Meggie felt the breath on her face, a girl whispered, "How come you called me ma'am?"

After a while, Meggie felt gentle hands working at the knot of her blindfold. "Don't see no sense in you having to wear this all the time. So dark outside now anyhow, don't make much difference. Guess Germaine's got too much else on her mind."

Meggie murmured, "Thank you." She blinked and peered into the gloom at Pansy beside her. The girl seemed to be her keeper and friend at the same time. She could barely make out the bulk of a large trunk that took up space on one side of the jiggling wagon. The other girls were merely dim shapes lounging in the straw. Two whispered behind their hands. Another had curled into a ball and appeared to be asleep. "Let's get this canvas offa here before I smother," the girl said who had complained of it earlier. She began to claw and pull on it. Helping hands crumpled it up and flattened it at the back of the wagon. Meggie involuntarily took a deep breath. Several of the girls sighed with relief. "Germaine won't like it," one of the girls warned. An answer came immediately. "She ain't gonna know if you don't tell her."

They rode for hours, the wagon creaking and swaying. Occasionally, the girls fell sideways onto one another as the wagon lurched over a rock or root. The air grew increasingly chilly. The girls huddled together, some asleep. Meggie dozed, whimpering in her sleep now and then.

Just before dawn, the wagon jerked to a stop. Sharp footsteps struck the hard clay of the road. Germaine appeared as a dark shape. She began to prod and slap whatever flesh she could reach. "Get up. Hurry now. You're not that tired. Who took this canvas off? You want us all in jail? Everybody out. You need to go to the bushes? Go now. Don't fall in the creek. Get yourself a drink and run back to the wagon. Pansy? Pansy? Get that vixen off the wagon and see to her."

Pansy answered sleepily and Meggie felt her steadying hand as they climbed off the wagon together. What a relief to stand on level ground. Meggie raised her arms to stretch and immediately rough fingers seized her below the elbow and forced her arms to her sides.

"Who untied this one?" Germaine demanded. "Where's her blindfold?"

"I-I didn't think you'd mind," came Pansy's meek reply. "It was dark and I—"

Meggie heard a slap and Germaine's "Who told you to think for me?"

Pansy sobbed, "I-I'm sorry, Germaine."

"Get moving, now. Everybody back in the wagon in five minutes. Raoul? Raoul!"

"Right beside you, Germaine."

"Well, why didn't you say so? Fix this canvas. These girls think they can ride without the canvas in broad daylight?"

They were moving again. Under the canvas, the air grew hot and muggy. The girls grumbled. "Where we going?" "Can't see a thing." "I'm suffocating." "Betcha Germaine wouldn't sit here like this." "I'm hungry. Ain't we gonna get any breakfast?" "I gotta use the bushes again. She think I can wait all day?"

Abruptly the wagon stopped, throwing them forward in a tangle of arms and legs. Germaine appeared at the end of the wagon. "Everybody out," she ordered. "We're coming to a town. Raoul will bring back something to eat. Listen now, see those trees over there. You march right over and don't make a lot of noise. Get behind the bushes so you can't be seen from the road."

Meggie looked at Germaine in surprise. She wore a faded print dress with a tear in the sleeve. On her head was a gray wig done up in a straggly bun. A wisp of her own hair, dyed flaming red, peeked out at the temple. She had drawn age lines in kohl around her mouth and a frown between her eyes. She caught Meggie's stare and gazed back in defiance. Meggie quickly looked down at her lap.

Raoul came around the corner with hard rolls and a granite coffeepot. From a gunnysack, Germaine produced a tin cup for each girl.

Trouble began immediately. Carla said, "Which cup is that darkie girl drinking from? I ain't usin' that cup after she's done with it. Don't care if it's washed. Make me puke."

Meggie cringed. She kept her gaze on the ground. Pansy nudged her elbow and handed her a steaming cup of coffee. "Don't pay no attention, Meggie. Don't pay no attention." The other girls stared at her. Two of them giggled behind their hands until Germaine said, "Be careful what you say, Carla. Erlina's worth more than a wagonload of the rest of you."

The two gigglers straightened their faces and leaned toward Germaine. "No fair, no fair, Germaine, if we—"

Germaine applied a swift slap to both their cheeks. "I make the rules, girls. Have you forgotten? You can go back to where I found you if you want. Remember how that was?"

One of the gigglers began to cry. The other snorted through her nose, sent Meggie a vengeful look, and turned away.

"Back to the wagon, girls," Germaine ordered. "Make it quick. We have a long way to go."

CHAPTER 44

Meggie lost track of the days. The girls grew more and more agitated as they huddled under the canvas. Several times, Germaine had to separate brawlers. Rest stops and meal times were short interludes as the horses pulled the jouncing wagon along increasingly rough trails. They left the sage plains and prickly thickets behind. Stolen peeks from under the canvas revealed low hills and stands of yellow pine. Occasionally, they were close enough to glimpse the chimneys and shacks of some remote town's front street and wondered why Germaine did not stop there. Once in a while, the girls heard a rushing stream over the creaking of the wheels and most scrambled to the back of the wagon to see it.

Meggie did not join them. She had her place in a corner, protected from kicks and pinches on two sides. Pansy sat beside her, fending off most insulting remarks. The value Germaine had put upon her made the girls scorn and hate her.

One other, who kept aloof from the rest as well, did not taunt her. They had been on the road five days and nights shut up under the canvas when Delia leaned toward Meggie. She whispered, "You never told me how come you called me ma'am."

Most of the girls were asleep. When Pansy's eyes drooped and her head settled on her chest, Meggie whispered back, "I'se used to calling other people ma'am. Allas had to. It's a sign of respect. And where I come from, you'd better be sure you pay respect or it's a whipping for sure."

"A whipping? Were you a slave? Are you a runaway?"

Meggie put a hand over her mouth. She'd done it again, spilled the whole thing. Her tongue couldn't stay out of trouble. "Please, Delia, please don't tell nobody. I shouldn't have told you."

Delia patted her arm. "Do not worry, little friend."

When they were out in the sunshine for morning exercise, Meggie had studied Delia's glossy black hair and almond-shaped eyes. She had noted Delia's high cheekbones and quiet reserve toward the other girls. "Where you from?" she ventured timidly.

"I used to live in an Indian village near one of the towns where there was a gold strike. That's when I first saw Germaine. My mother was Cherokee. My father was a prospector. When I was two years old, my father disappeared. I was only twelve when my mother gave me to Germaine because she was dying and could not take care of me herself. I have been with Germaine for five years."

Meggie whispered, "You like Germaine?"

"Germaine does not expect us to like her, but she gives us food and a place to stay out of the cold."

Meggie asked, "How come Germaine wears that old dress and that gray wig?"

Delia chuckled, "Don't she look funny, though? She wears it for a disguise. If anybody stops us, she pretends to be a farmer's wife and Raoul is her husband. It's quite funny because neither one of them can hardly tell the difference between a pig and a cow. She thinks we'll be safe this way. We're supposed to be a load of hay or something."

Meggie probed deeper. "But, why wouldn't Germaine want folks to see us?"

"Well, not every town likes us. Didn't she tell you?"

"No, they blindfolded me and kidnapped me right off the street."

Delia laughed quietly. "I thought you would have guessed. We stop at dance halls. We sing and dance and pretend we're having a wonderful time. Some folks call us sinful. They say we lead the men a-astray. I've had rotten tomatoes thrown at me."

"Tha's awful."

"It ruined my dress one time. And then if some man wants us to, we go upstairs with him and we—"

Meggie interrupted. "Oh! No, no, Delia, I ain't never—"

"Sh-h-h. Not so loud, Erlina."

"I ain't Erlina. My name is Meggie. And I never, never—"

"If Germaine tells you to, you'd better do what she says or—"

"No, Delia, I'll die instead."

"It's better than starving."

Meggie shook her head, although Delia could not see. A shudder danced along her spine. She whispered, "Ain't you ever thought of running away?"

The wagon lurched and their shoulders touched. Meggie felt Delia's shrug. "Where would I go? What would I do?"

Meggie thought of Massah Robinson and Arlo. "Betcha you could do lots, same as me, if you had to."

The girls were silent. Delia would have to decide for herself what she would do. Inwardly, Meggie vowed, "I am not Erlina." *That Germaine woman can't make me be Erlina. I ain't escaped slavery under Massah Robinson just to get shut up in more slavery, just a diff'runt kind.*

Delia began to snore softly. Meggie chewed a thumbnail and screwed her eyes shut. She'd find a way to run from Germaine. She had to. She would not let some saloon man paw over her. She whispered Juba's name. "Juba, dear Juba, I got myself in another mess. And if you're still alive—oh Juba, please be—I'm gonna find you, you hear? If it takes the rest of my life, I'm gonna find you."

Germaine followed a routine. They'd stop on the outskirts of a small town. She sent Raoul to scout it out. Sometimes, he came back shaking his head. On they traveled to the next settlement. The girls remained cloistered in the wagon, granted only occasional brief strolls in the open air. They ate stale bread and cold sausage and drank bitter coffee. They fought over blankets as the trail led upward and nighttime temperatures dipped. The wagon now wound through forests of tall, green-needled trees. The air was pine-scented.

Then, one evening, when they were wearied to the point of exhaustion, when it seemed the bumping along in the creaking wagon would never cease, the wagon stopped. Germaine poked her head under the canvas. "Not one peep out of you, you all hear? Raoul will be back in a few minutes."

The girls waited, casting anxious glances at one another, scratching sweaty bodies, tapping fingers mindlessly against the wagon's sideboards. Abruptly, Germaine's head appeared again. The girls all jumped. Germaine had shed her disguise. Her hair gleamed a brilliant copper against the lowering sun. She wore an emerald green dress of satin with velvet piping on the collar. "We're unloading. Drag the trunk out. Stay close behind me."

The girls followed Germaine single-file, clumping over a board-walk. Then there were climbing risers oozing pitch as the trunk scraped an outside stairs to an upper room.

When they were assembled in a row, Germaine said, "New town, same songs, girls. Pansy, you teach Erlina the dance routine." She pointed down the line. "You two, open the trunk and shake the wrinkles out of the dresses. Erlina's is crimson with gold trim. Don't anybody try to take it away from her. Washroom's down the hall."

Raoul poked his head in the door. "I'm making the poster now, Germaine."

Germaine's skirts swished as she spun toward him. "Good. Performance is at nine o'clock." She turned back to the girls. "We'll bring you up something to eat before then." She opened the door and walked out.

CHAPTER 45

One-two-three-kick. Whirl and whirl. Three steps back, three steps forward. Whirl and whirl. Over and over, the girls repeated the routine on the dance hall platform. From behind the curtain, Germaine's voice was gruff. "Smile, girls. Erlina, get that frown off your face or I'll slap you. Smile, smile, smile. They're loving it. Keep it up. You're not tired. Let your face show you enjoy pleasing the men. Smile, girls. Easy money. Extra bonus. Come on."

Meggie wanted to sit right down where she was and rest her feet. The shoes Germaine gave her pinched her toes. The light cast from lanterns hung about the platform glared in her eyes. The smoke from a roomful of pipes and cigars drifted toward the girls and clogged her throat. Some of the men crowded the platform. They reached out, grasping at the girl's dresses. Meggie saw a sea of leering eyes and open mouths. To her ears, the men's lewd calls and whistles melded into the braying of a hundred donkeys.

When Meggie whirled too close to the edge of the platform, a stocky man in a blue chambray shirt and red suspenders swung an arm out and grabbed her skirt. "Ha! I got her. Look, boys, I got her."

Meggie tried to pull away from him. "Let go, let go!"

The man hung on. The other girls bumped into Meggie and shoved her as they continued their routine around her. Elbows prodded her. Hands pushed. The girls complained, "You're in the way. You're holding up the line."

Meggie lost her balance and almost fell off the stage. The man whooped, "Lookie there, this girlie's about to fall right into my arms."

Meggie swatted at him. "Let go, let go. You'll tear my dress."

"Tear your dress, girlie? Maybe I tear it all the way up. C'mon, give Curley a kiss."

Germaine appeared beside her. "Not now, Curley. Wait until the dance is over, then Erlina will be pleased to see you." Deftly, she disengaged the man's hand from Meggie's dress. She whispered to Meggie, "What did I tell you, Erlina? You are a huge success. Go to your room when the dance is over. I'll send Curley along."

Meggie felt as if someone had stabbed her in the chest with an ice pick. Send Curley up? To her room? She performed the rest of the routine woodenly. When once more Germaine called, "Smile, Erlina," from behind the curtain, Meggie stretched her mouth. But it was no smile.

All too soon the music stopped. The girls, chattering and giggling, crowded backstage. "Did you see that fella with the black moustache?" "Ooh, I caught the eye of the most handsome—" "Just the same, I miss Dooby." "That one was drunk." "You should have seen the wink he gave me."

Meggie pushed through the ruffles, the swishing satin, crinoline petticoats and raced to the dressing room. She unbuttoned her dress as she ran. She could hardly breathe for the terror that claimed her. *Must hurry—can't let him—* She yanked at buttons that refused to yield. The hated shoes flew across the room. In the clutter and heaps of clothes the girls had left when preparing for the stage, Meggie found her dress, the one Sal had given her. She yanked it over her head. *Hurry, hurry.* She paused a moment, listening first one way, then another.

What'll I do? Climb out the window. Grab a sheet. Tie a knot. No time for a sheet. Break the pane. Jump. Too far? Someone was coming along the hallway. Someone wearing boots. Meggie pulled her dress around her. No time to button it. She rushed to the window, lifted the sash, and climbed onto the sill. The only light was a lamp shining through a downstairs window and a lantern hanging from a porch post. A few feet below her, a lattice covered with ivy clung to the side of the building. Meggie tested the lattice with her foot. She heard the door to the room open. A man's voice boomed, "Here's Curley, my girlie, come to—" She heard an expletive.

The lattice broke. Meggie held on and followed it to the ground. She landed with a splintering crash, tangled in vines and leaves. She looked up. Curley hung out the window. "Hey, girlie."

Meggie picked herself up. No broken bones, only bruises. She ran. Already out of breath from the panic that assailed her, she searched for a place to hide. She heard Germaine's bellow. "That vixen, I'll tan her good. Hurry up with that light."

Meggie dodged between shacks, over piles of refuse, searching, searching for a place to hide. She heard running feet behind her. Germaine's loud exclamations punctuated the air. Curley's plaintive "here, girlie, here, girlie," followed like a refrain. The lights of several lanterns reached toward her and at times shone ahead of her, their beams crossing on the sides of buildings or tall weeds.

Meggie paused to knead the stitch in her side. She couldn't go much farther. Was there no place to shelter her? Then she saw it. A wooden rain barrel sitting at the corner of a leanto. She climbed into it, shuddering as the cold water rippled over her knees, her waist, and finally her shoulders. She hunched down and closed her eyes until only her nose remained above the surface.

Footsteps pounded the dirt and ran past her. "Now, where'd she go?" "See any sign?" "You, over there, hear anything?" "Raoul, why didn't you keep better track of that girl?" "Wait till I get my hands on her!"

Something brushed across Meggie's face. She put her hand up and felt soggy fur. It was a drowned rat floating on the surface. She poked her head above the water and pinched her lips over a scream. "Oh Lawd, get me out of here," she breathed. She could hear the searchers further on, arguing, calling to one another. With both hands, she felt for the rat and scooped it onto the ground. Her stomach lurched.

They were coming back. Their voices grew louder. She heard Germaine's accusations and the mumbled comments among the men. She forced herself under the water once more. The search party passed by on the other side of the street. Their voices died away. She waited. A door slammed in the distance. A dog barked. Music from the dance hall wafted on the night air. A drunk hooted and guffawed. Meggie heard glass breaking. Two men on horseback rode past. "I'm for home now, Jim. Light and sit sometime." "'Night, Amos."

Meggie waited until she could not bear the rain barrel's murky water another minute. She shivered violently. Carefully, slowly, she climbed out and stood, dripping. She stumbled away from the buildings. Her knees felt like jelly and she fell repeatedly as she staggered through a ditch and up an incline. Covered with mud and quaking with cold, she sat in the weeds, and rubbed her arms and legs. Below her, the dance hall was still brightly lit. One by one, lamps in the houses went out. She heard the livery stable door close. The rising moon followed the silhouette of a lone horseman riding leisurely out of town.

A lone horseman—an involuntary shiver shook her body—a lone horseman . . . Should she risk it? Could she do it?

CHAPTER 46

The horse she led out of the livery stable was a docile nag with a bony spine. There was no time to strap on a saddle. Besides, she didn't feel right about stealing somebody's saddle. At least, she had the horse blanket. Her nerves prickled like needles under her skin and her muscles twitched with every step, expecting someone to raise the cry, "There she goes!"

She kept close to the deep shadows under the trees lining the street. "We gotta walk, horse. Don't you start skittering 'round. Just walk—slow—walk." Frequent glances over her shoulder revealed no one watching from a doorway or running to catch her. Music from the dance hall gradually faded.

They plodded along until they were almost a half mile from town. Then Meggie kneed the horse and said softly, "Giddap." It responded with a jolting trot. "Good girl," she said, being careful not to catch her tongue between her teeth.

Although the ride was rough, she was glad she took the horse. "Yeah, I stole you," she admitted. "But how else could I save myself? 'Sides, you ain't no race track wonder."

They followed the trail until they came to a fork in the road. "Whoa, horse, whoa." Again, she listened for pursuers. All was quiet. She studied the moonlit terrain.

An old nursery rhyme flitted across her mind: "Eenie, meenie, minie, mo, catch a nigger by the toe . . . My mother told me to choose—this one." How often had she heard the little white girls in their ruffled pinafores recite as they played on the lawns of the massahs? They had not realized nor cared that the hateful words wounded the very souls of their young black slaves.

Meggie raised her eyes to the tops of the trees where the moon hung suspended between the branches. "Juba," she whispered. "Juba, where are you?" The heat from the mare's flanks had dried and warmed her legs. A shiver crawled over her still damp shoulders. "North," she said to the horse. "When Juba left the wagon train, he must have gone north."

Trying to track the wanderings of Germaine and Raoul's wagon hidden under the canvas was impossible. But out in the open, Meggie had an instinct for true north. She turned onto the left fork in the trail and walked the horse along a rocky ridge. A coyote slunk across the track in front of her. An owl skimmed the air just over her head and pounced on a field mouse in a clump of grass.

The old horse never broke stride. "Glad you don't shy, horse." It seemed fitting to talk to her. It was a sort of getting-acquainted time. She even said, "Thanks for coming with me," and felt her muscles relax a little as she managed a grin.

Once more, she paused to listen. There was only the wind lowing in the trees and the distant cry of a nighthawk to break the stillness. Her dress had dried. She no longer felt chilled.

They climbed steadily and after a while, they came to a woods. Meggie led the mare just inside the trees, its hooves cushioned on a dense carpet of pine needles. Soon, the mare pricked her ears and increased her pace, then Meggie too heard the sound of rushing water. They found a quiet pool where rocks enclosed the tumult and both drank. She wondered how many miles they had come.

They kept on, climbing higher. Meggie's head began to nod. Each time, she jerked herself awake. Finally, she lurched to the side and almost fell off the horse. "I'm tired, horse. Awful tired." She dismounted, led the mare deep into the trees, and tied her to a low-branched pine. "Hope we're safe here. You rest a while." She patted the mare's neck. "I gotta get some sleep." She laid the horse blanket at the base of a tree and her eyes closed even as she curled up on it.

Bird song and squirrel chatter woke her. Sunlight lay in wavy ribbons on the ground between the trees. "Oh my, didn't 'spect to sleep this long." She led the horse out of the trees and stared at the incline they had climbed during the night. Somewhere, farther down and to the west, lay the town. "Don't even know its name," she murmured. "Don't ever want to know."

About a mile distant across the valley, she spied a column of dust and saw a horse and buggy leisurely traversing a road.

The man and his buggy looked tiny. Tiny, just like her, in this vast country with huge open spaces and mountains so high the snow never melted. How could she ever find Juba? It was like—*what did white folks say?*—like trying to find a needle in a haystack. Well, Juba was no needle. He was about as solid as a man could get. She closed her eyes and brought to mind the warmth and strength of his arms, his kisses. The remembrance made an awful hurt and yearning well up inside her and she began to cry, deep sobs that shook her whole body.

Meggie found herself praying. "Oh Lawd, oh Lawd, where is my Juba? Please help me find him."

CHAPTER 47

The horse was about played out. Meggie could see that. The mare had begun to limp and favored its left front leg. Meggie was about played out as well. In the past several days, she had found a few green plums and wrested two wild onions from the ground. They had made her breath stink and her stomach rebel. She was thankful for the numerous streams of water they found. She had tried peeling back the tough outer skin of cattail stalks and chewing the inner fiber. It was barely palatable.

More and more, Meggie found herself dozing as she rode. Once, when she awoke, the horse was standing still. "Hey, you old nag, we can't get anywhere that way." But what was her destination? "I don't know where I'm going, old horse. Just going, that's all."

They left the thick forest behind and followed a stream down a hill. Before them spread a basalt outcropping. The rocks were sharp underfoot and held the mid-day heat like an oven.

Meggie heard the warning rattle before she saw the snake. It struck at the horse's leg. Terrified, the horse jumped sideways, throwing Meggie off. She rolled down an incline and tumbled among the jagged rocks. Her momentum was broken by a large boulder that whacked her shoulder hard. When her head quit spinning, she raised up painfully to see where the horse had gone. She spied it, already a quarter of a mile away, running with a ragged gait to accommodate the sore leg.

"Here, horse," Meggie croaked. She hadn't the strength to call out. The mare wouldn't have paid attention anyway. Resigned to the loss of it, she mumbled to herself, "Oughta come back here. I need you, you old nag." The lump in her throat ached. Her shoulder sent out sharp pains. She wailed her misery with a parched mouth. A person couldn't even have a decent cry when they were so dry of tears. With a sigh, she leaned against the boulder and panted. *Wish I could just sit here and never—get up—again.*

An inner voice scolded her: "I ain't letting you give up now, girl. You gotta find a town or a farm or something 'cause you're starving, you hear? Now, get on your feet. Stand up proud and tall. You lost the horse, but it weren't never really yours. You got two good feet. Use 'em."

Meggie staggered up and picked her way down hill, grabbing at bushes to steady herself. Finally, she came to the corner of a fence line. Hallelujah, fences meant people somewhere. A cow trail followed the fence until it angled to one side. And there, a hundred feet off was a road. Meggie stood in the middle of it. The road began to sway and blur. She shook her head to clear it. The road tilted. *Whoa, there.* Her knees hit the hard packed dirt. She blinked and rubbed her eyes and tried to rise. The road tilted again and rushed toward her. She began to shiver. Just before she fainted and hit her head on the ground, a thought crossed her mind: *Sure would like a crust of bread to chew on.*

A pair of matched bays pulled the jade green carriage. Silver ornamentation on their harnesses sparkled in the sunshine. Scrolls of gold filigree graced the sides of the carriage. The curtains were open to the clear, warm day. The driver's livery was the same green as the carriage with gold braid on his cap and jacket. Inside, a lady wearing a broad-brimmed straw hat adorned with an ostrich plume, smoothed the fingers of her silk gloves. Her midnight-blue satin dress rustled slightly as she tapped her foot on the floor of the carriage. She hummed a tune, keeping time with her foot and occasionally glancing out the window.

Ahead, beside the road, there appeared to be a castoff bundle of rags. The driver directed the horses to the opposite side of the track as they passed. The lady gazed languidly at the bundle, then abruptly sat forward. "Jepson!"

"Ma'am?"

"Back up. Back up, Jepson."

"Yes, ma'am."

"Stop. Stop, I say."

"Yes, ma'am."

"Jump down, Jepson, and help me alight."

Jepson did as he was told. The lady marched around the carriage and studied the object in the road.

"My Lord in heaven, it's a girl, Jepson. A girl lying in the dirt."

"Yes, ma'am, but we dasn't delay. Let the wench lie."

"Jepson, what are you saying? This is a child in distress. I will not leave her."

"But, ma'am, we know nothing about her. Most likely inebriated. She may—"

"She's a child of God, Jepson. That's all I need to know."

"Yes, ma'am, but I would be careful, ma'am."

"Help me get her into the carriage, Jepson."

Jepson stepped back a pace. "She may have a dreaded disease, ma'am. She may—"

The lady bent to touch the girl's arm. "Enough, Jepson. Anyone can see she's half starved and hurt."

"Yes, ma'am. But do be careful of your dress." And as the lady brushed aside the dark hair that had fallen over the girl's face . . . "Your gloves, ma'am."

"Stop your twaddling, Jepson. Gloves, indeed. As if I didn't have too many pair as it is. Help me get her into the carriage."

Jepson curled his upper lip and hesitantly lifted the girl, holding her as far from his body as possible. He placed her in a reclining position upon the velvet cushion of the carriage. Her head lolled to one side. Her eyelids fluttered.

"Beg pardon, ma'am. I shall have the interior of the carriage cleaned as soon as possible."

The lady lifted her skirt slightly. "Help me in, Jepson." She seated herself beside the girl. "Now then, how far are we from Rock Lake City? I trust they have a doctor in the town."

After dusting off his own gloves and the front of his jacket, Jepson settled himself on the leather driver's seat and clucked to the horses. "I think we are about twenty miles from the city, ma'am. As to a doctor, I wouldn't know, ma'am."

"Of course, you wouldn't, Jepson. But we shall see, shan't we?"

"Yes, ma'am."

The lady removed her gloves and took one of the girl's hands in her own, rubbing it gently. "I would think if we are to partake of the horse races and the lake excursions, surely the city would have a doctor."

"Yes, ma'am." And to himself Jepson muttered, "Probably the town butcher."

"What's that, Jepson?"

"Nothing, ma'am. Only a little clearing of the throat, ma'am."

Two hours later, the carriage and its occupants entered the town of Rock Lake City. Jepson, lip still curled, still obeying orders, carried the girl into a hotel where she was tucked into bed. A doctor who also served as a dentist and barber examined her.

"Malnutrition and exposure," the doctor said. He shrugged. "If I were you, ma'am, I'd let this one take its natural course. You want a body servant, you can find a healthy one for very little output. Just like cats and dogs, no use wasting time on a sick one." He shrugged into his coat and left.

"Nonsense," the lady said. "Jepson, order up chicken soup from the hotel kitchen, then go away for a while. I'm going to give this poor child a sponge bath."

Jepson, eager to get out of the room, did as he was told. He wandered the town and found an empty stool at the Coyotes Whelp, where he was the object of much whispered observation among the locals.

Meanwhile, the lady carefully washed the girl and coaxed a little soup between her lips.

The girl opened her eyes and whimpered.

"There, there," the lady said. "Francesca Montworthy knows how to take care of girls. Another spoonful of soup, dear. That's good. I've had forty years of experience, you see. My boarding school for young ladies has an excellent reputation. That's it, another spoonful. You'll soon be fit as the proverbial fiddle."

Lady Montworthy leaned back to observe her charge. The girl's skin was the color of dark honey. Her ebony eyes would soon show the luster of good health. "Your name, dear?" she inquired.

"I-I'm Meggie." The girl's voice was a mere whisper. "Oh, Ju-Ju-Juba," she began to sob.

"There, there, don't worry, dear. We'll sort it out in good time. You can tell me all about it after you finish the soup."

Lady Montworthy plied the spoon again and Meggie obediently opened her mouth. Her eyes drooped and she drifted into sleep.

Lady Montworthy smiled. "Look at those thick lashes," she murmured to herself. "And those long, delicate fingers. Why, I wouldn't be surprised this one could be a pianist if she had the chance." She sighed. "But, in this world, she'll not likely have the opportunity. Surely, she's a runaway slave. It's a miracle she traveled this far."

CHAPTER 48

Over the next several days, Meggie began to respond to Lady Montworthy's loving care. The kindly woman offered sympathy as Meggie told her story. "You may never find your Juba, Meggie," she said, gently affirming the realities. "This is a vast country."

"Yes, ma'am," Meggie conceded. "But I can't quit hoping. I—I'se come so far—"

"Yes, indeed. You certainly have. But, right now, I believe a little diversion might be in order. You can't continue traveling the country alone without provisions or even a destination in mind. How would you like to be my companion?"

"'Scuse me, ma'am, you—you mean for me to be your servant?"

Lady Montworthy, who had been reclining on a brocaded horsehair sofa, sat up, full of indignation. "I should say not! Don't you see? I'm a bit lonely. I resigned from the girl's boarding school a few months ago. And I said to Jepson, 'Let's travel the countryside for a while. I need to breathe the fresh air of wide open spaces. Jepson's been with me for years. He's a good man, but—well, how would you describe Jepson, Meggie?"

"You want me to—oh, ma'am, I couldn't say—"

"Yes, you can. I'll tell you. Jepson's a stuffed shirt."

Meggie had no idea what that was. "Ma'am?"

"And from the look on his face, one would think he had a steady diet of sour pickles."

Meggie laughed. She couldn't help it. Yes, that was Jepson, all right.

Lady Montworthy stood. Her silk dress rustled as she crossed the room and rang a bell. A white-aproned maid appeared at the door. "Send up some hot tea, please," Lady Montworthy said. The maid nodded and closed the door.

"Now then," Lady Montworthy said, when she and Meggie were settled with their dainty teacups, "tomorrow there is to be a parade in Rock Lake City and after that, I understand the local people are conducting a fair, complete with a . . . ," she paused and her eyes twinkled, ". . . a horse race. Do you enjoy horse races, Meggie?"

"Don't know, ma'am. Never seen one."

"Then we shall begin your enlightenment of horse races. But first, we shall procure you some clothes. You need several dresses, obviously. Excellent tea, don't you think?"

Meggie wasn't sure what "diversion" or "procure" or "enlightenment" meant, but she understood "several dresses" very well. And as to describing Jepson a "stuffed shirt," she must be careful not to smile too broadly. Lady Montworthy made her head whirl with all her pronouncements. Was she a guardian angel? For certain, Meggie would have died on that road if Lady Montworthy had not come along.

CHAPTER 49

Well over a year had passed since Juba crouched behind the slave shacks on the plantation and pleaded with Meggie. That was the spring of '84. Now, it was autumn of '85. A year and a half since he had talked to Meggie, since her kisses had dried on his cheeks. As he went about his morning chores, he wondered what made her presence seem so near this particular day. Maybe it was because he could finally see himself getting ahead. How he would have liked to take her hand and say, "See, it's been hard work, but freedom is worth it. Worth every drop of sweat, every blister and callus." It hadn't been easy. He'd wanted to quit lots of times. But whenever there'd been a crisis, he had dug in and hung on. Had to. He quit running a long time ago.

Might as well quit daydreaming now too, because he would never have a chance to hold Meggie's hand in this life. He sure hoped her chilluns took after Meggie. Arlo was an ugly brute.

Juba leaned over the fence and poured skim milk into the hog trough. He grinned and watched his three slick porkers slurp the milk. They squealed and jousted one another for dominance. "You hogs are the greediest critters on earth," he told them. "Eat up. You'll be ready for market soon."

"*Meggie.*" Juba looked up as if someone had spoken. He shook his head. Gotta think on things to be done today. He had a five-gallon can of cream cooling in the bubbling spring water. He'd take it to the restaurant in Rock Lake City today. With faithful Bess and a heifer to calve in a couple of months, he'd have to invest in another cream can to hold it all. The restaurant paid him premium price. "Best cream we ever bought," they said. "Must be the way you cool it." And Juba would just grin at them. Not even those store-bought iceboxes folks were beginning to brag on could match what God had placed deep in the land, flowing endlessly from its source in his pasture.

Juba turned from the hog pen and sauntered by the chicken coop where hens cackled over fresh-laid eggs. He angled toward his cabin. No more dirt-floored shack with strips from a ragged shirt stuffed in the cracks to keep the wind and snow out. Toby had helped him in the spring. They'd notched logs, raised and chinked them, put in a floor, even added a couple of windows. With two hand-hewn chairs and a table, Juba felt proud every time he walked in the door.

"Meggie." *Cut it out, man. You got work to do.*

Yessir met him on the path. The pesky cat that had shown up one cold morning rubbed against his legs. Yessir adopted it right away, even though Juba had said, "You sure we need a cat?" Juba bent to pet it. The cat did keep the mouse population at an acceptable level.

Juba washed his face and hands, and shrugged into a clean shirt off the clothesline. He hitched Jack to the wagon and backed it down to the creek. He hoisted the cream can into the wagon, sloshed gunnysacks in the cold water and draped them, dripping, over the can to keep it cool on the way to town.

He swung around by the cabin, jumped down, and brought out a bucket of eggs wrapped individually in old newspaper. His arrangement with the mercantile, trading groceries for eggs, had paid well. Hadn't their customers let it be known all over town that the mercantile had the best tasting eggs?

Privately, Juba wondered if they knew their eggs came from a black man's chickens. Probably not. How about the cream? Would cream from a white man's cow taste better?

He rode to the restaurant first. The white-aproned cook met him at the back door.

"Howdy, Juba."

"'Lo, Ben. Something sure smells good in there. Whatcha cooking?"

"Porkypine pie and kangaroo dumplings."

Juba slapped his knee and laughed. "Good thing I'm eating at home then." He carried the cream can inside and set it down beside Ben's big cooler. There was water on the floor where the melted ice from the icebox overflowed its tray.

The cook reached into his apron pocket and brought out four bits. "How's that?"

"Just right. The cow thanks you and I thank you." Juba slipped the coin into his overall pocket and picked up the washed empty can from Monday's delivery. "See you in a couple of days, Ben."

He jumped into the wagon and tickled the reins over Jack's back. The wagon wheels creaked as Jack pulled forward. Juba headed for the mercantile. Ordinary day. Pleasant routine. Down the street, a crippled man with his crutch beside him on a bench picked out "Old Folks at Home" on a banjo.

"Meggie." Not again. Why was her memory bothering him so much today? Some inner part of his being must be clawing away the layers of protection he had so carefully laid over the old wound.

In the mercantile, he bought coffee, pinto beans, three cans of tomatoes, a pound of eight-penny nails, and a bottle of turpentine. After his two dozen eggs were subtracted from the total, he carried his purchases to the wagon. His foot was on the wagon step, his mind already on the work left to do at home. He shifted his weight and glanced across the street. It was a familiar motion, one he had performed countless times.

"Meggie." He saw her!

Juba's breath caught. He blinked. He froze. An inner voice said, "Aw, man, you're just fooling yourself. Wishing so hard your mind's playing tricks. Settle down. Settle down." But no, through the press of the crowd milling on the boardwalk, he caught another glimpse of her. Juba jumped off the wagon step. He ran across the street, legs pumping fast, and almost collided with a lumber wagon.

The driver cursed, "Get outta my way, you idiot."

Juba paid no attention. "Meggie, Meggie!" he shouted. "Meg—"

On the boardwalk, he bumped into people. "Watch where you're going, fellow." "You trip me and I'll have you flat on your back." "Hey, black man, forgot yer place?"

Juba mumbled, "Sorry, sorry, excuse me," as he wove a path through the crowd. *Gotta get to Meggie. Gotta let her know I'm here. Please, God, help me.* "Meggie?" Meggie?"

He was drowning in a sea of people. More folks than he had ever seen in Rock Lake City, and they all blocked his way. Why? Where'd they all come from? Then he remembered: They were in town to see the fair and the horse races down at the old stockyards.

He stood on tiptoe and searched frantically. "Meggie?" He let out a pent-up breath. His shoulders sagged. He had lost her. Doubt again attacked him. *Mind's playing tricks. Just wishing I'd see her. Wanting to so bad. Have some sense, man. No way in the world I'll ever see her again. No way in the world she could be here.*

A parade marched up the street. Horns blared. Drums thumped a counter rhythm to Juba's heartbeat. He stood in the middle of the boardwalk while people crowded around him. He searched their faces. "Mister, have you seen—" "Please, lady, I'm looking for—" "She's about this tall and pretty and—"

No one listened to him. He might as well have been a fence post. The crowd, like a cresting wave, washed around him and merged together on the other side of him. Everyone wanted to see the parade. He was an obstacle in their midst.

Had he dreamed the whole thing? What if he was hallucinating? He stood dejected as the world went about its business without him. He was dimly aware of bodies jostling and brushing past, elbows poking and feet trodding on his toes.

Slowly, slowly, shoulders slumped, he shuffled back to his wagon. Every joint in his body hurt. His head was about to split open. His tongue clung to the roof of his mouth. *Probably got a high fever, man. No wonder I'm seeing things. Go home and lie down. No, no.*

It was Meggie. He was sure of it. His Meggie. He sat on the wagon seat, staring at nothing until a tug at his arm roused him.

"I say there, fella, you all right? You've been sitting here for an hour or more. Better move on if you've got your business done. This town's mighty crowded today."

Dull-eyed, Juba looked up at the constable. "Oh, guess—I just been—"

The constable eyed him sternly, "You been drinking?"

"Uh—no, sir. No, sir, I—never mind. I'll go."

Somehow he got Jack moving and sat unheeding, the reins slack in his hands, as Jack took him home. Lost in his own muddled thoughts, Juba did not notice Hank leaning on the fence as he turned into his own lane. He did not hear Hank mutter, "I'll fix you yet, nigger boy."

Jack stopped in front of the cabin and Juba looked around. What was the good of all his toil and sweat to hang onto this homestead? He saw his farm with different eyes. What he had been so proud of this morning looked pitiful, even laughable now. He had strained at a gnat and accomplished nothing. He rubbed his thumb over his calloused hands and carried the groceries into the cabin. Had he bought tomatoes and beans and coffee? He couldn't remember, but there they were.

Juba sank onto his cot with a sigh and stared unseeing at the floor. Yessir crept close. He laid his head on Juba's knee. From long habit, Juba caressed the dog's head. "You know, Yessir, right now I'd like to turn the cows loose. Get me a jug of water from that spring out there and take off. Just leave the place. Go somewhere else. Don't care how far."

Yessir whined.

"Yeah, you could come along. Guess I can—" He choked on the words. "—guess I can count on you not walking out on me." Tears blurred his vision and he had to pull his ragged bandana handkerchief out of his back pocket.

CHAPTER 50

In the middle of the night, Juba awoke with a start and sat bolt upright. "Meggie?" Her voice had been so plain, as if she were in the cabin with him. He swung his legs to the floor, fumbled with a match, and lit the kerosene lamp. "Oh, Lawd, I've been dreaming. She was right here—so close—" He shivered. The last of the coals from his supper fire winked briefly when he lifted the stove lid. He poked at them, balled up a piece of paper, and laid on some chips. When he reached into the woodbox for a small stick, his fingers trembled and he dropped the stick on his foot.

"Ow, ow!" He shoved the wood into the firebox and slammed the lid down. "Can't do anything right. 'Bout broke my toe." He sat on his cot, rubbed the offended foot, and felt mighty sorry for himself.

After a while, as the fire crackled and the room warmed, Juba turned the damper in the stovepipe and blew out the lamp. He lay on his cot and watched the firelight flicker on the ceiling.

He knew what he'd do. He'd go home, back to the plantation. And whatever it took, he'd persuade Meggie to come away with him. If he had to fight Arlo or if Pilcher put him in chains—or shot him—

so be it. Anything was better than this hurting, this everlasting hole in his heart. He dozed and at daybreak, the rooster roused him.

Toby rode in after breakfast. Juba was mucking out Jack's stall. Toby poked his head into the barn. "Hey, Juba, want to see a good horse race?"

Juba leaned on his pitchfork. "Yeah, guess so. Whereabouts?"

"Down at the old track. They cleaned it up a bit. It's to go along with the fair at Rock Lake City. Oughta see the huge pumpkins. Wainwright took his prize bull. Got a blue ribbon on it. You ever see it? Say, betcha you could have won some prizes too."

Juba threw a forkful of manure-soaked straw past Toby. "Whoa there, I can't keep all this important information in my head. You're a walking newspaper."

Toby dodged the pitchfork again. "Well, I'd rather be a newspaper than the target for what you're shoveling. I'll wait around the corner."

Juba called out, "Give me about five minutes. Ol' mule deserves a clean house just like the rest of us."

Toby kept up a continual monologue as they rattled along toward the racetrack. Juba tried to listen, but his mind wandered back to the moment yesterday when he thought he saw Meggie. He muttered "yeah" or "that so?" or nodded when he hoped it was appropriate.

All at once, Toby pulled on the reins, skidded the wagon to a stop, and glared at him.

"What's the matter?" Juba asked.

"That's what I'd like to know. I've asked you a question three times and you just nod your head."

Embarrassed, Juba said, "Sorry, got something going round and round in my brain. Guess I was wool gathering."

"Well, what's eating you?"

Juba half turned and gazed over the side of the wagon. He mumbled, "I'se bothered 'bout hearing things, seeing things. You'll think I gone loco."

"Won't know for sure until you tell me. What things you been hearing?"

The horses switched their tails. Off in the trees, a squirrel set a branch to swaying. Swallows, wearing feathered blue-black tuxedoes, swooped low over a mud puddle and lifted toward their nests under the eaves of an abandoned barn across the road.

Toby pressed on. "I asked you a question. What things you been hearing?"

Juba fidgeted. He took a deep breath. "I—I was doing my chores yesterday—just like always. Kept hearing somebody whispering Meggie's name. I even turned around to see who was behind me. Nobody there. See? I tole you you'd think I was loco."

Toby asked, "You been hearing things other times?"

"No, just yesterday."

Toby clucked to the horses and tickled their backs with the reins. The wagon began to roll forward. "And what you been seeing?"

Juba groaned. "Do I hafta tell?"

"Yeah, you have to."

"Lawd, help me. Well, after I got the chores done—"

"When?"

"Yesterday."

"All right, go on."

"I went to town, leaving off the cream'n'eggs an—" Juba paused and rubbed his eyes. "I—I was fixing to come home and I looked up and I saw—I saw Meggie! Right there, on the boardwalk. She was with a fancy-dressed old lady. And by the time I got across the street, she was gone." He rested his elbows on his knees. His long slim fingers covered his face. Muffled sobs came from behind his hands. "She—she disappeared. I couldn't find her."

Toby said, "Hm-m." They came to a crossroad and turned onto a well-traveled track. He said "hm-m" again. "Ever hear of telepathy?"

Juba sat up and wiped his eyes. "Tele-what? Naw."

"Telepathy. That's when one fella knows what's going on with another fella, even though they're miles apart. That might explain it."

"Explain what?"

"Explain why you heard Meggie's name. Maybe she was thinking of you the same time you were thinking of her."

"You mean—kind of like a—a echo?"

"Yeah, I suppose you could say that."

"Well then, how'd you account for my seeing her in Rock Lake City?"

Sweet clover grew shoulder high beside the road. Toby snatched at a stem as they passed by. He chewed thoughtfully. "Lots of folks around now. The fair's drawing them. Times when there's a bunch of strangers you often see a fella that reminds you of somebody else."

They rode in silence for a few minutes. Then Juba blurted, "How many black folks you gonna see in a crowd in these parts? This ain't the south, you know."

"Well—"

"C'mon, Toby, walk down the street. Right here. Rock Lake City. How many black folks you apt to see?"

"You got me. Maybe two or three."

"I saw one, Toby." He held up a finger. "Just one, Toby. Her."

They bumped around a curve and down a hill between boulders. Before them spread a flat grassy plain. In the center of it, makeshift corrals held an assortment of farm animals. Their owners bustled about with buckets of water and forkfuls of hay. They trundled wheelbarrows of dirty straw and poured old coffee cans full of grain into troughs. One barefoot boy of about twelve stood proudly beneath a string wound between two poles. On it fluttered a blue ribbon. At his feet, two spotted hogs snuffled in the straw. One scratched his back on a protruding board.

Toby pointed. "See? What'd I tell you? There's Wainwright's bull. Over there. Ain't he a big one? Hope he don't knock the fence down."

Juba shook his head.

"What's wrong now? Still seeing things?"

"No, just looking at all the people."

Toby laughed. "Betcha some of them came from fifty miles away. Fair's a big attraction. Couple hundred folks milling around here."

They parked the wagon beside the shade of a poplar tree and climbed down. Toby looked up into its branches. "Did you know, Juba, Wainwright's old man planted this tree? One of the first settlers around. Built the cabin somewhere over there, I think. No, maybe closer to the creek. Don't matter. Snow caved it in a couple years ago."

They walked toward tables laden with netted gem potatoes, yellow-cored carrots and ten-pound cabbages. A little girl sat by a box holding three kittens. A cardboard sign said: "Free."

Juba smiled at her. "How many didya give away?"

The girl clutched a kitten to the front of her dress and shrank away from him. She hid behind her mother and peeked out. The mother twisted her apron with reddened hands. "Don't pay m'girl no mind. She never seen a darkie man before." Her bottom lip trembled.

Juba shrugged and walked on. He mumbled to Toby, "I eat little white girls for breakfast. Like 'em best with cream'n'sugar."

Toby pulled on his sleeve. "Over there's the race track. Let's go see if a race's about to start."

They were surrounded by a crowd surging toward the track. Swept along and jostled, Juba endured elbows and shoulders vying for a place ahead of him. He was soon separated from Toby. Once he turned, glimpsed Toby in the crowd and heard him call. He was rewarded by a punch in the back and a rough voice yelling, "Keep moving, black man."

At last, the people pressed together around the oval track. Shut out behind an unyielding wall of overalls and calico, Juba lingered near the back. Nearby, a drunk swayed as he swigged from a half-empty bottle. He eyed Juba warily. Another man with red eyes leaned on a crutch made from a forked limb. One leg was encased in a grimy bandage. Juba motioned for the man to stand in front of him. The man shook his head. "Better off here. They'd trample me."

Juba grunted and muttered to himself, "Keep to the rear, all you maimed, muddled, and black." He stood on tiptoe and stared across the track at the people on the opposite side. He saw gentlemen in waistcoats and top hats. Beside them, stood ladies with voluminous dresses and parasols to guard their creamy skin from the sun. A wry smile played about his lips and he shrugged. On his side were the farmers and laborers, the sweat-stained shirts and gingham aprons. Even the white folks separated themselves into classes.

The starting gun sounded. Juba glimpsed a fleeting flash of horseflesh streaking away. The crowd shouted and cheered. They pounded one another on the back. They shook hands and shoved and clapped.

Since the horses were barred from his view, Juba stared again at the more proper segment of society across the track. His eyes widened. His mouth dropped open. He blinked. "Meggie!" He blinked again. There she stood, in a pretty dress of pale blue, beside an elderly lady in some shiny dark material. Meggie shaded the woman's face with a ruffled parasol.

"It's Meggie! It's Meggie!" Juba shouted. He could not stop himself. The words bubbled up from within him. "It's Meggie. It's Meggie!"

A gray-bearded man directly in front of him turned around. "Shut up", he said. Others cast frowns at Juba and pointed over their shoulders. "Stupid nigger." "Darkie making trouble."

Juba waved his arms, and jumped up and down. "Toby," he called. "It's Meggie. She's here. Toby. Toby!" He tried to move forward. "Excuse me, sir. May I pass? Pardon, lady, please let me through. I need to— Toby! Toby! It's Meggie!"

Juba did not see the fist that landed on his chin or the two men who grabbed him from behind and threw him down. They pinned his arms across his back and ground his face into the dirt. Somebody yelled, "Turn him over."

Twisting and kicking, he heard a curse as his foot connected with a soft belly. "Why, you filthy nigger."

Juba spit the dirt from his mouth and shook his head to clear his vision. The race was forgotten as a circle of angry men and women leaned toward him. He tried to get up, but they shoved him down again. They shouted expletives as their fists flailed the air and pummeled his body.

All at once, between the legs that encircled him, Juba glimpsed the crippled man. He saw the man raise his crutch and slam it down upon the head of one of Juba's assailants. The burly bully crumpled to the ground. The crippled man quickly sidestepped those who turned to him in astonishment and melted into the crowd. Next, Juba saw the drunken derelict, not to be outdone, weave and duck until he stood in the circle. Still grasping his bottle, the little drunk waved his arms and, seemingly by accident, struck one of the attackers on the nose. The man cried out, while the drunk dove between the circled legs and ran away, giggling.

Juba again struggled to rise. A boot slammed into the side of his head. He groaned. The world reeled and began to grow dark. Voices faded. He was falling, falling into soft gray velvet. A refrain echoed in his mind: *the maimed, the muddled, and the black.*

Toby found him there. The races were over. Stragglers from the crowd cast suspicious glances at the man lying on the ground. They skirted a wide path around him and hurried away. Toby knelt, pulled his handkerchief from a hip pocket, and gently brushed the dirt and blood from Juba's face.

"Juba, Juba? Can you hear me?"

Juba grimaced and slowly opened his eyes. "Toby?"

"Yeah, it's me. What happened? Who beat you?"

"Beat me? Oh-h—"

"Looks like they got you good." Toby steadied him as he tried to sit up. He grabbed the front of Toby's shirt. "I saw her. Toby, I saw her!"

"Hold on, hold on. What're you talking about?"

"Meggie. I swear it. Right over there. She was—"

He let Toby help him to his feet. "Can you stand? Let's get you to the wagon."

Juba's legs buckled a time or two as Toby pulled him along. "She was—she was holding a pink umbrella for a—"

"The wagon, Juba. Let's get you to the wagon."

Juba glanced wildly around. "Have to find her. Can't let her get away—"

He lurched sideways and Toby caught him. "Look, fella, you're in no shape to look for anybody. Let's go home, clean you up, and—"

Juba wasn't listening. "She's gone, she's gone. Just like last time," he cried.

Toby helped him into the wagon and clucked to the horses. "Everybody's gone, Juba. Race is over."

CHAPTER 51

It was past midnight. Half awake, Juba coughed. He smelled smoke. He opened his eyes and sat up. He saw the reflection of flames through the window on his cabin wall. Smoke poured in through the open sash. *Smoke?* He leaped out of bed and ran outside. Fire crackled and climbed the walls of his barn. He stood there in a stupor, unbelieving. He turned. Tiny flames flared at the edge of his front stoop. He stamped them out with bare feet.

"Oh, Lawd! Jack. Bess." Juba sprinted to the barn and darted inside. Smoke shimmered like gray gauze before his smarting and tearing eyes. *Can't see. Where's Jack's stall? Where's the gate hook? Can't find the gate hook.*

Inside the stall, the frantic mule turned in circles and kicked the wall. Juba fumbled for the hook and dropped it. He blindly groped the surface of the gate and rammed a sliver in his finger. *Where is it? Where is it? Lawd, help me!* He bent over, head near his knees, and sucked in air. The hook scraped against his ear as he straightened. He grasped it, pulled it up, and flung the gate open. Jack's big body loomed before him. He slapped Jack hard on the rump. The mule charged through and knocked the gate off its hinges.

Eyes streaming and lungs straining for air, Juba ran outside and sucked in a couple of deep breaths. Bess and the heifer were still in the barn. He had to go back for them. He held his arms in front of his face and searched through the billowing smoke. There they were, lighted by the flames that licked the inner wall. Bess snorted and pawed the straw. She tossed her head wildly, catching Juba in the ribs. He waved his arms. "Get out, get out, you fool cow," he hollered against the roar of the fire. He doubled over, retching. He had to get her out. He couldn't lose Bess. Yessir appeared beside him. The dog barked and nipped the cow's heels. She bolted through the door, bellowing and kicking, and ran toward the pasture. The heifer followed.

Juba stumbled outside to the three-sided hog pen he had built against the barn wall. The hogs crowded into the far corner of their pen. They squealed in panic as glowing embers landed on their backs. Juba gripped the latch with trembling fingers and flung their gate open. They bumped against him, knocked him on his backside and ran away into the night.

It was too late to save the chickens. Juba watched in horror as the roof of their shed caved in with a whoosh. Sparks lit the night sky. Sooty tears ran down his face. "Oh Lawd."

He looked toward his cabin. He had stamped out the tiny flames by his front stoop. But now, the back wall and the roof were on fire. He raced toward the cabin and skidded to a stop. "No!" he wailed as the wall fell inward. Fire licked across the roof. Flames shot skyward and the roof collapsed. All the work. All the pride. All gone. All burned up.

Juba sank to the ground in despair. He had no strength left. Yessir, trembling, leaned against him and licked his cheek. Juba took the dog's head in both his hands and cried, "It's all gone, Yessir. All gone. Oh Lawd, whatever happened?"

It was then he heard the scream. Terror and hopelessness were hedged in that scream. "What?" Juba staggered to his feet. "Did you hear it, Yessir?" He heard the scream again, an eerie sound wavering in the smoky air. "It's coming from the barn," he yelled.

Half the barn was already a blackened shell, highlighted by glowing timbers.

Nothing could be alive in there. Juba raced around to the back, not knowing what he was searching for, what he would find. The scream came again. At close range, it made Juba's skin prickle. Then he saw Hank Duvett writhing on the ground, his chest pinned by a charred timber. A tangle of wire wound around his legs.

As Juba lunged toward the trapped man, the back wall of the barn burst into flame. The intense heat singed Juba's eyebrows. Muscles bulging, veins standing out on his temple, he heaved the timber off Hank's chest. It fell slantwise into the hot dust. Tiny swirls of smoke spiraled upward from it. The hair on Juba's arms curled and turned to ash. His hands were seared. Hank screamed, "Help me, help me!"

Juba grasped Hank under the arms. His knees buckled from exhaustion and fear. But he pulled and dragged Hank to safety, away from the flames, away from the fire that was destroying all his dreams. They watched as with a roar the barn disintegrated into an exploding storm of cinders and sparks and burning debris.

Juba laid Hank on the grass near the spring. He untangled the wire from Hank's legs and wadded it into a ball. Hank sat hunched over, staring at the ground. Firelight flickered over his face. Juba collapsed on the ground. He covered his face with his hands. Muted sobs racked his body. Neither man said a word. The only sounds were the crackle of the fire and the occasional snap and thump of another board burned through and falling to earth.

After a while, Juba stood up. He stumbled to the spring, and dipped his head and arms in the cold water. Although he was dripping and shivering, he walked proudly, head up, and stood before Hank. He had left the last trace of the submissive slave far behind. The fire devouring the buildings was no match for the fire blazing in his heart. He dared Hank to look him in the eye. Hands on hips, he said, "It's the middle of the night. Whatcha doing on my farm, Hank?"

Hank's face showed clearly in the light from the still-burning buildings. He was the one who cowered and lowered his gaze to the ground. "Guess you already know why."

"Got a good idea. Want to hear it from you."

Hank could not meet his eyes. He muttered, "Whatdaya think? Just trying to clean out the trash. Ain't no place for a nigger 'round here."

Juba forged ahead. "How'd you start the fire?"

Hank jutted his jaw. "Kerosene."

Juba stared at Hank. He saw the blistered lips, the seared flesh of his face, the scorched hands. He could only guess at the depths of hate Hank held for him. The hate that compelled him to destroy all Juba had worked so hard to build. He knotted his fists. The skin of his burned hands throbbed. He wanted to beat Hank senseless. He wanted to shout his disgust and revulsion, to shake Hank's scrawny neck, to squash him like a bug, to . . .

He took a deep breath. Surprised, he found himself looking at Hank with pity. After the fear and the struggle through the smoke and flames, the heartbreak and the surge of rage that shook his very core, here he stood, filled with pity for the man who had caused it all. He saw Hank for what he was. Just a small-minded man bound and enslaved by his own prejudice. A man to be pitied.

Juba sighed. He walked over to the tree where the tin cup swung from its leather strap. He took it down and squatted and filled the cup with cool, sweet water. He handed the cup to Hank. "Here," he said, "have a drink from my cup."

Hank looked up with bloodshot eyes. He scowled at the cup. He reached out with a smoke-blackened arm and slapped the cup from Juba's hand. It bounced and rolled away in the grass.

Juba's leg muscles quivered. It would be so easy to kick Hank in the face. He clenched his teeth and turned to pick up the cup. Bent over, his fingers closing around the cup, he whispered, "Let me hit him, Lawd. Let me hit him, just once."

He turned around. Hank had disappeared. A curtain of smoke lifted momentarily and gave him a glimpse of Hank tramping toward home. Juba hung the cup back on its tree branch. He swayed with exhaustion and grabbed hold of the tree to steady himself.

Five minutes later, Toby arrived. "Saw the flames. Came as quick as I could. What happened?"

"Hank."

Toby's mouth opened and closed. He stared at Juba, then at the smoldering ruins of the buildings. "Nothing left, is there? Not one thing." He shook his head. "What a shame." He touched Juba's arm. "You all right? Get the livestock out?"

"Yeah, all but the chickens."

"Look, fella, I'll run home, bring you some clothes. You sit right here till I get back."

Juba nodded, his face expressionless as he watched Toby's wagon rattle out of the yard. He found a charred bucket, its staves warped, hoops sprung, and sat, staring at nothing while a hundred scenes unfolded in his mind. As far as he knew, he did not move the whole time Toby was gone. Maybe he hadn't even breathed. It seemed only a minute until he heard Toby's wagon again.

Toby jumped down and handed him a jug of hot coffee and something wrapped in paper. "Isabel sent this along. And here's a change of clothes."

The flames from the burned buildings were dying down. Toby peered into the gloom. "Maybe I ought to take you home to Isabel. She's good about knowing what to do when folks are—"

"No, I'm all right here. Hafta start cleaning up soon's it's daylight."

Toby's hand pressed Juba's shoulder. "Then I want you to sit here and rest. You're still kinda in shock's my guess."

"Yeah, but I—"

"Thing is, I got some stuff to do. Take me a while. Promise you'll stay right here 'til I get back?"

"Yeah, I guess so."

Toby turned away. He yelled over his shoulder. "I'll be back soon's it's daylight."

Juba shrugged into the clothes. He sipped the coffee and stared absently at the singed hair on his arms. He rubbed his smarting eyes. All his work over the past year was for nothing. Everything he had gained was gone. No barn, no cabin, no hay for Jack and Bess. No seed grain. Chickens dead. His hands shook, and he almost dropped the parcel Isabel had sent along. He unwrapped it. Inside were two jelly sandwiches and a slice of apple pie. He ran a thumb along the edge of a sandwich. A sob caught in his throat. Toby and Isabel, hearts of pure gold. And then there was Hank . . . He couldn't eat just now. Maybe later.

As the sky began to lighten, the fast flowing spring turned silver. Juba stared at it. How many years had the spring been running? A hundred? A thousand? Maybe ten thousand, for all he knew. It had seen drought and plenty. Ruffians and pious alike had drank from it. Happy or despairing had tasted it. And the spring kept on flowing, offering cool sweet water to all, regardless. "Just like the Lawd," he mused. "Just like the Lawd."

Juba raised his eyes to his tin cup swinging from a branch as the morning breeze stirred it on its leather strap. The little barefoot girl way back there on his quest for freedom had handed it to him. Her father showed him hate; she and her mother showed him mercy.

Yessir came to stand beside him and laid his head on Juba's knee. Juba rubbed his silky head. "Just you'n'me again, Yessir. S'pose I might find ole Bess somewhere, if I want to look, wandering on somebody else's farm. She'll be so scared she won't give any milk for a week. An' Jack, he might be clear to that Oregon Territory I never got to see by now. Who knows how far those hogs'll wander. Coyotes might get 'em." He sighed. "Think we oughta pull out? Give up? Don't think I can be like this ol' spring, just going on, no matter what."

Rosy fingers began in the eastern sky and spread across the vast expanse. The rattling of wagons on the rutted road broke through Juba's muddled thoughts. He raised his head. A cloud of dust clung to the trail as far as he could see. He squinted into the rising sun and made out Toby's wagon in the lead. It swayed from side to side. It was loaded with timbers. Juba stood and frowned at it. "What's he—"

More wagons followed. Juba recognized some of his other neighbors as they drew closer. "What're they coming here for?"

Toby drew up beside the ruins of Juba's barn. "What's going on, Toby?"

Toby jumped down from the driver's seat. "Well, seems your barn was out of style. We aim to build you a better one."

Juba's head swam. He tottered forward a step or two. "Now, just a minute, Toby—"

Toby interrupted, "Why don't you sit back down till we can clear some of this stuff out of the way."

"But I—"

Toby went right on, "Need to hitch the horses and pull away these charred boards. Scorched hay'd make good mulch in the cornfield. We can get some of the boys to haul it out. Hey, Abe, bring your pitchfork? Let's make a—"

Juba's attention was diverted to the next wagon pulling in. He watched open-mouthed as another farmer wrestled two gunnysacks of seed grain to the ground and set down a wooden crate of squawking chickens. He turned as a third farmer said, "Whoa," then, "Howdy, Juba," and unloaded a hundred-pound sack of potatoes and a washtub brimming with cabbages. A young boy helped him carry a four-paned window and leaned it against the trunk of a tree. "For your new cabin," he said.

The dust from the wheels of a fourth wagon wafted over Juba. Astonished, he saw folks unload a rocking chair, a teakettle, and an iron frying pan. They added the items to a growing assortment on the ground. Several more wagons came to a halt. From the back of one, a fellow rolled a keg of nails toward the still-smoking remains of the barn.

"But, I—" Juba began again. No one seemed to pay him attention. They went about their business as if each had been assigned a certain task, clearing away burned debris, measuring dimensions for new buildings. On a plank table supported by saw horses, women arranged bowls of food, pies, and loaves of bread.

Juba heard a commotion in the field. He turned and squinted. His heart skipped. Coming across the pasture, two young boys coaxed along Juba's three squealing and snuffling hogs. Behind them, another led ol' Bess and the heifer toward home. Jack, snorting and with ears pricked forward, brought up the rear.

More wagons were coming up the lane. Far down the line, from the last wagon bumping along, Juba heard someone call his name. "Juba. Juba."

A shock stabbed his heart. He stood still. He heard it again. "Juba. Juba." The world whirled dizzily. He blinked and rubbed his eyes. He saw a woman climb out of the last wagon and run toward him. Her blue dress billowed around her ankles. *Could it be? Oh Lawd, could it be?*

A dear face. The face he had seen in his heart all these months. "Juba!" The voice he had heard in his heart, he would hold in his heart, forever.

She ran with arms outstretched. "Juba, my Juba!"

Juba stumbled forward. "Meggie! Is it really you? Meggie?"

Now he was running too, closing the distance between them. Running to hold her in his arms. Running to never let her go.

CHAPTER 52

Meggie fell into his embrace. "Oh, Meggie. Meggie. Am I dreaming?" Their tears mingled. His Meggie, his love. His lips found hers. Their heartbeats melded. Meggie caressed him and held his face in her hands. "Somehow I knew I'd find you, if I just kept going."

All of a sudden, he wrenched away. He stepped back.

"Juba? Is something wrong?" A flicker of hurt crossed her face.

"Yeah, maybe." He was shaking now. His knees turned to mush. The knife was twisting in his gut. "Where's your baby?"

"My what?"

"Your baby. Where's Arlo?"

Meggie frowned. "I don't have a baby, Juba. What are you talking 'bout?"

"Don't play with me, Meggie. Miss Lorinda said—"

"Miss Lorinda? Where ever did you see her?"

"In Independence last year. She told me you and Arlo—" The stricken expression on her face made him stop. Tears of a different sort streamed down her cheeks.

"Meggie?"

"Oh, Juba, you believed her? You believed that Arlo and me—that we had a baby? How could you!" She turned away. Juba saw her bowed head, the shaking of her shoulders.

He said to her back, "Miss Lorinda told me Massah mated you to Arlo right after I ran away. She said you were in the family way—a little buck, she called it, and you'd probably have another one next year. And I—I thought—maybe, that was why you wouldn't come with me. I wondered, Meggie. It hurt me awful bad, but I thought—"

Behind them, the steady rasp of saws and pounding of hammers set up a counterpoint rhythm to the calls of the men. "Hoist that beam up now, George." "Didya notch it?" "Hold it now." "Lem, could use that level over here." "Joe, lad, fetch me the adze." "Let's get this timber socked into place."

The background faded to a blur. Beside him, Juba heard Meggie sob. She stood hunched over, her head in her hands. His own tears smeared his face. "Meggie, hon, didn't mean to hurt you so. Oh Lawd, I jus' found you again and I've hurt you. Please forgive me. I didn't know. Miss Lorinda, she—" He clasped and unclasped his hands. Had someone plunged a knife into his chest?

Meggie put her arms around him and drew him close again. "I forgive you, Juba. Guess when you was out there in that wilderness all alone it was easy to believe something bad. Miss Lorinda tricked you, hon. That's what she did. Tricked you on purpose, just to hurt you."

Juba nodded. "I didn't want to believe, honest I didn't."

"I know, hon. Listen, Juba, you know Arlo's no good. Never will be. He's one of the reasons I had to run away. I never would have let him touch me. Never. Besides, I didn't want to live without you no more." She sighed. "I want you to meet Lady Montworthy. If it wasn't for her, I wouldn't be here."

"Who's Lady Montworthy?"

"She brought me to Rock Lake City. I was starving, and she came along and rescued me. She was on her way to the fair to see the races and I—"

Juba's face lit up. "You was at the races?"

"Yes, hon."

"Then you *was* there. You *was* there! Wait'll I tell Toby. Wait'll I tell—" He hugged her tightly. "Did you see me there?"

"See you? Well, 'course not. Didn't have no idea you—"

Juba could hardly keep from jumping up and down. "But how'd you—you came today. How'd you know?"

With a gentle finger, Meggie traced the scar on his temple and followed the smoky trail of tears down his cheeks. "We saw the flames and the smoke from the hotel. Lady Montworthy and me. Somebody said, 'Must be that black farmer's place. Juba Robinson, what he calls himself.' Oh, Juba, you shoulda seen me. I 'bout fell down. I kept saying, 'Juba, Juba.' An' Lady Montworthy said, 'Why don't you go out there and see, dear.' An' I tell you, I rushed around so fast and saw all these wagons comin' this way and I—Oh Juba, Juba! I love you so."

"We can get married, hon. We can get married. Toby's a justice of the peace. He can marry us."

Meggie was laughing through her tears. "Slow down, Juba. I can't keep up with you. Who's Toby?"

Juba kissed her cheek. "Toby's my friend. Best white man friend a fella ever had. He's—hey, Toby," he called. He grabbed Meggie's hand and pulled her along. "We'll find us a broom. We'll be married, right and proper."

Juba led her to where Toby was notching a log, chips flying in tangy half moons. "Meggie, my love, my darlin', nothing in the world can keep us apart now."

And Meggie looked into his face with shining eyes. "You'n'me, Juba. Just you'n'me for always."

CHAPTER 53

And so they were married. Together, they worked to restore and rebuild the farmstead. They weathered the frosts of autumn, and the winds and snow of winter. Finally, the day came when they sat on the doorstep of the new cabin and welcomed the warm breezes of spring.

"Look at the grass shooting up. Bet it's grown another inch since yesterday. And over there, Juba, a buttercup! Everything's sprouting up so fast."

Juba put an arm over her shoulder. "You're growing too, Meg. I better get started on that cradle I said I'd make you."

Meggie said, "Three more months till our baby comes. We got to make up our minds what we're gonna name our little one."

"If it's a boy, I know what name's I'd like, Meg."

Meggie grinned, "Reuben or Toby." She poked him playfully. "How far off was I?"

"How'd you know? I never said—"

"Wives just know stuff like that, hon. Easy as pie."

"Well then, what names you got picked out for a girl?"

Meggie traced a line on the knee of Juba's overalls. "Been thinking, it'd be nice to call her Reba Sal or Sally Reba. Which do you like best?"

"Reba'd be proud you named our baby after her. Never knew that Sal."

"Sal was kind to me, Juba, awful kind."

Juba stood and stretched. "That's fine with me. Whatever makes you happy. Better get moving. Gonna help Toby bring home more lumber for his new shed. Right handy having a sawmill nearby. More people moving in all the time. Place might get crowded after a while.

"Juba?"

"Yeah, Meg?"

"Heard any more about the circuit judge? Thought Toby said the judge'd be making his rounds through here pretty soon. Said he'd come in the spring, you know."

Juba sat back down. He took her hand and caressed it. "No use worrying over it, Meg. Toby said—"

"I know what Toby said. Don't want to believe it. Don't want to believe a judge would just laugh and shrug his shoulders. Hank oughta pay for what he did. He ought to be punished. He ought—"

Juba gathered her into his arms. He whispered, "Sh-h now, don't get yourself upset. We're doing all right. You gotta understand, lots of folks kinda afraid of Hank. Afraid if they open their mouths, he'd—Couldn't get 'em on a jury if you hogtied 'em. And then there's others that—"

"Yeah, I know about the others. Don't care one way or 'nother about us. Justice is justice, Juba."

"Sh-h, Meg, nothing we can do about it. You remember how Hank spread the word right away that he saw the fire and came over to help."

"Yeah, I know. Made me want to scratch his eyes out. Lying like that."

Juba plucked a blade of new grass and rubbed it between his palms. "Toby says Hank's still boasting to any who'll listen how he was working so hard to save the barn and got out just in time."

"Liar, liar!" Meggie clenched her fists. "If it wasn't for you—you're the one who saved him. Everybody ought to know it. Shoulda left him there. Shoulda—"

"Hush, Meg. You know the Lawd don't want us feeling like that."

Meggie leaned her head on Juba's shoulder. "But it's not fair. Not fair at all."

"I know, Meg. Never was. Maybe never will be. I don't know. Guess we'll just have to go on. Grow a callus over it and trust the Lawd. Now, you gonna be all right while I'm gone? You ain't gonna work too hard?"

"I'll take care, Juba. Need to get those taters in the ground though. I'll do that and then I'll rest."

"Good girl." He held her chin in his cupped hand. "Love you, Meg. Love you lots."

"Love you too, Juba. You know it."

They lingered over a kiss. Meggie watched the wagon rattle down the lane. She went into the cabin and came back with a knife and a bucket of seed potatoes. Carefully, she cut them, making sure there was an eye in each piece.

Juba had plowed and harrowed a spot near the cabin for their garden. Meggie grasped the shovel leaning against the cabin wall and began to dig rows of holes about eight inches deep. Into each one, she would drop a piece of potato, the eye pointing upward, then tamp the dirt firmly over it.

Yessir stayed close beside her. He wagged his tail, snuffed at the little dirt piles beside the holes, and pretended to look for mice. Meggie dug two more holes and straightened to rest her back.

Yessir growled. Meggie caught movement out of the corner of her eye. She saw Hank Duvett tramping across the yard. Yessir bared his teeth and growled again.

"Better shut up that worthless hound or I'll do it for you," he said.

Meggie laid a hand on Yessir's head. "Easy, boy," she whispered.

Hank came so close Meggie could see the gray hairs in his nostrils. Meggie stepped back. Hank moved forward again. He leaned over her. "See you're gonna populate the whole territory with little niggers," he sneered.

Meggie took a deep breath. "I'm kinda busy, Mr. Duvett," she quavered. "Please, I need to finish—"

"Your nigger's gone today. Kinda alone, ain't you?"

Yessir growled once more. He wedged his shoulder against Meggie's leg. She felt the rippling under his skin as he tensed his muscles and the vibration as his growl came from deep within his throat. Her hand on the shovel trembled. "Ju-Juba'll be back soon. I—I need to get these taters planted."

Hank's eyes swept the cabin and outbuildings. "Pity folks spent all that time helping to put up these shacks last fall. Never asked me. Nigger's a shiftless lot. Probably move on afore the year's out."

Yessir barked and bared his teeth. Meggie jumped. Hank tore the shovel from her hands. "Told you to shut that dog up." Yessir lunged for Hank as Hank hoisted the shovel high. He hammered it down on Yessir's head. The dog yelped, fell to the ground and lay still.

Meggie wrung her hands. "You killed my dog," she screamed. "You killed my dog!"

"Naw, just put him to sleep for a while. Quit yer screeching, woman."

Meggie backed toward the cabin. Tears streamed down her face. "Please go away, Mr. Duvett. Please leave me alone."

Still clutching the shovel, Hank plodded after her. His tone changed to a gravelly croon that sent shudders through her body. "Don't get so worked up, woman. Maybe I was looking for a little social time with you, afore your nigger comes peeking around the corner."

Meggie was almost to the doorstep. She glanced back to avoid tripping. "No, no!"

Hank grabbed the front of her dress. "Whaddaya say, let's go inside and get comfortable."

"No! Let go'a me. Let go'a me."

Hank twisted her collar. His hand brushed her chin. She clamped her teeth on one of his knuckles, biting down as hard as she could.

"Ow! No nigger woman's gonna treat a white man like that."

Meggie did not see the shovel descending. The handle struck her temple. She was blinded and sickened by the pain, and fell to her knees. Hank lifted her roughly, threw her into the cabin and across the bed. Meggie filled her lungs. She screamed again and again, and struggled as he tore at her clothes.

"Shut up!" he yelled. She glimpsed his doubled fist. This time he directed savage blows to her abdomen.

Meggie heard herself calling weakly for help and moaning as he continued to strike her. The room seemed to whirl. She gagged at the stink of Duvett's whiskey-soaked breath and gasped for air against the weight of his body. At last, she was falling down, down into a bottomless void where he could not reach her.

CHAPTER 54

Juba found her on the bed, crumpled in a heap like a broken doll. One eye was swollen shut. Her cheek was a mass of purple bruises.

"Meg! Meg! Oh, Lawd!"

After a frozen moment of shock, he bent and gently cupped her face in his palms. "Meg? Darlin' Meg, can you hear me? Meg?"

She groaned and tried to open her eyes. She whispered through cracked lips. "Ju-Juba, it—it was Hank. He—he—Juba, I—"

"Meg, oh Meg. There, there, easy now." A flash of memory ricocheted across his mind. He shuddered: Back at the plantation, helping Reuben to his bunk, rubbing tallow into the cuts from the whip, the unrelenting hopelessness, the anger that overwhelmed and could not find release. "Oh, Lawd," he breathed. "Ain't there no place on earth free from wickedness?" His voice cracked. Meg groaned.

Juba's jaw tightened. "Hold on, Meg. I'm gonna get Isabel to help. Hold on now. She'll know what to do."

"Don't leave me, Juba."

"Be brave, darlin'. Back soon's I can. Gotta get Isabel to help. Oh, Lawd, my Meggie. My Meggie!" Juba staggered out of the cabin. Inside him the fire he'd kept tamped down, the outrage he'd locked away, flickered and burst into flame.

The moment he'd walked into the yard and saw Yessir propped against the cabin, trembling and whining, his head covered with blood, a stab of apprehension had socked him in the chest. Immediately, his senses shouted, "Duvett!" And when he rushed inside and saw Meggie, his Meggie—

It seemed to take forever to hitch Jack to the wagon, his fingers all clumsy and stiff as sticks. And how come the road had stretched fifty miles to Toby and Isabel's farm? He pulled up in a cloud of dust and fell from the wagon. "Toby! Isabel! Help!"

They flung the door wide, hurried out, and listened to his breathless, tear-choked story. Isabel heard only a few words, turned, and limped back into the cabin. Toby stayed on the doorstep. He kept shaking his head in disbelief at the horror of it. Juba's legs buckled, and Toby caught him by the shoulder and steadied him. "Easy now, fella. Hold on, hold on."

Isabel appeared, clutching a cloth bag. "I'm ready," she said.

Back at his cabin, Juba helped Isabel from the wagon and she hurried to Meggie's bedside, ahead of Juba. She laid a cool palm on Meggie's forehead. "It's Isabel, Meggie. Don't be afraid now. I've come to help."

Juba hovered. "Is she—will she—?"

"Don't you worry," Isabel whispered. "I've taken care of lots of women. Helped set broken arms and birthed more babies than I can count and—"

"Birth? You don't think she—?"

"Sh-h-h, just meant to say I've had lots of experience. Now, I expect Jack's waiting for you to unhitch him and maybe something else needs taking care of?" Her mouth was a grim line. Her eyes were not smiling as she looked directly into his and nodded.

The turmoil within Juba had wound tighter and tighter. Yes, something else needed to be taken care of. And he'd best be at it. With a brief kiss on Meggie's brow and a squeeze of her hand, he struggled to keep his voice calm, "Rest easy, hon. Isabel's here. I'll be back soon's I can." He swallowed and stood, silhouetted by the lowering sun, as he paused in the open door. "Somethin' I gotta do."

Dusk was fast deepening into night. Juba covered the ground to Hank's place in double time. He found Hank pitching hay to his horses.

Hank heard him coming. His face screwed up as he backed into a fence. He whined, "I didn't do nothing! I didn't touch her!"

Without a word, Juba yanked the pitchfork from his grasp, threw it away, and rammed his work-hardened knuckles into Hank's jaw. Hank sagged and angled drunkenly against the fence.

Juba plowed forward. "Didn't touch her, huh? How come you know why I'm here then?" Juba caught him and pummeled him as he cried out his grief and rage. "You burned my buildings, 'bout wrecked my farm. I tolerated that 'cause you a white man and judges don't care 'bout a black man's property. But when you hurt my wife—," his voice broke on a sob. "You hurt my Meggie. Hurt her bad. Maybe you hurt our baby too. I ain't standing by no more. Not when you hurt my Meggie!"

Juba gripped Hank by the shoulders. Hank's head wobbled back and forth as Juba shook him and shook him until Hank's eyes glazed over. He heard the bones in Hank's neck protest. Juba's breath came in short bursts of anguished cries. Hank was a blur through the tears that flooded his face. "You're worse than a animal. You—you—"

As if he were wrestling a snake, the feel of Hank's body beneath his grip became a loathsome thing to his touch. Juba blinked the water from his eyes and gave Hank a mighty shove. With a grunt, Hank fell on his back. Wild-eyed, he rolled out of reach, scrambled to his feet and stumbled toward the field. Juba raced after him. It was almost dark now. Juba stubbed his toe on a rock, caught himself from falling headlong and ran on, Hank always an arm's length ahead.

Panting, tripping in the gloom, Juba tried over and over to seize the back of Hank's shirt. Time after time, his fingers brushed the fabric only to have Hank slip away. Legs pumping, muscles beginning to cramp, Juba strained once more, reaching, reaching. At last, he caught hold of a fold in the fabric. His fingers closed around it. He felt a sudden downward yank on his arm. He would not let go. The material tore as he held on desperately. Then, with his arm still outstretched, there was no weight to what he grasped. It was only a crumpled piece of cloth. "What! Hank. Hank?" Juba fell to his knees as darkness enveloped him. He heard a splash, a garbled cry. Like a blind man, he extended his other arm and felt nothing. Cautiously, he explored the ground in front of him. A mere three feet ahead, his fingers examined the edges of a sizable hole.

Juba lay there in shock and exhaustion. He was dizzy. His chest heaved as he sucked in air. He heard another sound, not quite human. Then all was quiet. After a few minutes, he scooted backwards, away from the hole, and patted the ground around him as if in assurance that it would not open up and swallow him.

"Musta been a well," he muttered. "Hank musta fell into a well." He pulled his handkerchief from his back pocket and wiped the sweat and tears from his face. "Oh, Lawd." He bent his head, folded his arms across his chest, and rocked back and forth. He hadn't known the well was there. He could not have directed Hank's footsteps toward it. The well had swallowed Hank. The well had meted out justice. And yet—Juba felt no triumph, no victory. His mouth tasted bitter.

After a while, he rose on shaky legs and found his way home. The lamplight from his cabin window shone on Toby's wagon parked in the yard. Just like Toby, come to be with him and Meggie.

Toby and Isabel stood by the bed. Toby put out a hand and said, "I came by so you wouldn't have to bring Isabel home and I saw— I'm sorry, Juba. Awful sorry."

"What? What you—?"

Isabel moved aside and Juba knelt beside Meggie. "Hon, I—"

They had tucked her into bed. Beside her, on the quilt, wrapped in a soft towel was the washed, silent body of their premature baby. Juba now glimpsed in the corner of the cabin, a tangle of soiled sheets and towels.

"Oh no, oh Lawd, no, no!"

Juba felt Toby's hand on his shoulder. Isabel seemed to be murmuring a prayer. He couldn't understand the words, didn't want to understand them. God was far away. God had not protected Meggie. God had let the baby die. God had let Hank—

Meggie plucked at his sleeve. "Juba?" Her voice was weak. "Juba? God knows how we feel. Juba, love—"

Juba gathered her into his arms and their tears mingled as together they cried out their sorrow.

Dimly, he heard Toby and Isabel say, "You need to be alone for a while. We'll be going now. We'll come first thing in the morning."

Juba drew a chair to the bed and stayed beside Meggie, holding her hand until she drifted into sleep. Then, eyes so full of tears, he could hardly see, he reached into the trunk beside the bed, brought out the little knitted blanket Meggie had made and wrapped the baby in it. Their baby, their little boy, never to draw breath, never to smile, never to cry. Their child, silent, forever sleeping. He stroked the tiny fingers and kissed the quiet brow.

Juba dozed in the chair the rest of the night. The next morning, before daybreak, he went to the shed and fashioned a tiny coffin from short pieces of lumber. He held it in the crook of his arm and stood in the doorway for a few minutes. He watched the sky turn from pearl to golden rays that shone in his face and made him squint. "Thought I'd be making a cradle, Lawd. Ain't—ain't gonna—need a cradle, now."

Later, with Toby and Isabel beside them and his strong arm around Meggie, they slowly, slowly walked to a shaded place beneath a lofty pine and buried the baby. Nearby, in the sun-warmed grass, a meadowlark's fluting tones carried over the fields.

Back at the cabin, exhausted from the ordeal, Meggie sagged onto the bed. She asked, "Hon—about Hank—where—what—where is Hank?"

With eyes swollen from weeping, face drawn, she searched Juba's expression, made him meet her eyes. But Juba turned his back and muttered, "It's all right, Meg. Everything's gonna be all right now."

And privately, within the walls of their own cabin, Toby Sandberg said to Isabel, "Wonder where the devil he ran off to. I ain't gonna feed his horses and livestock. Might as well get the sheriff to have a sale, haul Hank's stuff away."

CHAPTER 55

They'd loaded the wagon. Juba and Meggie sat close together on the driver's high seat. Meggie, still weak, had one arm around Yessir. His ear, where Hank's shovel hammered it, drooped like a limp rag. He had neither hearing nor vision on that side of his head.

Toby leaned on the wagon. He tried to keep his eyes from watering and to think of something cheerful to say.

"Thanks for buying out my patent, Toby."

Toby shrugged. "The least I could do. I'll take good care of the farm."

"Wish we didn't have to go, but—I don't see any other way, not now, not since—"

"I know, friend. Maybe some day, it won't be like this. Maybe some day—" Toby let the sentence dangle. Justice seemed far off. The way things were it might never come for Juba and Meggie. "Where you figure you're headed?"

Juba scratched his chin. "Not sure. Gotta go somewhere Meg'll be safe. Gotta get her away from here. Somewhere's don't have to be reminded every minute—don't know where—"

Toby squeezed Juba's arm. "You'll find the right place. I know you will."

Juba turned to Meggie. "Ready, Meg?"

"Yes, hon." She turned to say, "Bye, Toby."

Juba tickled Jack's back with the reins. The wagon wheels creaked. Toby, with a lump in his throat, watched them drive away. He turned toward the spring. There was the tin cup hanging from its limb. "Hey," he called, "you forgot your—"

They were too far away to hear him. He held the cup in his hand for a moment, then hung it back on the tree. "Let it stay there," he said. "Anybody comes along, can have a drink from Juba's cup."

CHAPTER 56

Three years later, Meggie stood beside the cracked window of the boarding house and balanced Reba Sal on her hip. She peered into the street where, day after day, the coal wagons rumbled by. The rattle and clank of chains and the thud of the horse's hooves churning the dirt of the street went on from morning until night. Dust filtered in through the window crack.

"Reba Sal, you's just passed your first birthday an' the dandelions already covered with coal dust. Pretty soon you'll be old enough to play outside. What am I gonna do? This ain't no place for a porch baby."

She heard the stomp of boots on the rickety porch. Juba came in and slammed the door against a swirl of dust. Reba Sal squealed. Juba squatted on his haunches and held out his arms to her as she toddled across the gritty floor.

"Got a letter from Toby," he said. He took the paper from his pocket, sat in the rocking chair, and lifted Reba Sal to his knee.

Meggie went to the stove and stirred a bubbling stew. "What's he say, hon?"

Juba flapped the letter to straighten it. He read:

Dear Juba,

Thought you might want to know we found Hank Duvett's body down an abandoned well on his property. Been there the whole time, I guess. Always wondered. Thought he ran away. We buried him yesterday. Just two people there. Hank, of course, and me, since I got paid for doing the service. Seems all the neighbors was too busy to attend. A squirrel up a tree scolded the whole time, so I cut it short. Two Quaker brothers bought the property. First thing, they filled in the well.

Lady Longworthy stopped by a while back with her fancy carriage. Asked if we was having another horse race this fall. Said she'd like to come. Wondered if I ever heard from you. Said she'd like to see Meggie again.

You sure spoiled the folks in Rock Lake City. They complain they haven't had any tolerable eggs and cream since you left.

Pansies Isabel planted around your baby's grave look right pretty, up there under the tree. The hollyhocks by your cabin wall are about six or seven feet tall. All pink and white and purple.

That's all for now. Isabel sends her love.

> *Your old friend,*
> *Toby.*

Meggie said in a choked voice, "Pansies. Hollyhocks." A tear rolled down her cheek.

Juba went to the water bucket in the corner by the stove and skimmed bits of coal dust off the top. He poured a cupful of water and took a couple of swallows. He grimaced. "Thermal underground sure keeping this stuff lukewarm. Ain't fit to drink."

He carried Reba Sal over to Meggie and put his arm around her. He had to wait while another coal wagon shook the floor as it rumbled by. "Wouldn't be surprised Toby left that tin cup hanging in the pine tree by the spring, hon. Let's go home. Go home and have a cool cup of water. Home."

"Hum," Reba Sal repeated as she laid her tiny fingers on her daddy's lips. "Hum."